A NOVEL BASED ON A TRUE STORY

HOLE
RIM TVERAS

Copyright © 2014 by Rim Tveras
All Rights Reserved

In accordance with the U.S. Copyright Act of 1976, the scanning, uploading, and electronic sharing of any part of this book without the permission of the publisher is unlawful piracy and theft of the author's intellectual property.
If you would like to use material from the book (other than for review purposes), prior written permission must be obtained by contacting the publisher: holethebook.com/diptera
The author and Diptera, his publisher, wish to acknowledge you, the reader, and thank you for your support.

The people, places, and events in this book are fictitious.
Any similarity to real persons, living or dead, is coincidental and not intended by the author.

Diptera
8945 West 103rd Street, Palos Hills, IL 60465
Diptera is a division of Peeps, Inc. The Diptera name and logo, EASY READ™, and the triangle with the asymmetric hole are trademarks and/or registered trademarks of Peeps, Inc.

First Edition

ISBN 978-0-9915276-0-1

holethebook.com
facebook.com/holethebook
@RimTveras

This is a Diptera EASY READ™ book. The typeface is Adobe Garamond Pro 13 point on 16 point leading. This combination facilitates reader enjoyment by increasing word recognition and reducing eyestrain, especially in low light conditions.

Printed in the United States of America

HOLE

A Novel by Rim Tveras

Chapter 1
Oak Lawn, Illinois 1957

"No, Marge—of course he sent her."

Through heavy Coke-bottle eyeglasses, Marcelline watched her laundry agitate in her shiny white Speed Queen wringer-washer. She leaned forward, resting her elbows on the squeaky-clean machine.

She was a short, stout woman with solid forearms and strong fingers. Her thin brown hair was twisted into perfect pin curls, each one criss-crossed with two black bobby pins. A mesh hairnet held everything in place.

She straightened up and put her hands on her hips. The cool basement air was fresh with the scent of bleach, vinegar, and Fels-Naptha laundry soap.

"Oh, maybe you think she just happened to be driving by, miles from her neighborhood, and said to herself, 'What a nice white store. I think I'll just drop in and buy my groceries. La-di-da.'"

She spoke in a low voice. Her enunciation was sharp

and clear—classroom perfect.

"I should have known, Marge. He got me again," said Marcelline, eyeing the room suspiciously.

"Satan, that's who. I know you're not Catholic, but you do know what sin is." She licked her lips.

"What did I do? I didn't do anything, Marge. I just thought to myself very quietly and politely, 'Why don't you shop in your own neighborhood?'" She looked toward her friend.

"Well, he tricked me because he made me think that. That's an Impure Thought. Venial sin, I think. It's a good thing today is Saturday. I can confess it at three o'clock."

She glanced at her waterproof stainless steel wristwatch.

"Yes. That means if something doesn't happen to me between now and three, I'll be safe because I'll be going to Heaven."

She tugged her hairnet down toward one ear, dislodging a pin in the process.

Marcelline wore a pink striped apron over a forest green floral print dress. Hand embroidered in white *I Love Lucy* script over a bright red heart was: Que Sera Sera.

"I've been first in line for the past three weeks. Father Lawlor greets me personally now when he comes into the confessional. He says, 'Hello, Marcelline,' when he opens my window. I say, 'Bless me Father for I have sinned.'" Marcelline raised her hand to her temple and expertly navigated the loose hairpin back into its proper position on her head.

"He's really nice, Marge … yes. He lets me lump all of

my venial sins … uh, huh … Impure Thoughts."

Her red, rubber-soled, canvas shoes squealed on the chocolate brown, enameled concrete floor.

"No. He doesn't ask for details. Not like Father Skriba.

"Oh yes! He wanted to know what I felt … you know, when I touched myself.

"Ughhh! Really creepy, Marge," she grimaced.

"Never! I don't go on the days Father Skriba is hearing Confession."

The wash cycle was over. She slipped off her watch and set it on the windowsill.

Marcelline was not on the phone, and Marge was not visiting. Marge, in fact, did not exist.

During the week, Marcelline worked as an accountant at a savings and loan. She never did anything indiscreet or immoral; nothing that rose or fell, depending on how one measured it, beyond the gravity of a venial sin. Her sins, if any, were sins of thought.

She wasn't too sure about the severity of her sin or whether it was a sin to begin with, but she knew from her laundry experience that a stain was a stain, no matter how faint. She did not want anything tainting her soul.

Marcelline confessed her sins under the Category: Impure Thoughts. It didn't matter what Father Lawlor made out of them because God knew. After performing the prescribed penance of five Our Fathers and five Hail Marys, all evil was erased from her ledger. Her soul sparkled like her pure white sheets and pillowcases drying on her backyard laundry line.

She was born nearly blind, and her young unmarried

mother wasn't able to keep her. Catholic Charities of Chicago placed her in a foster home. Her foster parents were devout Catholics and provided her with thick, heavy glasses. With her partially improved vision, she learned to read and discovered miraculous truths about Heaven and Hell, Jesus and Satan, and Sin and Salvation.

Her caregivers firmly believed that cleanliness and timeliness were next to Godliness. They stressed the importance of spending her time on Earth wisely to prepare her soul for her eventual meeting with Jesus.

On her wedding night and the nights that followed, Marcelline lay rigid in her bed with her eyes shut tight. Her cycle had been as regular as her monthly mortgage payment. When she missed her period, she rejoiced.

Goody Gumdrops! Thank You Jesus! She was pregnant. She would never have to have sex again.

Father Lawlor had explained that engaging in sex with her husband was not a sin. In fact, it was God's given request—with one condition: it had to be done the way God intended, and only to make babies.

Marcelline had no intention of having another child. That meant future sex would be a sin. Using any form of birth control was unthinkable. Compound one sin with another?

You're talkin' mortal sin for sure!

She knew about compounding. She worked with compound interest tables every day at the bank.

Stroke out or have a heart attack while your husband is wearing a condom? Holy mackerel! No meeting Saint Peter at the pearly gates for sure. Straight to Hell you go! No ifs, buts, or maybes about it!

Marcelline hated sex. To her, it was a dirty, degrading, disgusting, perverse activity. She told her husband she never wanted to see him undressed. With her Singer sewing machine, she sewed up the openings of his Fruit of the Looms so she wouldn't accidentally catch a glimpse of his *organ*.

She had instructed Joe to sit when using the toilet—every time without exception. The vulgar animal act of standing and peeing would not be tolerated. She threatened to divorce him immediately if he broke that rule. She knew God would understand.

One night, she dragged him into the bathroom after finding a yellow drop on the toilet seat. Had he peed standing up? No. He never did. The drop must have fallen as he stood up.

She accepted the explanation, sort of. Out of sight—but not out of Marcelline's mind. The memory of the nasty incident lived on. Joe always inspected the seat thoroughly and even wiped it with his hand to be sure he never missed another stray droplet. To do that was far more prudent than to risk the wrath of Marcelline's neurotic rage.

Marcelline was Celia's mother.

Celia's father was a strong, warm-hearted man, but he was unable to shield Celia from her mother. He couldn't even defend himself. Scrappin' Joe Bauer, who had landed his "Cat" in the Pacific waves spittin' distance from an enemy-infested coast to pluck a ditched Navy

F4F pilot out of his sinking aluminum coffin, kowtowed and tiptoed.

When his wife ranted about those "filthy sons-a-bitches", referring to every boy and man in existence, Joe would quietly slink out of the room and go to work at his drawing table set up in a corner of the basement. He had opened his trap to her in the past, but learned to keep his mouth shut after she had escalated her fury to Category: Eaten Alive. He would never again insert another mealy-mouthed comment regarding her irrational behavior.

Marcelline often talked to herself. Celia had observed her mother carrying on lengthy conversations. Oddly enough—with sexual content. Sometimes she appeared all aglow, smiling and flirting with an invisible man, cackling, standing provocatively with her hands on her hips, gazing up as though *he* were tall. She would pose coyly in front of the bathroom mirror while she waited eagerly for *his* response.

Celia found Marcelline's behavior confusing. It contradicted her preaching about the offensiveness of sex and the nastiness of boys and men. Celia got into the habit of making loud noises before entering a room to snap her mother out of her perverse conversations.

During the summer of Celia's fifteenth birthday, her father died of a massive heart attack. Her mother sent her away to live with an older woman in another suburb. Marcelline made monthly payments for Celia's room and board, but never visited.

Celia didn't bring much in the way of baggage. Her

belongings consisted of a JC Higgins bicycle, a Victrola 45 record player, a worn out copy of Elvis Presley's *Heartbreak Hotel*, a few hit singles, and some clothes and personal effects.

Her most treasured possession was a small bottle of *Muguet de Bois* perfume by Coty that her dad had given her shortly before his death.

She was an outcast looking to start a new life in a new home in a new town. She would transfer to a new school and, hopefully, make new friends.

Chapter 2
Palos Hills, Illinois 1957

She was a lonely girl; a bit on the shy side. She had naturally blond wavy hair, green eyes, and long dark lashes. She looked fit walking down the hall in her five-foot-two, one hundred and three pound figure.

She wore what they wore: a grey tweed wool A-line skirt buttoned forwards; a long sleeved white blouse with a pink cable-knit cardigan sweater buttoned backwards; knee socks, and size five black leather flats. She smoked what many of them smoked: Newport mentholated cigarettes with filter tips.

The sophomore girls at Stagg High School weren't disturbed by the new arrival. She was short, quiet, and the boys had not been asking about her. The girls decided she was going to be okay.

In the high school's corridors, Celia saw boys enter and leave bathrooms regularly, but she was never bothered by it. Her troubles only began when she attempted to have a relationship. As soon as her feelings for a boy went a little deeper than *like*, she started feeling weird. When he excused himself to use the bathroom, her mind flipped.

It didn't matter where they were—on a movie date or in a pizzeria—when the boy returned from his innocent bathroom trip, Celia couldn't stand him any more. He didn't even look like the same person.

"What's wrong Celia?"

"Nothing. Take me home. Please."

"Are you alright? You were fine a minute ago."

"Yes. No. Just take me home."

It was over. She had banished that boy from her life. Boys who'd been terminated never understood why she seemed to like them at first, and later dropped them for no apparent reason.

Celia didn't understand the extreme change in her feelings. She knew she had liked the boy, then suddenly she hated him. She hadn't connected the dots until one Sunday afternoon in her friend, Bruce's, basement.

They were sitting on his family's gold corduroy sofa—one that had finished serving its time in the parlor and sat, stripped of its heavy clear plastic covering, on the green and beige tiled basement floor. They were watching Dorothy skip down the Yellow Brick Road on an old black and white Admiral television.

As much as Bruce hated to disrupt their cozy love-clutch, he needed to answer an urgent call. They'd been eating salty popcorn and washing it down with Coke, and his bladder wasn't going to be ignored any longer.

The bathroom door was next to the sofa, and for some reason, Bruce thought it would be cool to leave the door slightly ajar while doing his manly stand-up act.

Celia had never heard that sound before—not from a boy or a man. She knew what it was because the sounds she made herself were similar.

But this was different. It was the sound of a young man sending his strong, horrible stream crashing into the water below, turning it into a roiling frenzy of madness.

Immediately, she was thrown into a state of terror filled with thundering sounds, panic, and hatred. Her head pounded, her heart raced, and her brain filled with hot rage. She was halfway up the stairs before Bruce had zipped up his pants.

"Celia! Where are you going? Please don't go! Wait! What's wrong, Celia?"

He listened for a reply, but the only sound he heard was the slam of the screen door.

What Bruce didn't know was: she wished he was dead.

Chapter 3

Paramedics rushed her to the Emergency Room, unconscious. The doctors and nurses worked frantically to resuscitate her. They intubated her and massaged her heart. They flushed her stomach and analyzed its contents. The amount of undissolved medication indicated a lethal dose.

After she was stabilized in the ER, she was moved to a room in the Psychiatric Ward of Palos Community Hospital.

Celia had no memory of her trip to the second floor. She was wrapped in white blankets and wheel-chaired into an elevator by a staff nurse. She did not recall passing the uniformed cop sitting behind the entry desk in the hallway that closed with two sets of electronically locked double doors.

She was assigned a "shadow". One of the nursing staff was going to follow and monitor her every move.

She was stripped of all personal belongings except her blue jeans, blouse, and underwear. Makeup, mirrors, hair and hygiene supplies, belts, shoelaces, and other objects that could be fashioned into a weapon were not permitted on the floor. Some of the patients were alcoholics and would consume anything containing even a trace amount of alcohol. Mouthwash, cologne, and perfume were banned.

Her Newports were locked in the Day Room. She was permitted to smoke only under supervision after the shadow lit her cigarette.

The shadow studied Celia's body checking for bruises, cuts, and punctures. She even peeked under Celia's IV Band-Aids to make sure they weren't hiding other needle tracks. She was inspected daily for new flaws not matching the prior day's log. Detailed notes were charted regarding her behavior, demeanor, and interaction with staff members and fellow patients.

The Day Room was spacious and well lit with an orderly arrangement of sofas, round tables, and chairs. There was a pool table on the far end of the floor next to a metal buffet eating area.

The room was a comfortable seventy-two degrees. Tall, steel-barred, southwest windows allowed plenty of sunlight, but the arctic blue walls turned it into a teeth-chattering, bone-chilling ice chest for Celia.

Her only comfort came from three bulky blankets and Megan, a sixteen-year-old girl in for the third time due to parental problems and alcohol abuse.

Celia endured a battery of sessions with psychiatrists.

One doctor diagnosed her with Obsessive Compulsive Disorder. Another suggested Borderline Personality Disorder. Other colleagues considered Dissociative Identity Disorder.

The doctors weren't able to decide on a course of treatment. They were only able to reach agreement on one thing: Celia's symptoms were definitely uncommon.

Chapter 4

Dr. Lopez was a tall, bony woman with broad shoulders, long fingers, large flat feet, and knock-knees. Her dark skin was pocked with acne scars, but her heart and mind were unscathed.

They sat in two armchairs facing each other in a small private meeting room. After nearly an hour of pleasant chitchat, Dr. Lopez zeroed in on Celia's condition.

"You said your mother screamed and spanked you with a hairbrush after you wet your bed. Every night you were afraid to go to sleep. You knew you'd wake up shivering and scared on your cold, wet mattress, crying for your mother, only to be ripped red-eyed out of your bed by a raging monster to be painfully beaten … like the night before and the night before."

Celia caught the monster reference. She wondered if it was a slip or intentional. It didn't matter. Dr. Lopez was obviously in Celia's corner. For the first time in her life, someone was taking an interest in her, studying her, trying to understand her, willing to stand up for her.

She watched Dr. Lopez slowly, clearly enunciate her diagnosis.

"You were three to five years old at the time. It's quite likely she beat you even before then. You don't remember, but those attacks created deep trauma in your developing mind. Every night you were thrown into a frantic life and death crisis. You survived the deadly assaults, but the damage was forever imprinted on your brain."

Dr. Lopez paused to let her statement sink in.

"A similar condition is produced by using electrical shock on laboratory animals. Thousands of cruel experiments are performed daily putting the poor creatures into a constant state of pain, confusion, and terror. After repeated jolts of electricity, the animals are permanently altered and rendered useless for further research. They are destroyed and discarded.

"What your immature brain imprinted was pee or the act of peeing, fear of death, pain, and anger. Because you were too young to understand, your mind made only rudimentary connections. Peeing triggered fear and anger."

Celia listened intensely. She studied Dr. Lopez, watching each word as it was formed by her lips. She had never heard such things before, but the doctor's interpretation of her symptoms made the mystery of her problem understandable.

"It won't matter who or what is peeing. Males, females, or animals performing the act will prompt the same responses of panic, rage, aggression, and flight, in no particular order."

Dr. Lopez studied her patient. Celia looked like a young child with her eyes wide open, waiting to be told Santa was on his way, bringing her shiny new presents. Dr. Lopez hated what she had to say next.

"These connections can't be erased because this information is stored in the core region—the reptilian brain—far beyond the reach of reason and understanding."

Celia remembered standing near the edge of the hole in the ground at her dad's funeral. People had taken turns throwing dirt on his coffin with a shovel. Each shovelful had taken him farther away from her—

"The primal brain controls only what is required for survival. Fear, aggressiveness, and defensiveness, otherwise called the fight or flight response, are mechanisms hard-wired permanently in the brain." Another shovelful—

"This is the domain of automatic reactions. You've heard them called 'knee-jerk' because they are predictable. They are largely uncontrollable by the outer or cognitive brain, especially under conditions of stress when hormones are released into the brain." More dirt—

"This is a gross oversimplification of an incredibly complex and only partially understood landscape neuroscience is attempting to explore. But the short answer as of where we are today, is …"

This was the worst part: the stinking meat patty inside the bad news sandwich.

"… you can't be fixed with cognitive therapy, and

there are no drugs that can help you. You probably already know alcohol has little or no effect, or worse: it exacerbates the condition."

Celia tried to keep a brave face, but disappointment veiled her pretty features. Her lips quivered and her watery green eyes glossed over with sadness. She sat up with her back straight, hands grasping her knees.

Dr. Lopez continued.

"There is a positive side to all of this. As your brain developed, your later cognitive layers were able to transfer your primeval responses enough to remove *you* from that lethal combination of reactions.

"If that hadn't happened, you couldn't pee without bringing on intense self-hatred and emotional distress. You'd be living in constant fear of your own bladder. The flip side is that every boy and man is now the cause of your worst trauma and loathing."

"Yes. That's true."

"You mentioned an incident when you were very young, some neighborhood boys trapped you in a bathroom. Your memory wasn't clear, but you thought they'd put you in the bathtub and peed on you."

Celia winced as Dr. Lopez recounted the episode.

"Every time you entered a bathroom, your brain was cued to replay your early trauma. That, combined with your mother's insistence that all males are revolting and untrustworthy, confirmed your worst fears."

"It all makes sense now, Doctor. Well, not really." Celia frowned and stared down at her hands.

"It became easy for your creative brain to shift the

evilness of peeing to boys and men. You were vindicated and no longer bad when you had to pee. They were."

The lunch bell rang out from the Psych Ward's Public Address system, startling Celia.

"Thank you, Dr. Lopez. No one has ever explained any of this to me like you just did. At least now I know why I am what I am."

Her Popeye inference was accidental. It reminded her of early Saturday morning cartoon-watching with her father. Popeye the Sailor Man came on television at the same time each week, the exact time her mother left for her weekend shopping sprees.

Celia and her dad spent those warm and wonderful moments laughing and joking, imitating the corny shenanigans of the popular comic book hero. Celia had always thought her father resembled Popeye. They were both good-guy underdogs, had huge forearms, loved spinach, and smoked corncob pipes.

She wondered how her dad would have felt if he knew she was locked up in the psychiatric ward of a hospital, suffering because of the twisted teachings of his wife.

Dr. Lopez walked Celia back to the cafeteria and gave her a firm hug. She whispered, "We'll talk again in a couple of days."

Chapter 5

Dr. Lopez and Celia returned to the meeting room for the follow-up session. The Day Room nurse brought Celia her Newports.

"Celia, you said it doesn't bother you when men other than those you care about excuse themselves to go to the bathroom. You think they're disgusting and that's all there is to it. Your troubles start when you begin having romantic feelings for a man. That's when what should be a normal act of male peeing becomes a violent personal attack."

"Yes."

"It's similar to … well, this may sound confusing. Let me give you an example. Suppose a casual friend—a boy—is having sex with someone." Dr. Lopez folded her hands on her lap.

"You're indifferent because it doesn't affect you personally. It can only become a hateful act of betrayal if he is *your* boyfriend. It's like he's cheating on you by having sex with another woman. Are you following me, Celia?"

"Yes. Perfectly." Her eyes lifted then lowered again to follow the doctor's hand.

"You've probably never gotten far enough into a relationship to experience the actual pain of cheating. For you, Celia, the mere mention that your boyfriend has to pee brings on feelings of treachery. It's as if he's rushing off to the bathroom to cheat on you."

Celia watched the doctor's fingers play on the wide wooden armrest of her chair. It was the hand of a pianist striking notes on an imaginary keyboard. She didn't play one single note like someone using their index finger to emphasize each point. She used each finger, including her thumb, and played out in non-clinical terms Celia's strange dysfunction.

She felt the doctor had diagnosed her accurately. The symptoms were described, the problem was defined, the root causes named. It all made sense, but there was one bar the composer left out. What was the cure? The fix?

Celia wanted to know, but she didn't ask. She thought about what her new friend, Megan, had told her: *You wanna get out of this place, don't you? Then you gotta play the part. If they don't think they helped you get over whatever the fuck got you here, they won't let you out.*

Celia sensed impatience as Dr. Lopez readjusted her long bones and moved in closer to face her. This was a waiting game. She who spoke first lost.

Both women sat quietly. Celia lit a cigarette and

puffed out a perfect smoke ring. Dr. Lopez was first to break the silence.

"You probably have something you want to ask me at this point—"

"No. Not really, Doctor."

Dr. Lopez's eyes narrowed ever so slightly. She was about to offer Celia a remedy that did not exist to test her state of wellness. If her patient jumped at it, the doctor would have no choice but to recommend a longer stay in the hospital. It would mean Celia could easily succumb to her problem again, and her next suicide attempt might be successful.

"Celia, don't you want to know if something can be done to alleviate your condition?"

"Not really," she said and blew out a smooth stream of mentholated smoke.

"What do you mean not really?"

Dr. Lopez was puzzled. How could she not want to know if she could be helped? Maybe she needed to rephrase the question.

There was no need for a do over. Celia returned a flawless answer after her next smoky exhale.

"Well, I kind of see it like this. You know how you said my growing brain found a way to shift all the blame, loathing, and fears about peeing onto men? Well, I think my brain did something even better this time."

"Oh? Like what?"

"I don't even *want* men any more." Celia grinned as she spoke.

"There's a girl in my ward. I met her last week, and

now we really like each other, if you know what I mean."

Celia's shadow had documented the new friendship in her daily reports. Celia and Megan were described as inseparable. They were noted walking hand in hand in full view of everyone. The shadow had witnessed the two girls nuzzling each other on the Day Room couch. They'd even been seen kissing.

Dr. Lopez smiled broadly. Maybe she *had* been instrumental in this unfortunate girl's rehabilitation. Psychiatrists seldom witnessed positive outcomes, especially after a suicide attempt.

She believed Celia. In fact, it seemed like the most logical transformation her brain could have made for her own survival. The doctor scheduled two more sessions, then gave the department the go-ahead for Celia's release.

Marcelline refused to come to the hospital for an interview. "I didn't raise her to do this to me, Doctor."

After four weeks of lock down, written outpatient instructions were included with Celia's release papers. They were lengthy and ended with a specific stipulation:

INSTRUCTION TO PATIENT

*You must never allow yourself to develop romantic feelings for a man, or in layman's terms, fall in love.

*You must avoid places and activities that lead to dating and intimacy with men.

*Your mental health is of utmost importance. Maintaining it should be your top priority. Ignoring this warning will be detrimental to your well-being with unpredictable negative consequences anticipated.

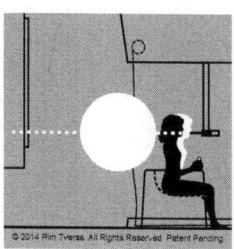

HOLE: Part One

Chapter 6
September 13, 1961

Dawn was wet and bloody red, surging across Lake Michigan, spilling down streets, outlining gutters and gingerbread, painting pink on chimneys and window boxes. It was daybreak in Chicago's Old Town Triangle. The night rain had stopped, leaving cobblestone streets and alleys shiny and dangerous like the slippery scales of an alligator.

A heavy man stood on the sidewalk looking up at the dark upstairs windows of the two-story coach house on the corner of Laurel and Ash. In the light of the electrified corner gaslight, he saw ghostly indications of three tall doorways filled in with brick and glass blocks. Above was a mechanical fire escape. A red entry door on the Laurel side displayed a large black 624.

The man walked to the door and pounded on it with the bottom of his fist. Seconds later, he stepped back when he heard deep, resonant barking. After a minute of woofing, baying, and growling, the door opened and a man in his early forties appeared holding back a large dog.

The man was tall with rough-hewn features, deep-set eyes, and a dark complexion. His long black hair was pulled away from his face, and ended in a tight braid down his back. An open shirt draped loosely over a fit, but not overly muscular body. He was barefoot and visibly annoyed.

"It is okay, Nixon," he said as he squatted, calming the dog with soft words and pats.

The heavy man displayed an open wallet with a shiny metal badge. "Detective Hogan. Palos Hills Police Department. I'm looking for a Mr. Peter Victor."

"I am Peter Victor, Detective."

"I'll need you to come with me to the station, sir. Your cooperation will be greatly appreciated."

The detective opened his jacket wide as he returned his wallet to the inside breast pocket, giving Mr. Victor a clear view of a revolver in a shoulder holster.

"Yes, I can go," said Mr. Victor, "but can you tell me what this is about?"

"I'd rather not talk about it here, sir. You're not under arrest. This is strictly voluntary. I must inform you, however, that if you refuse, there will be an officer with an arrest order showing up later today."

"Do I have time to get ready, Detective?"

"Yes, of course. Take all the time you need, sir. I'll wait for you in the car."

Mr. Victor climbed the long stairway to the apartment. Nixon was already upstairs announcing the news to an attractive brunette. He wiggled, wagged, and swished his tail as she lunged and grabbed him playfully.

"What? What? What is it, Nixon?"

Sara lived with Mr. Victor. She was an artist and modeled for his art students—often in the nude. She had shadowy eyes and thick black hair trimmed in a military buzz cut with a three-inch mop top.

She was wearing her usual—nothing—under one of Mr. Victor's work shirts. A pack of Marlboro cigarettes poked out of the left pocket. As she played with Nixon, her smooth skin flashed, revealing parts of her fine figure.

"What's going on, Peter?"

"I am not sure. There is a detective here and he wants to take me to the police station."

"Oh man, are you in some kind of trouble? Did you forget to pay your parking tickets?" she asked with a smirk.

"No. I do not think it is about traffic violations, but I am not worried."

"Do you have time to shower?"

"Oh yes, of course."

This is America, he thought. Shit, shower, and shave were as American as God, country, and the Fourth of July.

As Sara brushed and braided his freshly washed hair, Mr. Victor asked her not to cancel his art class and to have the students work on their sketching until he returned.

"I do not believe I will be gone very long." He kissed Nixon and headed for the stairs.

Chapter 7

"Ah, good. I was beginning to think I'd lost you," said the detective, smiling as he stepped out of his vehicle.

"I took a shower and shaved, Detective. You said I should take the time—"

"Yes, of course. It's perfectly all right, sir. I do apologize for this early morning call."

The sun was rising and the wind had picked up, drying off the tops of the ancient brick pavers; bringing out the rich dark red and brown earth colors.

Mr. Victor took a closer look at the stranger.

Detective Hogan was a plump man dressed in a moss green suit, white shirt, and gold tie. He wore a straw, cream colored Panama porkpie hat with a brown stingy brim and an orange striped sweatband. His hands were fat with thick, short fingers that tapered down to child-sized, manicured nails. His cream and brown saddle shoes were diminutive, making his roly-poly oval shape resemble a green olive.

And yet, as his jacket blew open, the nickel-plated Chiefs Special cast a discordant note into the comical composition; like seeing a fat infant gumming the drool-soaked, spluttered end of a fine cigar. Mr. Victor wondered why someone like Hogan was allowed to carry a firearm.

Only in America, he thought.

As Mr. Victor sized up his opponent, the detective did the same. Hogan noted that most of the darkness was gone from Mr. Victor's face. He was clean-shaven and wore a black suit jacket over a grey denim work shirt and an inch wide tomato red tie. Clean black jeans, black and white Converse basketball shoes, and a Mickey Mouse wristwatch completed the look.

To a designer, it would have been as telling as red, white, and blue to an American. The grey, tomato red, black, and white were the vanguard colors of the new design revolution in America. The building's Bauhaus grey exterior and Helvetica numerals on the tomato red door identified it as a design establishment, and Mr. Victor's attire declared him an integral moving part of it.

That wasn't how Hogan saw it. He made a mental checklist and began crossing off descriptions not applicable to his would-be detainee. Mr. Victor was probably not a civil servant, accountant, or insurance salesperson. No reputable company would keep a middle-aged man with long hair and inappropriate dress on their payroll. A suit jacket and sneakers? Only a musician or an ad agency executive could get away with that.

Hogan didn't overlook Mr. Victor's heavy foreign accent. Maybe that had been the reason for his oddball appearance. But this was Old Town. It was far more artsy and unpredictable than conservative Palos Hills on the southwest side of Chicago.

The detective opened the front passenger door of his unmarked police cruiser. He reached inside, picked up an aluminum clipboard with a clamped-on mess of dog-eared papers, and threw it on the back seat. He raked a collection of candy wrappers off the grey velour front bench seat, clearing a space for his passenger.

"Please have a seat, sir."

The large green Chevrolet didn't look like a cop car. It could have passed for a family sedan, except for some specialized equipment. It had a pillar-mounted spotlight for aiming at car windows, house numbers, and questionable characters. A two-way police radio and a gumball emergency flasher with a ruby lens cover were prominent on the dashboard.

Mr. Victor settled into the seat and closed the door. He noticed the scent of stale sweat, after-shave, and smoke permeating the fabric interior.

Hogan started the car and made a quick call on the radio. After the Ten Four, he hung up the mike, opened a fresh pack of cigarettes, and offered his passenger a Viceroy. Mr. Victor thanked him, but said he preferred his own brand: Kool.

Hogan pulled a lighter from his pants pocket and lit their smokes. He yanked the car away from the curb and headed west, tires roaring on the stony street—a charming, hoof-knocking, wheel-breaking Great Chicago Fire survivor.

"Where are you taking me, Detective?"

"The Palos Hills Police Station, sir. It's out on a hundred and third street, about a forty-five minute drive from here at this hour."

Chapter 8

The roar changed to a soft swish as Hogan's Wide Oval Whitewalls hit smooth asphalt on Halsted. He drove south, turned west on North Avenue, then south on Ashland. After pedal dancing through twenty-five minutes of rush hour traffic, he turned southwest onto Archer. Another couple of miles brought them to a White Castle restaurant on Kedzie. Detective Hogan whipped the car into the parking lot and pulled up near the entrance.

"Are you hungry, Mr. Victor? Do you like Sliders? If you don't mind, I'm gonna have some. This is my lunch time, and I've had a long morning already."

"No thank you, Detective," he answered, "but you go right ahead and enjoy your lunch."

"Okay. How 'bout coffee and a sweet roll?"

"A small coffee and sweet roll would be fine, thank you."

"I'll be back, sir."

As the detective stepped out, Mr. Victor felt the left side of the vehicle rise a few inches. He watched the oval olive trudge toward the aluminum framed glass door. The back of his suit was wrinkle-pressed by at least three hundred pounds of flesh.

He glanced at his watch. Mickey pointed to seven-forty. Four fingers and a thumb extended from each yellow-gloved hand. Until then, he'd been certain that Cartoon Mickey's gloves were white and only had three fingers and a thumb.

Hogan returned with four white paper bags and thrust himself into the car. A fragrant food waft filled the vehicle. Mr. Victor realized that what he'd thought was sweaty armpit stench was only the leftover scent of steaming White Castle hamburgers, a smell that lingered, especially in an airtight police vehicle.

The detective lined up the food sacks on the seat. One had coffees; another teemed with bakery goodies. Two bags had perfectly stacked double columns of little boxes, each enclosing a miniature square hamburger with chopped onions and Everything Sauce.

"Let's dig in," said Hogan.

As Mr. Victor reached for a sweet roll, the detective made another suggestion. "Before you commit, how 'bout a Slider?"

Mr. Victor felt rumbling in his empty stomach. He was not accustomed to having hamburgers for breakfast, but the aroma was strong and deliciously tempting.

"Sure, Mr. Hogan. I will have one."

Mr. Victor munched down three Sliders and a sweet roll. Hogan polished off eight burgers and two fruit-filled pastries.

The parking lot was abuzz with people and vehicles. Outside, the trademark White Castle fragrance mixed with acrid exhaust fumes and drifted into open car windows.

As the men sipped their hot coffee and smoked, Detective Hogan began his investigation.

Chapter 9

"So ... what do you do, Mr. Victor?"

"I teach art and design at the University of Illinois. I also work on my own art in my Laurel Street studio."

"Is that also your residence?"

"Yes. That is where I live and work."

"Does anyone else live there?"

"Yes, a young woman named Sara."

"How old is Sara?"

"Sara is ... nineteen."

"What is your relationship with Sara? Daughter?"

"Roommate—" He watched the detective's eyebrows rise and fall.

"—and you met Nixon, my Chocolate Labrador Retriever."

"Heh, heh, yes. Magnificent dog, sir. Is it male or female?"

"He is a boy."

"Oh, I love dogs. I have two Yorkies myself ... but they're no match for your Nixon. Great name, by the way. Almost beat JFK. Your dog could have been President Nixon. Would you have nicknamed him Prez? Do you think he'll run again? I mean the Vice President, not your Nixon! Heh, heh."

"I did not name him, Detective. Nixon was the name on his adoption papers from the shelter."

Hogan dragged on his cigarette and turned his bulky body, moving closer to his subject. "Do you have many students, Mr. Victor?"

"Oh ... about forty-three."

"Are you related to any of your students?"

"No, sir."

"Have you had a relationship with any of them?" Hogan's intense blue eyes locked on to Mr. Victor's.

"So ... have you had sex with any of your students?"

The fat, happy Buddha who had been generously doling out food and drink was now serious as a cobra coiled and ready to strike.

Mr. Victor tried to calm his swelling paranoia. He never had sex with a student. He had worked hard to help them develop their skills and to excel in their creative—

He thought of Robyn.

She had been after him all of the past semester, talking to him after class, inviting him to have coffee with her in the student cafeteria, even saying how young and *with it* his nice long hair made him look. Once, she brought a painting to school and asked if he would critique it in her car. She claimed it was too large to bring in, and too difficult to maneuver through the crowded corridor.

The painting wasn't a class assignment. Robyn had painted it for extra credit. She explained in graphic detail how she'd produced the effect by coating her naked body with special paints and rolling herself on the canvas. She directed Mr. Victor's attention to some of the pertinent points by drawing with her finger.

"See, here's my right boob ... and ... there's my nipple! And that's my beaver—shaved, of course."

She asked if he might have time to come over to her house while her parents were away to watch her paint and hopefully give her some suggestions.

Mr. Victor never made the time. He wondered if Robyn had told the police that he did. He remembered giving her a "B" grade for the course, which had made her very unhappy. She thought she deserved an "A".

He would have to admit he saw the painting, but only in her car. He thought she drove a pink and grey Chevrolet station wagon.

His adrenalized, rambling imagination cut to a courtroom. A tough young female prosecutor was giving him the third degree. In her mind, every human with a penis was a crime waiting to happen—

"You said you remember your student, Robyn, purposely directing your attention to the 'nipple' detail and, as you said, the 'beaver'. You claimed that Robyn showed you the painting in her car—a station wagon. Perhaps a pink and grey Chevrolet.

"We checked out your story, Mr. Victor. Robyn's neighbor has a pink and grey Chevrolet Nomad wagon. You probably

saw it at Robyn's house during your visit and thought it was hers.

"Robyn only owns one vehicle, sir. A green Toyota Corona sedan—"

"Mr. Victor, I asked you a question. Did you have sex with any of your students?"

Hogan's stare stabbed at Mr. Victor, pinning him into the corner of his seat.

"Of course not!"

Chapter 10

The remainder of the trip was quick and quiet. The men entered the station without words. There were two staircases inside the lobby. One went up half a floor to the Desk Sergeant's office. They went up the steps and stopped in front of the big desk. Detective Hogan took a set of keys from the Sergeant and led Mr. Victor down the other stairway into the lower level of the building.

They made their way down a long hallway with green and black asbestos floor tiles laid out in a checkerboard pattern. They passed several doors, each with a metal identification number that started with a "B". Hogan stopped at the end of the hall in front of B-17 and unlocked the door. When they were both inside, the detective closed it firmly.

Mr. Victor quickly surveyed the contents of the room, his eyes peeled for a large canvas painted with bright organic shapes in red, magenta, lime green, and black.

A grey metal shelf stood against one wall holding two cardboard boxes sealed with bright red tape. EVIDENCE—EVIDENCE—EVIDENCE was printed repeatedly on the tape in bold black letters. Neither of the containers was large enough to hold Robyn's artwork.

Oddly, there was a good-sized painting sitting on a table in the corner of the small room, but it wasn't Robyn's.

Mr. Victor was keenly aware of Detective Hogan standing behind him. He could feel his piercing blue eyes watching, studying him intensely. His nerves were still on edge and his breaths were shallow. And yet, he saw nothing in the room in any way troubling. He began to feel a thaw coming, melting his icy, self-made fear.

He returned his attention to the painting. It looked like oil paints on a stretched canvas. The image wasn't anything special—a yellow sky darker at the top and gradually lightening toward the bottom. About one third of the way down, soft white clouds appeared and continued downward.

It must have been the work of an unknown and most likely, never-to-be known artist. It had no artistic worth and could have easily been hanging in a discount furniture store.

He didn't see a signature but noticed a small round hole near the lower right-hand corner where artists often signed their work. On the table was a piece of paper sticking out from under the painting. It was wrinkled and looked as though it had been stained with coffee.

"What do you know about this painting, sir?"

Mr. Victor inhaled a deep breath of stale evidence room air and let it out audibly. This wasn't about Robyn after all.

"Nothing, Detective. I have never seen this painting. I do not recognize the art or the artist."

He waited for the detective to open the door, lead him upstairs, clear his name, apologize for the inconvenience, and drive him home.

Hogan walked over to the painting. "The artist who painted it died early this morning. There was a note."

He pulled the piece of paper out from under the painting and handed it to Mr. Victor. It felt damp and cold.

As Mr. Victor glanced down at the wrinkly slip, his face drained to white. The note read:

Please deliver this painting to—
Mr. Peter Victor
624 West Laurel Street
Chicago, Illinois
I painted it. It is my gift to Mr. Victor.
—Celia Bauer

Chapter 11

"She died from a gunshot wound. Her body was found in a basement storage area next to the laundry room in her apartment building. A tenant happened to be in the hallway around 3:00 a.m. when she heard a shot. She ran back to her unit and called the station."

Hogan's cold blue stare stayed focused on his subject.

"The wound looked self-inflicted. The bullet exited the back of her head. Powder residue and blood indicate the gun was fired inside her mouth."

Mr. Victor stood motionless, clenching the note. A solitary tear trailed down his cheek.

"Look closely at the painting. There's a small hole near the bottom on the right-hand side. The bullet was lodged inside a box filled with clothes. We think the painting was propped up against it before the shooting. There was blood, cranial fluid, brain tissue, bone fragments, and some hair stuck to a piece of corrugated cardboard. I'm guessing the cardboard was used as a shield to keep the painting clean. The note was lying in a pool of blood on the floor. We rinsed it off."

Hogan stepped back from the canvas. He raised his arm and pointed to the red-taped EVIDENCE cartons on the shelf.

"The cardboard shield, weapon, bullet casing, the recovered fired projectile, and the clothes are all in the boxes."

Mr. Victor only half-heard the detective. Celia was one of his favorite students. He'd always felt protective towards her, almost like a father. She was a young and deeply troubled artist who, despite her vulnerabilities, presented a fun, confident exterior. She was talented, beautiful, and very unusual.

Hogan took the note from Mr. Victor and laid it back on the table. He led him upstairs into a well-lit room with two green vinyl office chairs facing a large grey metal desk. Through his blurred vision, Mr. Victor was able to make out a glass ashtray, a stack of horizontal letter trays, and some picture frames with photos of a woman and two girls. An engraved brass nameplate read: DETECTIVE WINSLOW HOGAN.

The detective pulled several printed forms out of a drawer and asked for Mr. Victor's identification. His Driver's License would do. He left to use the copy machine returned minutes later. He began to interrogate his *person of interest* and make notes in a spiral-bound notebook.

People didn't kill themselves without reason. Was

Celia mentally ill? Did she use drugs? Was there a boyfriend in the picture? A girlfriend? Did he have any idea what happened?

All Mr. Victor could say was no.

Hogan was frustrated. He wasn't getting anywhere with this peculiar college professor. The evidence clearly pointed to him—the painting, the note, the fact that he knew her, that she was his student.

Hogan sprang up from behind his desk, threw off his jacket, and landed in front of Mr. Victor. He stood, eyes glaring, his weapon threateningly close to Mr. Victor's face.

"Were you in love with Celia?"

Mr. Victor hesitated. "I love Celia, Detective. But I am not in love with her."

Hogan turned up the volume. "What exactly do you mean? Is that a yes or a no?"

"Yes, I love her. No, I am not in love with her."

"I'd expect that from a fourth grader, not a grown man. Let me repeat my question. Were you in love with Celia?"

The narrow brim of Hogan's hat bumped Mr. Victor's forehead. The detective's breath was strong with the smell of onions and coffee. He spewed spit particles as he spoke. The detective's jolly caricature was long gone—replaced by a relentless interrogator.

"I have loved Celia like she was my own daughter, Detective. I was never her lover."

"Have you ever touched her? Or kissed her?"

"No, sir. Never."

"Then why in Hell would she have killed herself? Can you explain that?" Hogan loomed over him, his enormous gut ready to crush Mr. Victor into his chair.

"I do not believe she died because of me, Detective. I do not know why she died. I do not know why she gave me the painting."

"Have you seen the painting before?"

"No, sir."

"What does the painting mean?"

"I do not know."

"It must have meant a great deal to this girl if she was willing to shed her life's blood on it."

"Yes, yes, yes. I know, I know, Detective."

Hogan put his meaty hands on Mr. Victor's shoulders and gave him a shove, sliding him and his chair back on the tiled floor.

"What do you know? You better tell me right now!" Hogan shouted. "This is serious! A young girl is dead! What do you know?"

"Detective, I was only agreeing with you. The painting must have been very important to her. I did not know she painted. I do not understand what it means."

Hogan wasn't convinced that Celia was just his student, but that didn't mean Mr. Victor was responsible for her death. He turned to his desk, picked up a large white envelope, and pulled out a stack of glossy black and white photos. "These came in from the photo lab while we were downstairs."

He handed the photos, one by one, to Mr. Victor. The pictures showed the dreary storage room where the poor girl had drawn her last breath. A mutilated face lay in a nest of sweet blonde curls encircled by a dark shiny pool. Her eyes were wide open, staring into nothingness. Her mouth was a craggy black hole.

Mr. Victor sat up in his chair and thought: *That does not look like Celia!*

"The gun automatically reloaded because the magazine was full. The slide came forward after it recoiled. It knocked out her front teeth and wrecked her lips."

"Her arms—"

The girl's arms were covered with dark slashes. Some were parallel; others crossed each other.

"Those are self-made injuries."

"I do not understand, Detective."

"We see it a lot. That's what some people do to deal with extreme emotional pain. They try to get relief by replacing their mental pain with physical pain. Young people do it more often than adults because they don't have as much experience in handling their emotions. But ... it doesn't always lead to suicide."

Mr. Victor tried to convince himself that the girl in the pictures was not Celia, but in his gut, he knew. He gagged, bent over, and heaved his partially digested meal into the detective's steel wastebasket.

Chapter 12

Detective Hogan slid the photographs and notebook into a manila envelope and filed it in his desk drawer.

"The girl will have to be identified. So far we have a body, an unsigned painting, and a note with both your names on it. The note isn't dated and proves nothing. The weapon isn't registered. We'll search her apartment and car later this morning. Celia Bauer's records show that she has a living mother. Marcelline Bauer will be called to identify the victim."

Mr. Victor was shocked, his ravaged brain aching. He wanted desperately to deny the experience. He hadn't seen Celia's body, and the art was unfamiliar. The note looked like it had been written by Celia, but maybe it happened to be on the floor where the *other* girl's blood soaked into it.

The face didn't look like Celia's. Mr. Victor hadn't seen her since Luke's farewell party three weeks prior, but her arms had always been free of cuts and bruises. Hogan hadn't mentioned the little airplane pendant that Celia always wore. The girl in the photos didn't have any jewelry on her neck.

Hogan said the body was in the Cook County Medical Examiner's Office. An autopsy would be performed to determine the cause of death and rule out any possibility of foul play.

"You'll have to be photographed and fingerprinted, but you're not being charged. It's a precautionary procedure to eliminate you as a suspect should any unexplained fingerprints show up."

"I understand."

After they had finished in the photo and fingerprint room, the detective drove Mr. Victor back to his studio. He opened the passenger door and let the broken man out of his car.

"You may be called back in if we need more information. Don't plan any trips."

Hogan felt no sympathy for the professor. A young girl was dead. Mr. Victor was disheveled by her death, but he'd get over it. The girl would not. All Hogan wanted to do was go home, grab his fat wife and daughters, and love the shit out of them.

The sight of the familiar bright red door brought Mr. Victor no comfort. As he opened it, the door bumped something. There was a large, flat cardboard package lying on the tile floor inside the entrance. It was marked URGENT.

He carried the parcel upstairs, laid it on the coffee

table, and collapsed on the futon. It was after one o'clock and class was over. Most likely the students were gone.

"Hey, Peter! You're finally back!" Sara called from the kitchen. She walked into the living room and sat down cross-legged on the hardwood floor. Nixon plopped down and laid his head between his outstretched front legs; his big brown eyes looked up. Sara put her hand on Mr. Victor's arm.

"What's wrong?"

"They think Celia is dead."

"What?" Sara shouted in shock, her face twisted.

"The police are saying she killed herself this morning."

He was hoping, waiting for Sara to say Celia had been there earlier or that they had spoken on the phone. He felt Sara's hands grip his forearm hard.

"Oh, my God! Peter! Why? Was there a note?" Sara moaned.

He shook his head. The lines around his eyes deepened with fear and pain. "Not one with any explanation. She left a note saying she was giving me a painting she had made for me."

"God. I'm so, so sorry, Peter. I don't understand." Sara buried her face in the crook of his elbow. Her tears soaked into the wool fabric and left dark stains on his sleeve.

Chapter 13

URGENT scrawled on the package meant another rush job. Mr. Victor knew Dave would be calling. As much as he didn't want to, he knew he should open the package.

There was no sender information. Dave usually omitted a return address in a last-minute dash to get the package out and into the hands of a messenger—typically a nimble black man who could weave a bicycle in and out of downtown Chicago traffic like a mechanized minnow.

The cardboard box contained an expandable red rope artist portfolio filled with sketchbooks and folders with typed pages and watercolor renderings on illustration boards. It didn't appear to be another graphic design job. It looked more like an architectural project.

Mr. Victor glanced at the cover letter. It wasn't on Dave's letterhead and was written in longhand.

His heart skipped, then began to race.

Dear Mr. Victor:

I am dedicating the enclosed project to you.

I started it for my Architecture 103 class but thought it might be too radical for the university.

I have since dropped out of architecture but continued to work on it in my spare time.

The project became a collaborative effort when I brought your ideas into it. I especially like your theory that we are holes in the universe. As a working title, I am choosing to call it HOLE.

I hope you will forgive me for not involving you in the project earlier. I trust you will understand. I am handing the entire effort over to you because I won't be able to take it further.

I want to emphasize HOLE is not a suicide machine. There are many cheaper and easier options available to the person whose only intention is to terminate their own life.

HOLE is a tool—a means and a method to enable the artist, which I believe exists in everyone, to create a personal, final, worthy, and enduring art form.

See what you think.

Celia

Chapter 14

Mr. Victor picked up the first typed page.

INTRODUCTION:

I think there is a great deal of confusion associated with suicide. I believe people who kill themselves are not craving death. They only want to end their pain.

Physical pain can often be helped with drugs. The greater pain by far is mental. Pain that has no remedy. Pain that cannot be understood by anyone except the person who feels it every minute of every day. It is never-ending, hopeless anguish with no fix in sight. Mental pain can become unbearable.

Seeking remedy through suicide is not an easy path. Everyone fears death. Facing the unknown is worrisome for the staunchest believers in a happy afterlife. Suicide is not an option allowed by any of the major faiths. For a Catholic, trading in a lifetime of earthly pain for an eternity of agony in Hell's fires, never to see God's face, is no bargain.

Irrespective of their beliefs, for an artist, suicide poses a dilemma. Making art is an act of creation. Suicide is largely seen as an act of destruction. Artists, who are creators by their very being, find themselves in a quandary.

I created HOLE as a solution.

Rather than distressing about the destructive, and therefore repugnant, act of terminating one's life, they can focus on the creative aspect of making art.

HOLE allows the artist to shift his or her purpose from destruction to creation. Death is no longer the object of the artist's desire. Art is.

To paraphrase something you said, Mr. Victor, "Death, like art, is not the destination. It is the journey."

The apparatus I invented for HOLE allows the artist to direct their effort on making their art, knowing it will be finished in the way he or she intended. Professionals will handle all of the artists' wishes. Details will be meticulously managed. All arrangements will be made ahead of time.

The method, means, and apparatus are new, novel, and much improved over anything existing or used in prior art. If an artist without extraordinary means attempts to achieve a similar outcome by doing it himself or herself, they will not be guaranteed the same level of success.

First, they cannot be sure the weapon they choose will produce the exact result they are looking for; i.e. a clean hole in their art where they would normally sign their work.

Second, they may unknowingly choose an inappropriate location to carry out their operation. This will cause problems for others. Unsuspecting visitors happening upon the scene may thwart the artist's efforts.

Third, the artist will have no control over the final disposition of their most precious work. The piece may be discarded by law enforcement or destroyed by a family member who wants to obliterate the act and the art forever.

HOLE eliminates worry and time wasting. The artist can feel confident knowing their art will be on permanent display in elegant surroundings. Their final statement will be treated with the dignity it deserves for the passion put into it and for the ultimate price paid.

I know many will call this suicide. I think suicide is an ugly word which robs exceptional individuals of respect. The term itself is a label of judgment that blots out who the person was and distorts what they wanted to say. I reject the word and all of its prejudiced meaning.

I do not wish to promote or popularize suicide with HOLE. Many will argue that a reasonable person will see death as the inevitable outcome. To them I say art is the highest purpose of the artist—not their death.

When Michelangelo sculpted his David from solid marble, chips were inevitable, as was the destruction of a huge block of stone, but the piece has been admired and valued for centuries. I doubt anyone grieved over the loss of the stone. Likewise, aside from families and friends, I doubt many will mourn the artist who used HOLE.

I believe there is an artist living within each of us even though most people spend their entire lives pretending to be "normal".

They conform for the sake of appearances, for their children, their spouses, friends, associates, and bosses. They suppress and deny artistic thoughts in their quest for comfort and tranquility. They would rather be ordinary than unsettling.

Art, by its very nature, is disruptive. Many artists choose to live in hiding. Few dare to come out and expose their inner selves to the scrutiny of strangers.

I would like to insert a caveat. HOLE may not be the best solution for everyone. It is intended only for serious artists with full understanding of the finality HOLE brings to their art. When considering HOLE, artists should not allow themselves to be influenced by anyone. They should be guided solely by their own discretion.

ABSTRACT:

To provide a novel and improved method whereby a person can add value to their art by effectively putting their unique signature in the form of an impression or HOLE made by a projectile fired from a specialized device, the projectile having passed through a portion of their body before making contact with said art.

The method is generally described as a means of causing an impression or HOLE in artwork after inflicting gross trauma to the self-internal brain thereby, in most instances, causing immediate loss of consciousness, exsanguination, and rapidly ensuing death; this means self-activated by use of both hands simultaneously without assistance by others.

The Method and Apparatus is more particularly described by the following and Exhibits A and B.

BACKGROUND:

There are many needs not adequately met in society. One is the need to correct mistakes. Many lives are mistakes from the very beginning. They should never have been. Other lives start out well and on a seemingly good path but turn bad along the way. Many cannot be fixed. When appliances are broken beyond repair, we think nothing of discarding them. Because we attach a great deal of sentimental and emotional value to our human lives, we find that to be difficult. Sometimes nearly impossible.

This is understandable. You can always buy another toaster. You cannot buy another you. But you may not want to be another you.

Killing oneself has largely been cast in a negative light. The various religious institutions and governments probably started that kind of thinking. They wanted to have and maintain complete control over their subjects. Allowing the membership to make decisions about their own lives would take away too much of the power they wanted to retain for themselves.

I think each person should be allowed to make that choice. I look at it as a personal responsibility. It is a decision that should be made by someone who wants to remain in charge of their final destiny. I do not see it as weakness or a cowardly act as it is often portrayed. I think it is the exact opposite. I see it as a noble act deserving of dignity and respect.

The weak and cowardly person is one who accepts what is happening to them. The one who suffers with the pain of a terminal disease to the end. The person who struggles with a mental condition that has robbed him of the ability to contribute anything of value to himself or others. Or one who is living a life totally empty and unsatisfying on any level.

In my opinion, no one should be judged on how they came into existence. It is not of their doing. However, they should be able to choose how they exit. That option is not always available, but when it is, people have an obligation to consider it.

I created HOLE to change hearts and minds. I want to make ending one's life relevant. I want to liberate it. To put it on a pedestal. To be uplifting for the human spirit. To make it elegant. To leave a lasting memorial worthy of the act itself.

DESCRIPTION:

Dramatic architectural spaces will vary by design. They will be located in congested cities, rural landscapes, on wooded mountainsides, and in open fields. They will be inviting spaces open to visitors. Inside will hang paintings. Each one will be made by a different artist.

A plaque made of durable material, i.e. stainless steel, polished stone, etc., will hang near each painting. The artist's statement will be etched into the surface. The message can be something special or nothing at all. It can be a letter, a note, a poem, or a word or two. If the artist wishes, their plaque can be blank, or display their name only, or be anonymous. There will be no editing or censoring.

Each artist will make their own painting. The art can be as plain as a freshly painted wall, or as busy as an Impressionist landscape. It can be in any style; graffiti from a New York subway train or the wall of a concrete underpass. Or it can be just a scribble.

All artwork will share one unifying element—a small hole near the lower right corner. It will be their signature, and their work will not hang unless it is signed. The hole will be the result made by the projectile that went through their body and caused instant death. The artist will perform the act themselves in a special room made for only that purpose. No one else will be in the room with them.

PROCESS:

The artist will sit in a special chair. The seat will be kept warm at body temperature and will be pleasant to sit on with or without clothing. The artist's work will hang on a supporting fixture behind them. There will be other art on the walls from artists before. There will be a control panel with speakers, a microphone, and adjustable push button controls for room lights, music, and intercommunication.

The artist can smoke if desired. Using the panel of room controls, they will be able to adjust the lighting, listen to music, and speak to the attendant. The walls will be soundproof and the door will be locked from the inside. No one will be able to enter, but the artist will be able to exit at any time if he or she does not want to finish the process.

When ready, the artist will push the START button, which will bring down a white linen curtain from above. It will surround the artist like a shroud. A pipe-like mechanism on a robotic arm will descend and stop in front of the artist's face. The muzzle will be positioned to aim at the lower right hand portion of the artwork.

The panel will light up, and a pleasant female robotic voice will ask if the person wants to continue or cancel. If they click the CANCEL button, the mechanism will ascend and disappear into the ceiling. The shroud will lift. The room lights will go on, the music will stop, and the artist will be free to leave immediately.

If they click the CONTINUE button, the voice will prompt them to lean forward and put their open mouth over the muzzle. There will be two upright handles on the armrests of the seat. On top of each handle will be a button. The artist will be instructed to hold the handles in each hand. Both buttons will have to be pushed simultaneously. If they let up on either button or back away from the muzzle, there will be no action. The voice will repeat the instructions as many times as necessary until the performance is completed.

There will be no time constraints. There will be plenty of time to think, ponder, and reminisce without being rushed.

IMPORTANT:

Before each step, the artist will be verbally given the option to CANCEL or CONTINUE the process. Many will not have the nerve or will power to carry through to the end. They will be free to leave and return at another time if they choose.

For those who CONTINUE, there will be no further instructions. The art will have been signed, and the door will unlock.

POST-PROCEDURE:

A doctor will enter the room first, check vital signs, and sign the Certificate of Death. A copy will be attached to the Certificate of Authenticity for the art.

The linen shroud will be detached from the ceiling unit and used to carefully wrap the body, which will then be taken to a pre-arranged location.

The room and artwork will be relatively clean. The shroud will contain most of the blood and tissue spatter. The chair seat and base will be thoroughly rinsed with water from a hose. Drains in the seat and floor will allow remaining debris to flow down the drain with the water. A chemical rinse will be applied to remove and destroy any biological residue after the initial water wash.

THE FUTURE OF HOLE:

Laws of supply and demand create value. Prices rise when supply is reduced. If supply becomes a single unit, the price becomes whatever the market will bear and goes to the highest bidder. There may be no limit to how high the price of an artists' work could be driven.

The value of a Van Gogh piece with the distinctive HOLE signature—proof positive it was his last creation—would now be astronomical. Imagine if Hemingway had made a painting for HOLE instead of loading his shotgun. That work today would be tremendously expensive, and highly sought by collectors.

The artist will have pre-designated beneficiaries. If he or she were famous or wealthy before death, the beneficiaries may opt to auction or sell the work, and endow their favorite charity with the earnings.

If the art is auctioned or sold outright, it will be removed from the facility after all commissions and financial obligations are paid. The facility may also act as a gallery or museum, which will also contribute to creating and maintaining personal interest and monetary value for the institution.

Regardless of his or her motivation, there will be one requirement for each artist. They must create their art. It cannot be purchased or something they made prior and brought in from home. It will be mandatory that their final piece be made by them in the HOLE studios.

The reason for this is to clarify and verify that the artist is sure about their decision to use HOLE. The artist will have no choice but to interrogate themselves and second guess their choice while creating the last and most meaningful art of their life.

The shattered girl whose fiancée left her at the altar will not be able to off herself on that night. She will have to work in the studio first and create her art. She may discover talent she never knew she had. She may decide that her life does have value, and that she doesn't need a man's attention to justify her existence. She may suddenly want a life all her own, and then walk out the door and never look back.

COST:

There will be a fee to consider. It will be discussed and agreed upon by the artist and the attending HOLE Administrator before the art is made or any other process begins.

The studio will not be considered a cheap way out of life. The HOLE process will advocate a solution for those who have considered all other options. HOLE is particularly tailored for people living with incurable mental or physical pain, paralysis, terminal illnesses, dementia, etc. It is for people who wish to free their loved ones from being financially ruined from their ongoing hospital bills, medical costs, and nursing home facility expenses. Old folks who want to preserve their dignity in death by foregoing years of bedsores, diapers, and other elderly deteriorations, might choose to paint an apple. Or a pet or a favorite food. Gutsy Grandma will go out with a bang and inspire for years.

MY FINAL NOTE:

There is no question it will take guts to choose this option. Having that cold piece of steel in your mouth will be a grim reminder of the finality you are face to face with. It could be a deal breaker for those who come with the strongest intentions.

You will have to summon strength you never thought existed, and find courage you never knew you had.

But courage is not reserved for comic book superheroes. And it's not found in people. Or in places. Until that needful moment when it shows up.

Celia Bauer

Mr. Victor gathered up the typewritten pages, set them aside, and began to examine the illustration boards.

Chapter 15

The drawing marked as Exhibit A was an illustration of the machinery of HOLE. It was a chilling presentation in graphic detail depicting the gruesome invention.

He studied the drawing with revulsion and detached fascination. It was difficult to imagine that it could have been Celia's brainchild.

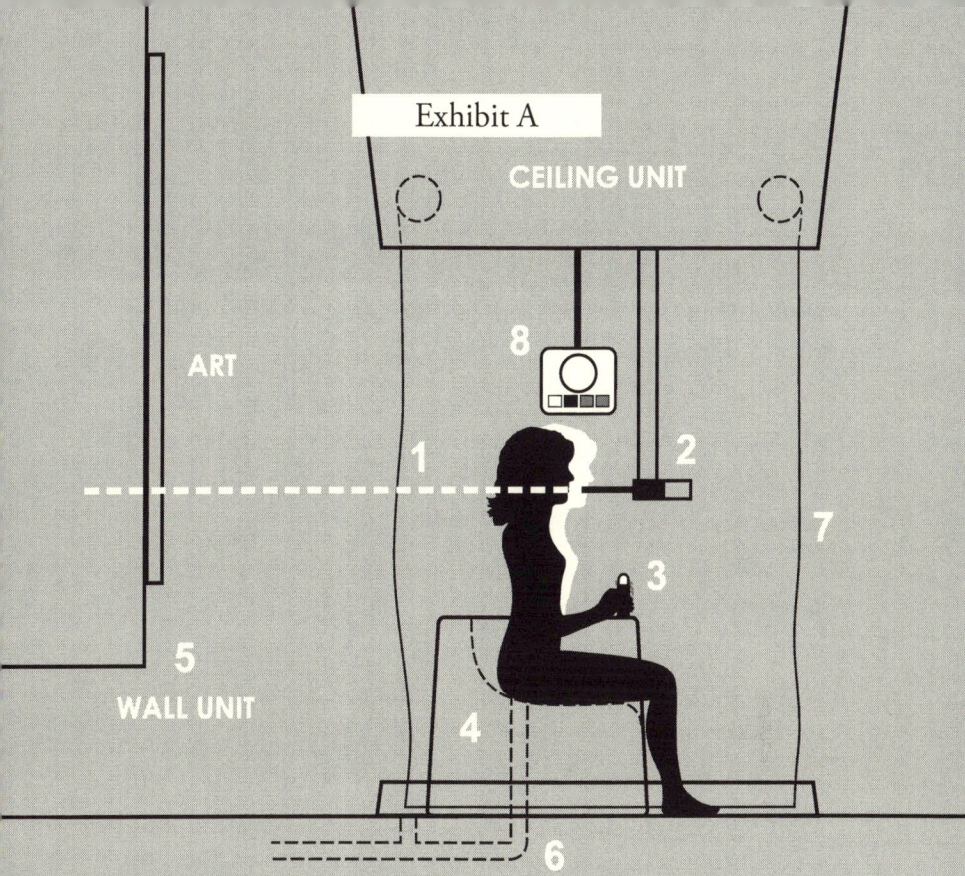

Exhibit B hit him hard. Suddenly there was a connection. But more than that, it was an indictment. Celia had used *his* words and ideas as part of her HOLE concept. His story was enmeshed with hers. The illustration was the certificate—proof that he had caused, or at least contributed, to Celia's death.

The watercolor illustration showed a plan, an elevation, and an isometric projection. It was similar to an in-ground pool. Three equal walls met in mitered corners to form a perfect equilateral triangle—*his triangle*.

The cast concrete walls rose out of the ground about twenty inches and were capped with polished granite. It was a good height for a seating bench around the pool. With names engraved on its surface, it would be an enduring, elegant memorial to the departed.

SOURCE, SYSTEM, and EXPRESSION—*his words*—were etched on the corner capstones. One word at each corner reading counter-clockwise in that order. On the floor of the pool was a circular well about ten feet in diameter. With a few inches of water over the triangular floor, the round recessed area would look like an underwater black hole—*his description of the HOLE in the Universe*.

About three feet below the top were horizontal rows of bronze tubes sticking out of the vertical inner walls, each about a foot long and spaced two feet apart. They looked like gun barrels. Water would flow from the tubes and fall in an arc to the pool below.

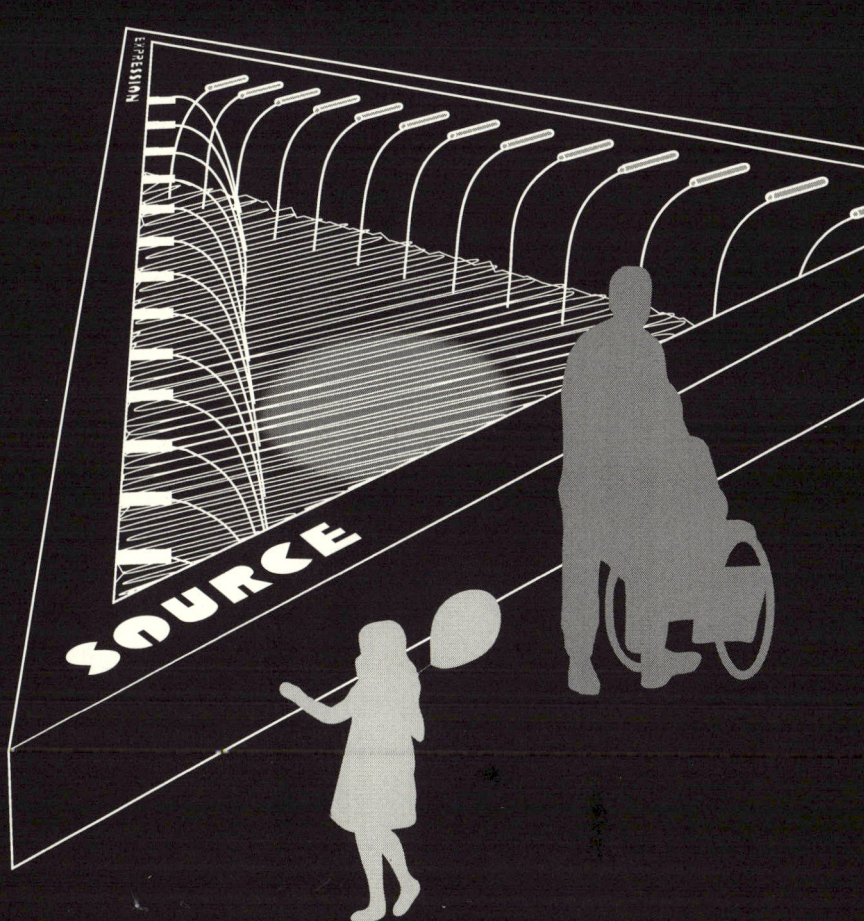

He placed the pages, illustration boards, and Celia's cover letter back into the portfolio, tied the string closure, and slid it back into the carton marked with Celia's URGENT request.

He didn't see the note attached to the small white envelope stuck in the bottom of the corrugated container. Handwritten on the envelope was:

Please give to Luke.

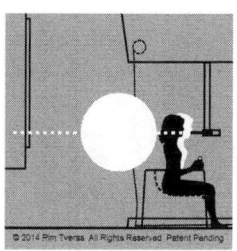

HOLE: Part Two

Chapter 16
Vienna, Austria 1944

"Lukuti, čia Viena," said my mother in our native Lithuanian language. Lukuti was an affectionate term for Lukas. Her words meant, "Little Luke, this is Vienna."

I was a blond, blue-eyed four year old in the summer of 1944. My mother and father carried three suitcases, a briefcase, a purse, and me off the train. That was all we could take because that was all we could carry; fleeing from our country—trying to save our lives.

As we stood on the platform, an old woman walked by and said, "Verfluchte Ausländer," in a language I didn't understand. I saw hurt and tears in my mother's eyes. My father wrapped his arms around her and kissed her. "Nu, Lialia, Lialia, neklausyk tai durnai bobai." He said to ignore the stupid woman.

My mother was thirty-two with kind Baltic blue eyes and thick, wavy chestnut hair—without a doubt, the most beautiful woman in the world.

My dad was forty-one, dark haired, and handsome. He had told us the Americans and the British were bombing factories and military installations all over Europe, but not civilian cities. And certainly not Vienna, the centuries-old center of art, music, science and culture for all of Europe. He said we'd be safe there.

It was nighttime when we first heard the sirens. They were loud and the wailing went on and on forever. My mother said not to worry when my dad scooped me up from the bed. It was just a practice alert.

I felt his breath on my cheek as he ran down the long hallway, holding me tightly in his arms, my mother at his side. The stairs were jammed with people. They were pushing their way out of the building, headed for a stairway that went under the street.

In the cellar, a man stood reciting to a small group surrounding him. After a sentence or two, he paused, and his audience repeated his words in unison. When the walls trembled, his speech became frantic. He was shouting.

"Pupuliuk, the man is praying," said my mother. Pupuliuk meant "little bean".

I didn't know what he was saying or why he was praying. In the dim yellow light, I saw men, women, and children clutching each other. I heard whimpers and cries but didn't know why they were crying. My mother and dad weren't crying. I felt safe and warm as they held each other with me squeezed in the middle.

"Those are potatoes falling into a root cellar," my mother said when we felt tremors. She was smiling, but

I knew it was just a story she had made up so I wouldn't be afraid.

I heard sirens again—long, shrill, and steady. After they had stopped, the sound kept ringing in my ears. People stirred, gathering their things, and we all filed out through the single exit.

Outside, the street was strewn with bricks and dirt. Through the smoke, I saw fires in the distance. I didn't think they were practicing, but I wasn't worried.

Back in our room, I watched my mother take a dainty handkerchief wrapped around a small bar of scented soap from her purse. She dampened the cloth, rubbed it on the sweet soap, and gently wiped my face.

My mother's purse was magical. I watched her slender fingers work the purse clasp. I waited to hear the click when it opened, and to sniff that special soapy smell I knew so well—my mother's scent. It let me know everything was going to be all right.

Air raid alarms went off every other night. We slept fully dressed in our socks, shoes, and overcoats, huddled together in our single bed in our cold room in the Pension Pohl—ready to run at the first sound of the sirens.

In early spring, we moved to a farm near the village of Weixerau in Southern Bavaria.

Chapter 17
Weixerau, Bavaria 1945

Green fields were sprinkled with tall red poppies and bright blue cornflowers. Flying and climbing insects inspected wildflowers and weeds. A bumblebee crash-landed into a gangly yellow buttercup and tugged it down. It sprang up easily after the heavy visitor departed.

On the ground, tiny animations scurried over open dirt patches and blobs of twiggy leaves and brush. Caterpillars crawled, crickets jumped, and beetles ran, disappearing and reappearing in and out of tunnels and spaces—a world of fables and fantasies.

Ants gathered food, packing it away in their cellars while grasshoppers fiddled around outside, enjoying the sun, squandering summer's gifts, missing opportunities. They would learn their lesson when winter brought starvation and regret. That's what my mother had told me.

A creek meandered through the meadow. Dragonflies flitted over the water, their see-through wings flashing in the sun; bodies glistening with iridescent blues, greens, and reds.

I lay on my stomach in the deep, soft grass gazing into the watery world as the bright sun illuminated life underneath. Long leafy vines swayed in the currents. Minnows darted, tadpoles kicked, and snails slid over the stony bottom.

I dipped my hand in the stream. It was warm and tickled as it flowed over my fingers. I lifted a golden snail out of the water and placed it on my arm. It must have been afraid because it didn't move. After a while, it moved its strange eyeballed tentacles—retracting, extending, curling, and bending. I studied the fantastic creature, then put it back exactly where I'd found it.

"We must thank Jesus for keeping us safe and ask him to continue watching over us, Lukuti."

My mother showed me a small gilt-edged picture of Jesus she kept inside a miniature prayer book.

"Why is his hair long, Mamyte?"

"Nu, that is how men wore their hair. Jesus was here a long, long time ago."

Jesus was an unshaven man with light blue eyes and wavy blond hair that was longer than my mother's. A ring of golden light floated behind his head. He was pointing to an object in front of his chest. It looked like a burning cross on a heart wrapped with a thorny vine. It was dripping blood.

"What is that, Mamyte?"

"That is Jesus' heart, pupuliuk."

"Why is that awful thing wrapped around his heart?"

"It is because his heart hurts. Many people are bad. That is why Jesus' heart hurts."

"Does your heart hurt too, Mamyte?"

"Sometimes it does. But do not worry, Lukuti."

Every night my mother knelt beside our bed and whispered to Jesus. She said it was important for me to do the same. I didn't even have to speak. I could think the words and Jesus would hear me.

I didn't know how Jesus could hear me talking or thinking. I didn't understand why I should kneel when I couldn't even see Him. He probably couldn't see me either, but I did what my mother asked.

After a while, talking to Jesus didn't feel weird. I believed that He heard me every night. I could almost see Him sitting on the other side of our bed, and I knew He would still be there after I drifted off to sleep.

My mother explained that when Jesus was young, His parents, Joseph and Mary, had taken Him and fled their country to seek shelter in an angry, foreign land. They had left their home and everything else behind just like we had.

"Nu, you know, Lukuti, people were not always kind. They told them they had no room. Maybe they should go back to where they came from. They could only sleep in the barn with the animals.

"There was one nice man who let Jesus stay in his house—like our Mr. Schohner. We are living here because Mr. Schohner wanted to help us. It is because of you, pupyte. If you were not with us, I am sure he would have turned your father and me away."

She held my face tenderly with her soft hands and kissed me. She pulled back and looked into my eyes.

"Pupuliuk, there is a place called Heaven. It is far away, high up in the sky past the sun and the moon and the stars. Jesus is there. So is Algytis." She started to cry after she said my little brother's name.

"You can talk to him, too, mano mažyti." Mano mažyti meant "my little one".

"Algytis will hear you like Jesus hears you," she whispered and ended her words with a smile and more kisses—the way she always did.

I didn't understand how Algytis and Jesus could be in Heaven and hear me, but I believed it.

My mother said Jesus was my special connection to Heaven, but I began to think of Jesus more like a space between my world and me. It seemed the more I thought about Jesus, the less I cared about the world all around me.

The war ended that summer. We stayed on the farm through the following winter, and in the spring we moved to Landshut, a town about ten kilometers to the east.

Chapter 18
Landshut, Bavaria 1946

The Displaced Persons camp in Landshut was a group of four apartment buildings surrounding a courtyard. The Lithuanians were the largest group of DP's and were housed in the longest east building. The Ukrainians occupied the west, and the Latvians were in the north. The south building was used for storing food and supplies and had rooms for classes and activities.

One man in our camp rarely spoke. He was a strange sight to my eight-year-old eyes. He had long black hair and always looked like he needed to shave. He shunned people and avoided conversations. Some parents told their children to keep their distance—maybe he was dangerous.

He constantly smoked, and the fingernails on his left hand were stained in shades of yellow, orange, and brown. His dark eyes glowed like his smoldering cigarettes. When he looked my way, they seemed to burn right through me.

His name was Petras Viktaravičius.

There were about three hundred Lithuanians in our camp, but I think I was the only one who talked to him. Once, he gave me some paper and a set of watercolor paints in a small black metal box. Another time, he taught me how to use my pocket knife to make a whistle from a freshly cut willow branch.

He never had much to say except, "It is not like you think it is."

"What is not like I think, Pone Viktaravičiau?"

"Nothing is like you think, my son."

"My son" was an expression many older people used when talking to boys or younger men, but it had an odd ring to it when he said it to me. He sounded as though he was talking to his own son, but I never thought to ask Mr. Viktaravičius if he had a family.

The United Nations Relief and Rehabilitation Administration supplied our camp with food, cigarettes, blankets, candles, and thousands of flannel ear-warmers. The women discovered they could make their wood floors shiny and beautiful by rubbing them with the sides of the candles and buffing them with the ear warmers.

Some adults attended classes for language and other skills to prepare them for life in the USA. My mother trained to become a Certified Seamstress. She received a diploma with her name neatly hand-lettered in light blue ink.

The Americans appointed my dad the official Food Service Supervisor for our camp. I think it was because he was a colonel in the Lithuanian army and had executive skills. He was in charge of rationing food to families.

The women in camp held a catechism class in our storage building. One woman was a nun so she really knew what she was talking about.

They taught us about God, Jesus and Mary, souls and saints, angels and devils, and Heaven and Hell. They talked a lot about sins. They said I wasn't good—that I was born with sin. Original Sin was the permanent stain on my soul left by Adam and Eve when they had disobeyed God.

The nun said Confession would remove my sins and leave my soul clean. If I died, my soul would go straight to Heaven. I couldn't wait to be old enough to go to Confession and receive my First Holy Communion.

My friend and I became altar boys. We set up a cardboard box in his apartment and pretended it was an altar. He had a book with the priest's words and our responses written in Latin. We learned the words and the moves needed to assist the priest in serving Mass.

I didn't feel the changes as they happened. I had forgotten that I had been an ant, a horse, and a dragonfly; that I had lived in the pond as a frog, crawled up the banks as a turtle, ran as a rabbit, and circled high in the sky as a hawk.

I only thought of myself as *me*.

I had a soul that made me special, different, and better than all the animals. I would live as Lukas, and after I died, my soul would go to Heaven to live forever with God, Jesus, Mary, and the angels.

My life had taken on new purpose and meaning. I

was put on Earth to serve God, live according to His will, ask Him to feed me daily, beg Him to forgive me for my failings and discourage me from doing bad things, and hope He would keep me away from all evil.

That was my new world, one I had never seen or imagined, but it became the only world. The world I had once felt a part of—the one filled with awe and amazement—was gone.

Chapter 19

A short walk away was a US Army camp filled with new wonderments—all Made in America.

I think the soldiers knew we were from the DP camp. They smiled as my friend and I approached the gate. They didn't speak Lithuanian, but we communicated well enough with body movements and hand gestures. They invited us in and gave us chocolate and chewing gum. Even better—they let us rummage through their garbage dump and take whatever we wanted.

It was the gateway to mind-boggling treasures—current issues of American magazines and comic books. We grabbed as much as we could carry and lugged it all home. It didn't take long for the other kids to find out about our newly discovered gold mine.

Competition became fierce. Our parents didn't allow us to go alone, and when five of us went it was awful. We ended up squabbling like crows over a dead mouse, so we made a plan. Rather than fighting over who saw what book first, risking grabbing and tearing pages, we agreed to go in pairs. We chose partners with dissimilar interests. I found a friend who liked superheroes and *Archie,* and didn't care for *Walt Disney's Comics* or *Red Ryder*—my favorites. As our collections grew, we filled in missing issues by trading.

None of us knew what the word balloons meant, so our imaginations invented the stories. I had an advantage. My mother was learning English and was able to translate some of the dialogue. Thanks to her and Walt Disney, I learned many words and phrases. American comics were the founders of my English language.

From American magazines, I learned about World War II aviation. I was already very good at drawing. In no time at all I was drawing and painting B-17 Flying Fortresses, P-51 Mustangs, RAF Spitfires, German Me 109's, Japanese Zeros, and even the curvy Consolidated Catalina PBY Flying Boat.

Another dumpster treasure was readily found on American food cans. They were decorated with the world's most beautiful labels. We saved the colorful paper wrappers from the empty cans and used our mothers' scissors to trim out the images.

Fish, cows, strawberries, tomatoes, corn, cherries, peas, and plums became our currency. To us, it was better than cash. We based value on beauty, condition, and rarity. A shiny, gold-embossed image of *Elkay Red Alaska Sockeye Salmon* might have ten times more purchasing power than the dull red *Fern Park Tomatoes.*

Then something unbelievable happened: American soldiers began showing movies in our storage building.

I sat beside the projector man and watched him take a reel of film out of a can and thread it into the machine. When he turned it on, the screen came to life. It painted in vivid black and white light, action, and sound, the fantastic land where cowboys and Indians roamed.

On October 18, 1950, my parents and I boarded the US troop ship General Black in the seaport of Bremerhaven, Germany. I was thrilled. We were finally bound for New York, USA.

Soon I would be in the land of Donald Duck, Mickey Mouse, Hopalong Cassidy, Red Ryder and Little Beaver, The Lone Ranger and Tonto, the Daisy Official Red Ryder BB guns, Hershey's Chocolate, Wrigley's Doublemint Gum, Coca-Cola, and beautiful, delicious American food.

Chapter 20
Chicago, Illinois 1950

He who writes on shithouse walls
  Rolls his shit in little balls
  He who reads these words of wit
  Eats the little balls of shit

Boys' Bathroom
Nativity of the Blessed Virgin Mary
Unknown Author

Nativity was the first school I attended in America. It was run by the Sisters of Saint Casimir, an order of Lithuanian Catholic nuns. It was right across the street from our apartment on the corner of Sixty-Eighth Street and Washtenaw Avenue.

The three-story brown brick school building stood like a factory with its tall, steel-framed windows. The parish church was inside the same building. I smelled floor wax and incense as my mother and I walked through the silent halls looking for the principal's office.

It was grey and chilly in November when Sister Mary Francetta introduced me to her second grade class. I was almost eleven years old and should have at least been in fifth grade, but the nuns thought it would be better to place me in the lower grades first, and promote me as I learned English.

Some of the kids came right up to make friends. Others kept their distance, gawking at my wool shorts, knee socks, sandals, and suspenders. I was four years older and a head taller than everyone else, wearing shorts two weeks before Thanksgiving. After a few snickers on the first day, most of them turned out to be good sports.

Two girls were especially eager to teach me how to speak English. They couldn't wait to tell me a new word, jumping in front of each other, trying to steal my attention away from each other. They pointed to objects in the room, pictures on the walls, and to parts of their bodies. Getting a strange large boy to mimic sounds correctly must have been pretty exciting for them, and Sister Mary Francetta was pleased with our progress.

Girl, eye, hair, hand, desk, map, flag, Jesus, angel, Mary, Indian, pilgrim, cross, corn, and pumpkin were words I learned fast. One of the girls said "turkey" and showed me a crayon drawing pinned on the wall. I knew that couldn't be right. Turkey was a country, not a bird. Maybe the girl didn't know what she was talking about, but her friend said yes, yes, yes—she was right. I wondered if there was a shortage of words in America.

By springtime, I was moved to sixth grade where I belonged. By seventh grade, I had my first kiss with Indre. She made the first move and excited me in a new way I had never felt before. Later, she became Duke's girlfriend, but I never forgot the kiss.

I remember when my dad quit his job as Clockmaker at Marshall Field & Company and started a watch repair service in our apartment. He'd assured my mother and me that growing a small business of our own was a far better idea than working for someone else.

I was twelve when my dad gave me an old Elgin pocket watch to disassemble. I had no trouble taking it apart. Unfortunately, he had to help me reassemble it because I couldn't figure out how to put it back together.

As I sharpened my skills, my dad set up my own watchmaker's workbench next to his. Every day after school, I spent a few hours working with my father as a professional Watch Repair Technician. As we worked, we listened to classical music on station WFMT on our new Zenith FM radio.

It wasn't hard work, but I was weighed down with heavy responsibility. I worried about every watch I repaired—praying it would run perfectly—hoping the customer would return with more business—wishing they'd spread the word about our fast service and low prices.

My friends never understood what I was experiencing. From their part-time jobs, they went straight to the park and played cards. They lived carefree lives like the grasshoppers while I worked and worried about the survival of my family's business.

I may not have had it the easiest, but I certainly had it the best. I loved my life in America, fully realizing that my loving, hard working, and very uncommon parents had made it all possible.

Chapter 21
Navy Pier, Chicago 1958

The University of Illinois at Navy Pier was the college of choice for me, but it wasn't my choosing. It was the state school, a commuter inner city school, and the only college my parents could afford. It was chosen by Necessity—the evil goddess of need—forcing me to dash my dreams, alter my plans, lower my expectations, and settle for seconds. She callously sweated my brow while grinding my greatness into the dirt with her fickle foot.

Navy Pier was never meant to be a school. It had been built as a dock on Lake Michigan to bring in ship-borne commerce and provide entertainment to the bustling city of Chicago. During World War II, the US Navy built double rows of classrooms in the north terminal building that stretched over a half mile into the lake. They used it to train aircraft mechanics, machinists, and carrier pilots.

After the war, the classrooms with the three thousand foot long corridor began their new life as the Chicago

Campus of the University of Illinois.

I enrolled in Architecture. As an architect, I could use my drawing skills, although I wasn't especially interested in buildings. My preference was to draw military aircraft, but I needed a real profession—something I could build into a career with a decent income. Fixing watches and drawing airplanes wasn't going to cut it.

I studied the map in the registration booklet in search of my Architecture 101 classroom. It was at the far end of the pier on the second floor above the student cafeteria.

The room was spacious with good lighting and huge windows looking out onto Lake Michigan. Drawing tables were covered with doodles, writings, cuts, scratches, pinholes, masking tape, and ink stains. Tall metal stools were scattered between the tables. Some kids sat and smoked. Others strolled around, smoking, sizing up the competition.

I was amazed that smoking was allowed in class. At Saint Rita High School, smoking had been strictly forbidden in, or even within, sight of the school. It was an all boys school run by Augustinian priests who believed that physical pain and deprivation were a necessary part of teaching and learning.

I remember being called into the Student Counselor's office after I was caught smoking behind the football stands. Father McArdle clutched my shirt with both hands as he pummelled sense into my rib cage. He pulled me to him and then punched me away like a paddle ball, never letting go of my shirt. He used his massive fists for punctuation. Commas were light hits, periods were heavier. Exclamation points and question marks were breath-stopping, bone-bruising wallops.

Goodbye, Saint Rita. It's been a real slice.

I counted thirteen students: three girls and ten boys, including myself. They had long hair, medium hair, and crew cuts. Some guys were clean-shaven. Others were trying to grow moustaches, goatees, and sideburns. There were blue jeans, tee shirts, sweaters, windbreakers, suit jackets, Army jackets, and even a full suit with tie.

Under the tables were street shoes, sneakers, loafers, wedges, moccasins, sandals, and motorcycle boots—with and without socks.

I wondered why the girls were there. I had never heard of a woman architect. They must have enrolled in the Liberal Arts program and chose the drawing course as an elective.

I wore a blue poplin dress shirt, grey Sears and Roebuck slacks, brown leather shoes, and a tweed sport jacket.

James Dean had worn a jacket and tie on his first day of high school. My friends said I looked a lot like him. After I saw him in *Rebel Without a Cause*, I knew what they meant. Emma, my girlfriend, had even called me "Jim" after we left the show.

Well then, there now.

Unlike me, Jim came from a dysfunctional home. Even through the wartime years, my family life was stable and loving. I hadn't suffered teenaged angst like Jim.

Hollywood wanted us to believe every parent was incompetent, and every young person was a victim. What

I'd taken away from the movie was an affirmation of my good looks and a desire to own a car like Jim's black Mercury Coupe. I wished my dad had bought us one of those aging beauties after the Buick expired instead of the almost new, three year old Ford.

This must be what college is all about—learning, freedom, and smoking.

I took out a Lucky, fired up my Zippo, and lit up.

Chapter 22

I stared at my class schedule. It was ugly. Classes that could have easily been packed into a three day week were scattered across all five like a gap-toothed, grinning idiot. Except I was the idiot who'd registered.

I was in the Art 112 room. It was the same room I had been in the day before for Architecture 101. I found the same stool I'd used twenty-four hours earlier. I noticed the other students did the same. It was as though we'd made friends with our stools, desks, and workbenches. Maybe we came back to them out of loyalty. Or habit. Or returning to our places on the planet. Or some other stupid reason.

At 9:05 a.m., the instructor still hadn't come in. Some of the students were studying a notice tacked to a bulletin board. I dragged on my cigarette and sauntered over to take a look.

It was a printout of the class. There I was: Lukas

Norkus. Then I saw the instructor's name—

I couldn't believe it. It had to be him. How many people could be named Petras Viktaravičius?

I hadn't seen him since Landshut, and I never thought I'd see him again. I was surprised to learn he was an artist, but to imagine him as my teacher ten years later in America—Chicago, no less—was dumbfounding.

I watched his eyes scan the room as he walked in at 9:10 a.m.. There was no cigarette dangling from his mouth, and he looked much younger than I'd remembered. He was clean-shaven and wore a black suit. His hair was long but neatly braided down his back. He had a narrow, bright red wool tie over a grey denim work shirt. His shoes were Converse Star gym shoes, the kind the Harlem Globetrotters wore while showing off their basketball antics timed to the whistled tune of *Sweet Georgia Brown*.

His eyes stopped on my face. I was amazed that he recognized me. He smiled instantly, then walked up to the blackboard and wrote: Art 112—Petras Viktaravičius.

"You may call me Mr. Victor," he said to the class, and began to describe the nature of the course.

That was the first time I heard him speak English, and the first time I heard the name Mr. Victor. His accent wasn't as heavy as my parents' but was quite evident. His sentence structure also set him apart from Americans—he didn't use contractions.

After Mr. Victor dismissed the class, he walked over to me.

"Labas, Lukai," he said.

"Labas, Pone Viktaravičiau," I replied.

"Labas" meant "Hello". "Pone" meant "Mister".

My birth name was Lukas Norkus; Mr. Victor's was Petras Viktaravičius. Like many immigrants, we had simplified our names to make them more easily pronounceable and indistinguishable from the native population, sort of. With a slight modification, I became Luke Norkus. He'd gone whole hog when he made up Peter Victor. Our school registrations were recorded in our ancestral names. We wouldn't have recognized each other otherwise.

We shared a big hug. There was no time for a longer reunion. I had ten minutes to run a half mile back down the corridor to Rhetoric 101—not an easy trip, running and elbowing through the crowded corridor.

As we separated, I didn't see the burning cigarettes in the hollows of Mr. Victor's eyes. I saw tears.

Chapter 23

By semester's end, I was one of Mr. Victor's best students. It wasn't because he'd known me from camp or because we shared the same nationality. It wasn't even because I was exceptionally talented.

From the time I was a young boy, I was trained to work hard. My dad had taught me that it mattered. Not only was it necessary for getting ahead—sometimes it was needed for survival. My work ethic fit right in with what Mr. Victor was teaching.

He told the class that talent wasn't measurable, and more importantly—that it didn't matter. He said what could be seen was effort, what could be evaluated was performance, and what could be felt was passion.

He never failed to make a memorable impression on the class when he ripped a student's sketch out of their drawing pad and threw it on the floor.

"This is shit! You are not using your arm as I taught

you. You are drawing from your wrist and your fingers. You are making noodle soup. When you draw from your arm, you are teaching your body to follow your eye and your brain. Your long muscles are learning. When you make sweeping motions, you can begin to control them."

We got his point after he had us draw a cube in perspective—in thirty seconds. There was no way we could do that by noodling.

When a student grasped the concept, Mr. Victor held up their drawing to the class, inviting everyone to view the work. He always made sure those who worked hard were recognized and rewarded.

"This is not a course designed to teach art. That is only what they call it in the catalog. It is about learning how to draw. Everyone here can learn to draw. It is a skill that is attained by doing."

He watched the faces waiting for an explanation. "There is no art taught in Art 112 or in this school or in the world, people.

"Art cannot be taught. Art is something that can be achieved, but only by those willing to put all of their passion, skills, and effort into it. You must stretch beyond your reach, push past your bounds, work harder than you ever expected—and never believe what you create is art."

I didn't understand what he meant. I don't think anyone else did either.

Mr. Victor and I grew to know each other well as the year went on. The school cafeteria was right below Art 112, which made it convenient to meet for snacks and chats during breaks and after classes. In the spring, we watched seagulls through the windows while we ate, drank coffee, smoked, and talked.

He asked me why I chose Architecture and if I had considered Industrial Design. He said he was a designer, not an architect.

He went on to explain that design was similar to architecture but not restricted to buildings. Artistic skills were necessary to create everything from automobiles to furniture to toys to toasters.

That was it—the fertile field where I would sow my restless creative seeds. I decided to switch my major to Industrial Design. I'd have to forfeit a few hard-earned credit hours in Architecture, but I felt the loss was worthy. It was a small price to pay for admission into the brave new world of Industrial Design.

Near the end of the semester, Mr. Victor asked me if I would like to work for him part time in his new home and studio.

"Of course I would! Yes! Thank you very much for the opportunity."

"Do not thank me, Luke. It is nothing. You can try it and see if you will like it. I will see you Tuesday. Yes?"

"I'll be there, Mr. Victor."

Chapter 24

I realized I had missed my turn at Larrabee when I saw the Halsted Street sign. I turned right on Halsted and after a few blocks, found Laurel on my right. Victorian era homes with ornate decoration and leaded glass windows lined the narrow street. The cobblestone pavement was straight out of a Dickens novel. I thought my car would shake itself apart before I reached Ash Street.

The building on the left fit the description. I parked and went around to the front door. It was unlocked.

As soon as I stepped in, a big brown dog came bouncing down a long wooden stairway. It was happy and panted in appreciation as I scratched and rubbed its floppy ears.

"Labas, Lukai," I heard from the top of the stairs.

"Labas, Pone Viktaravičiau."

"It looks like you and Nixon have already met. Come upstairs, Luke. I will show you the apartment. Be careful on the steps. It is a good idea to use the handrail."

Mr. Victor switched to English after his initial salutation. It was consistent with the way many Lithuanians greeted each other, and it was done instinctively.

I smelled paint, plaster, and freshly cut wood. The steps were covered in a layer of sawdust. Nixon was already at the top when I started climbing. He left swirls and a hazy white cloud in his wake.

The upstairs door led to a spacious living room facing Laurel Street. Heavy black lines were drawn above the traditional curved archway leading to the dining room and kitchen. They marked where changes were to be made. The opening was destined to be rectangular and modern.

Further in were three bedrooms, a bathroom, and another room with windows and a door leading to a flat roof. All the walls and ceilings were painted white. There were no baseboards, door jambs, or window trim; their edges had been replaced with crisp metal corners. Big white glass globes hung from the living and dining room ceilings. The apartment had the sterile look of a modern art gallery being readied for its opening.

He went into the kitchen and poured coffee from an aluminum percolator into two heavy white mugs. He added milk to one. He knew how I liked my coffee from our chats in the school cafeteria.

"Who else lives here, Mr. Victor?"

"Only Nixon."

"How long have you had this place?"

"It is my third year here. As you can see, I have not done very much. It is hard to get things done without help. Now that you are here, we can make progress."

"This is really nice."

"You are looking through the eyes of a designer focused on a future vision, Luke. The building is not usable. I will agree it is going to be a good place to live and work. Come. Let us go downstairs, yes?"

I felt newly finished concrete under my feet. Stacks of construction lumber and wallboard were piled up near one end of the huge space.

Mr. Victor gave me a brief overview of his intended plan for the studio. I'd never done that kind of work, but he said it would be fun.

"We will be learning together, Luke."

Juggling my work hours between school and my watch repair job at home, I learned how to use power tools, finish walls, build furniture, and do plumbing and electrical work. Mr. Victor taught me to lay brick and glass block, filling in three large door openings that had originally been built for trucks.

We painted everything white. I hung fluorescent lighting and built four large worktables and six art easels similar to those in the Art 112 classroom. Mr. Victor brought in stools, lockers, and three huge slate blackboards from a public school that was being torn down by the city.

We mounted the blackboards side by side on the long wall and added an inviting conversation cluster with two black futons, three tomato red Herman Miller chairs, and a paper Noguchi lamp on a low glass table.

To complete the studio, we set up two drawing tables and a cabinet for storing flat art.

Mr. Victor and I worked side-by-side—like master and apprentice—as he taught me graphic design. By the start of summer, he was ready to invite students into his new Laurel Street studio.

Chapter 25
Navy Pier, Chicago 1960

"Honestly, if I had to live there one more day, I'd have lost my fucking mind!" Sara vented to her classmate.

By the time she had enrolled in the University of Illinois' Foundation Art Program, she had bailed from her life as the daughter of a conservative Circuit Court Judge and his loyal wife.

"They made me attend their dinner parties. They made me play my cello for their guests. They put me on display like some fucking Shirley Temple imitation." She dragged long on her Marlboro.

"I love my parents—I really do. But they wanted me to go into law or medicine or even something as fucked up as the pharmaceutical industry." She studied the cigarette in her hand, rolling it between her fingers.

"They didn't understand me at all. I don't think they'll ever really know who I am." Sara squinted as she took the last drag, and crushed her cigarette in the ashtray.

"It's like we're from different planets. I was fucking suffocating."

Her classmate listened and understood perfectly. The life of a princess wasn't all it was cracked up to be.

Sara's parents had always stressed the need for education and cultural development. It had been their life mission to raise a successful, well rounded, well educated, only daughter. By the time she was in second grade at the North Shore Jewish Day School, a private school for exceptionally fortunate children, the sounds of her half-sized cello filled her fine home.

There were no sounds from television. The Steinbergs believed that the idiot box offered nothing of value to their precocious child. Dostoyevsky and Tolstoy were familiar names. Sara had never heard of Lucille Ball or Dick Van Dyke.

Her father was Chief Judge Seymore B. Steinberg, an influential figure in the state of Illinois. Her mother had been in charge of everything else in Sara's life, including the nurturing of love and respect for her parents.

"Daddy? What is daddy? Oy, oy, oy. We do not use *that word* in this house, my darling. We say 'Father'."

Mrs. Steinberg never made capricious claims. Her requests were logical and simply stated. "Daddy is what those *other children* say. They do not have fathers like *your* Father."

The Steinbergs had the means and intention to send Sara to the University of Chicago for medicine, or to Loyola for law, or even to the nearby Northwestern

University School of Pharmacy, but Sara would have none of that. She was going to be an artist.

Her parents had no choice but to back off. After years of dedicated effort, they had to accept a bitter reality: they didn't know their daughter at all.

Sara left her family, childhood friends, neighborhood, comfortable home, wardrobe, and her cello. She refused to suck up to her folks to get the shiny new high school graduation Jag or Benz like some of her brown-nosing schoolmates. She left carrying a suitcase, her art, and her integrity.

As her final declaration of independence, Sara cut off her beautiful long hair and changed her name. The name on her birth certificate was Sarah Zaina Steinberg. Her new artist name would be Sara Stein. She moved into a tiny two-room apartment in Old Town, a short walk to Mr. Victor's home and studio.

She was barefoot when Mr. Victor found her sitting on the stone stoop of his front door. The soles of her feet were black from the hot, dirty Chicago sidewalks.

"Hello, Sara. Are you here to see me?" He knew her from his drawing class at the university.

"I need to talk to you, Mr. Victor. Is this a bad time?"

"No, no. Let us go inside."

He unlocked his front door, and they were immediately greeted by Nixon. He almost knocked her over when he jumped up to lick her face. Mr. Victor started to reach for Nixon's collar, but Sara stopped him. She welcomed the animal's affection.

"I have a problem."

"What can I do to help?"

"My landlord hiked up the rent last month, and my roommate moved out. I can't afford to stay there any longer."

"Do you need money?"

"Oh, no, no. I don't want to borrow money. I wanted to ask if I could crash in your studio. Somewhere out of the way, like a broom closet, or maybe in the basement. It would only be for a few days until I get a job and find another place to live."

"There are extra rooms upstairs, but do you need to get permission from your parents?"

"Oh, I turned eighteen last spring, Mr. Victor, but I'd rather stay downstairs. I don't want to impose."

She glanced up. "I'm usually only around at night. I promise I'll stay out of your way. You won't even know I'm here."

Mr. Victor smiled. If Sara could have read his thoughts, she would have seen three little words—one of Mr. Victor's pet expressions: *Only in America.*

"That sounds fine to me, Sara."

Without further discussion, Mr. Victor, Sara, and Nixon piled into his red and grey Volkswagen Micro Bus and drove to her apartment to get her things. They returned with one suitcase and a zippered artist portfolio.

Chapter 26

"Hi, I'm Sara," she said, extending her hand over my drawing board. "You must be Luke."

I nodded and took her hand. It was cool and dry and didn't feel like a girl's hand. Her fingers were slender and her nails were trimmed back, which made the fleshy pads round off the tips like a boy's.

"Mr. Victor told me a lot about you, but he didn't tell me you look just like James Dean."

"I don't think he knows about James Dean," I laughed. "He doesn't go to the movies. He told me about you, too. He said you were going into fine art, but he didn't tell me you look like Elizabeth Taylor." She broke into a bright, toothy smile.

"Wow, Jett and Leslie. Not bad for a start," she said.

I didn't know what she was talking about, and it must have been obvious because she added, "Oh, I thought you meant the movie *Giant*. They were in it together."

"No. I haven't seen that one. But that's cool." I wondered what she meant by "start".

"Want one?" she asked, taking a pack of Marlboros out of her left breast pocket. She wore jeans and a roomy, long-sleeved, grey denim work shirt. It looked like one of Mr. Victor's shirts. She had an unusual, rebellious hairstyle—one I thought I'd seen in an art magazine at school.

"Thanks, Sara, but I smoke Lucky Strike."

She put a Marlboro in her mouth and moved toward me. I grabbed a Lucky and my Zippo and lit our cigarettes.

"Have you been on the roof?" I asked.

"No. Is that an invitation?"

Sara wasn't shy, not like I was. But she was easy to talk to. Until then, I'd only been comfortable chatting with girls I wasn't attracted to.

"Yep," I said. "Mr. Victor won't mind."

Since I'd been working with him almost every day, I felt completely at home in the Laurel Street studio.

I let Sara go ahead of me up the stairs. She was barefoot—and shapely.

"Where's Nixon?" she asked, letting me know they'd met before.

"He's out with Mr. Victor."

"He told me you practically built this place, Luke. He's very impressed with you. He sounded like a proud father when he talked about you. He told you I'll be staying here, didn't he?"

"Oh, yeah. Sure." He hadn't told me, but I didn't want to embarrass myself or her.

We walked over to the low wall surrounding the patio. When we bent down to rest our elbows on the flat stone cap, her shirt parted slightly and I got a quick glimpse of her boob.

"Oh sorry, I didn't mean to flash you. I wanted to save that for later." She giggled as she buttoned the shirt.

The sight gave me an instant hormonal jolt. I pushed myself into the brick wall to hide the sudden rise in my pants. *Save that for later?* I wondered what she meant.

"How old are you, Luke? If you don't mind my asking."

"Twenty. And you?"

"I'm eighteen. I'll be modeling for Mr. Victor's drawing classes. I'm sure he told you."

What? I wondered what else he hadn't told me.

"He didn't go into any detail."

"Well, after I suggested it to him, he thought it would be very good for his students. He said it would be a nice addition to drawing circles and boxes."

Yes! I couldn't agree more!

"I asked him if he'd like me to model in the nude. I told him I wouldn't mind."

Woah, Nelly!

She took a long drag on her cigarette and studied me, watching for my reaction. I definitely had one going on, but I couldn't let her see it. I hugged the patio wall and stared down at the street below.

"What did he say?"

"He said, 'We will see.'" She imitated Mr. Victor's deep voice. "Is Mr. Victor German?"

"No," I laughed. "He's Lithuanian like me."

I wanted to change the subject. "Where will you be sleeping?"

"Probably on the futon downstairs. I won't be bothering you, Luke. I promise."

I promise you already are.

Chapter 27
Laurel Street Studio 1961

I was slumped over my drawing board with thoughts of Sara running through my brain when I heard clip-clopping. It took me back to the sounds of horse hooves on the cowboy radio shows I had listened to after school. It sounded funny inside Mr. Victor's studio.

I looked up and saw a short blonde across the room. She had come in with Shannon. I didn't see her face as she walked past, but I caught a glimpse of what was making the odd noise. The blonde was wearing Dr. Scholl's wooden soled exercise sandals.

I stood up and walked toward the girls. The blonde wasn't much taller than five feet and couldn't have weighed more than a hundred pounds. She wore a plain white, V-necked, short-sleeved knit top and jeans roll-cuffed at mid-calf.

Then ... I saw her face. And I took a deep breath.

She had big, almond shaped eyes and was a natural

blonde. I could tell by the short hairs on her forearms. They glistened like ten-carat gold. Her fine hair was wavy and below shoulder length, framing her face with wispy strands that fell in slinky spirals. Her lips were curvy like her figure. She had dark, perfectly arched eyebrows and thick eyelashes—a striking contrast to her blond hair.

I exhaled and felt dizzy. She was an intoxicating cocktail stupefying my senses.

Sara, Nixon, and I had been the only ones in the studio before the girls came in. Nixon was first to greet them and intruded his curious nose into the new guest's private business.

"Don't mind Nixon. It's the boy in him," said Sara.

The little blonde giggled as she redirected his attention by taking a rolled up strip of white paper out of her leather mail-carrier shoulder bag.

"Is it okay if he has some of these? There's nothing weird in them—just sugar—so they should be safe." Her voice was musical, and lower than I'd expected.

"Oh, he'll love those!" said Sara.

Nixon and I watched her hands and fingers flexing, peeling little candy buttons off their paper wrapper. They weren't primped and pampered princess hands. They were beautiful—like my mother's.

"Here you go, Nixon." She held four or five colorful dots in the palm of her hand. They were slurped up instantly. She giggled and wiped her hand on her jeans.

I looked away when she looked up, too shy to make eye contact. Our eyes did a little keep-away dance. As mine looked up, hers looked down. When hers looked up, mine looked down. She nearly caught me once. Almost, but not quite. Or—maybe she knew exactly what was going on.

I couldn't hold out any longer, and maybe neither could she. We looked into each other's eyes and held on tight.

Her eyes were *green amber*—the rare, pre-historic gift the Baltic Sea bestowed upon its sandy Lithuanian shores. The color was one-hundred-fifty proof Absinthe—the mind-melting liquor of renowned painters and poets—flowing into the creamy, delicious, dark chocolate outlines of her irises—

"Hi. I'm Celia."

"Hi. I-I'm Luke." I hesitated, then decided to add, "It's short for Lukas. It's Lithuanian. But you can call me Luke."

I heard myself stammering, tripping over myself. I sounded like an idiot.

"Hi, Luke," she said, smiling. "You can call me Celia."

I didn't know if she was being friendly or sarcastic. We'd only just met. Maybe she didn't like foreigners. Or maybe she didn't like me. Or maybe it was a secret code meaning she did like me. I didn't know why I was tormenting myself.

I noticed a silver chain with a PBY Catalina Flying Boat around her neck. It looked like a pewter Monopoly game token. I was probably the only guy in Chicago who knew what it was.

"Is that a Consolidated PBY on your neck?"

Celia's face lit up. "Yes! How did you know?"

"I've been drawing airplanes since I was a kid. I know almost every military aircraft. Why that plane?"

"My dad was in the Seabees in Guadalcanal. He flew them in the war."

Celia and I are connecting!

Was it coincidence, predestination, or just a lucky dog knowledge of aircraft? I knew "Seabees" stood for "CB", which was the abbreviation for "Construction Battalion". I felt a surge of confidence.

"It's short for 'Construction Battalion', right?" I spoke with authority and coolness.

"Yeah," she said, shifting toward me a little. "My dad said they did everything from making airplane runways to building barracks for the troops."

I lowered my gaze to the little plane for a just a second. The neckline of her shirt revealed a triangle of soft, creamy skin. The deep V pointed to the aircraft flying due south through a pass between two pert mountains.

I had run out of things to say. There was nothing left to add to the airplane story without sounding totally ignorant. Celia wouldn't be interested in the flight characteristics of the PBY, or that it could take off and land on a runway, as well as water.

She walked over to one of the art tables and leaned up against a stool. She took a pack of Newports and a 7-UP matchbook out of her bag and offered us a smoke. We gave her our little thanks-but-no-thank-you gestures. Everyone was loyal to their own brand. Celia lit her cigarette, and Shannon slid over a tuna can ashtray.

I was relieved when the girls started making small

talk. I had always been nervous making one-on-one conversation with a stranger. Maybe my fears went back to being called on in class by Sister Prudencia.

I watched Celia's lips move as she spoke. Her voice was deep and warm. She said she lived in Palos Hills and worked nights at Christ Hospital in Oak Lawn. On weekdays, she attended classes at Navy Pier.

Celia didn't chatter like other girls. The silent spaces she left pulled me in—filling me with a desire to get closer, deeper. I wanted to know what made her tick. My thoughts rambled. My brain scrambled.

I glanced down. Celia's left sandal was on the floor. The toes on her bare foot were free to play with the buckle on her shoe strap—

That is the most perfect foot I've ever seen!

My brain was in flames. I thought of Dalia. I thought of my parents. Though they'd never voiced it, I knew they preferred me in the company of a Lithuanian girl. I wondered what they would think of Celia.

She put her cigarettes back into her bag.

She was about to vanish, leaving me with only the fading flashbacks of her beauty—the PBY silently slipping over the horizon; the fleeting scent of her misty mentholated smoke; the sorcerous sound of her clip-clopping wooden soles—

I asked her in my coolest, most disinterested, by-the-way manner if she'd be coming back to Mr. Victor's.

"Maybe."

Chapter 28

Mr. Victor, Sara, and I were outside on the roof smoking and drinking wine. It was a warm evening. A gentle breeze from the west brought the sounds of merriment and beer hall smells from an open side door of the Tap Root Pub across the street. A jukebox played Johnny Cash's *I Walk the Line*.

Sara rolled a joint and passed it to me. Pot really wasn't my thing, but I took a few tokes out of friendship. When we went back inside, Mr. Victor said, "Sit down please. I want to show you something."

In the darkened living room, he pointed a flashlight at a puppet, a toy soldier, a potted plant, me, Sara, Nixon, Orphan Annie the cat, and himself. He clicked the light on and off and said, "If the light is not on it—it does not exist."

"Okay," said Sara. "I think I got it. This is about your 'Hole in the Universe' theory."

"Yes. What do you think, Luke?"

"What does the light mean? Is it like sunlight?" I asked.

"No. It is not about light. It is about something invisible that exists everywhere. It is the power of the universe flowing through everything and animating it. Giving it life. When the life force is not on it or through it, that thing—man, beast, or plant—ceases to exist."

"Far out," said Sara. "But I like it. Really cool, Mr. V." She sounded stoned.

"Yeah. I like it, too. I think the light is a good analogy for life. No light or life—no more—nothing," I said.

"Yes. No more nothing. Even though I believe that is incorrect English, Luke. No more nothing means there is something. Double negative—is that not so?"

That was pretty funny coming from someone who didn't use contractions in his speech. I had to laugh.

Sara took the flashlight from Mr. Victor's hand, stood up, and faced us. She lifted her left breast out of her unbuttoned shirt and bathed it in the bright light.

"I am a brrreast!" she shouted.

After what felt like minutes, she flicked off the light. "Now I do not exist!" She was imitating Mr. Victor's accent.

The image had burned into my retinas. A greenish spaceship flew around the room looking for a place to land. I blinked, trying to make it go away, but it only slid around on my eyeball. Eventually, the alien vessel faded out. Sara almost fell over laughing. Mr. Victor chuckled.

Still holding the flashlight, Sara laid down on the

black futon and whined, "Luke, come here." I hesitated.

Mr. Victor walked into the dining room and turned on a half-domed light that hung over the table. I glanced at him. He signaled me with his heavy black eyebrows to go to Sara. "You guys go ahead. I am going out for a while."

I didn't understand and I didn't know how to feel. Maybe the wine and the weed and seeing Sara's boob like that was messing up my mind. Mr. Victor had always been like a father to me. *What did he want me to do?*

"Wow. That is some good shit!" she said.

Her shirt was open down to her belly-button; her breasts took turns peeking out from the draped denim as she turned from side to side on the futon. The backlight from the dining room outlined her shadowed silhouette.

Sara shined the light under her chin and made a Dracula face. "I am a vampire! I vahnt to suck your bloooood!" She snarled with a Transylvanian accent and pushed in close, pretending to bite my neck. She smelled sweet.

"Look! Now I do not exist!" She was mocking Mr. Victor, but I knew it was all in fun. She had lived with him for about a year and had nothing but good things to say.

She clicked the flashlight again and placed her hand over the lens.

"I am a hand." The light was blood red through her palm. It became brighter glowing up through her fingers. Her nails were luminous. She was fascinated like a child with a kaleidoscope.

She pressed the flashlight under her breast and turned it into a fiery red ball. "Oh look! What are these?" Dark lines radiated through the translucent orb.

"I don't know."

Sara must have known what she was doing to me, or maybe she was just too wasted—either way, I was in an awkward predicament. I was used to seeing her naked when she modeled, but this was different. She was showing herself off in a provocative way, bringing attention to herself as a woman, exposing an unfamiliar but exciting dimension to the Sara I knew and loved.

My hormones were in an extreme state of upheaval, but so was my apprehension. I needed to think fast. The game was changing quickly.

She opened her shirt and slid the flashlight down her flat stomach. The circle of red light moved slowly toward the dark triangle between her legs.

"If I turn off the light, it doesn't exist. If something happens—it didn't happen."

I was getting shaky. I felt like I was in a high stakes poker game—and it was time to call or fold.

"Uh, I'll be right back," I said.

Chapter 29

I ducked into the bathroom, turned on the exhaust fan, sat down on the toilet seat lid, and lit a cigarette. I needed to sort things out quickly. But my mind was molasses. Being fast on the draw had never been one of my strong suits.

Sara was seventeen when she had taken Mr. Victor's art class at the university. She was eighteen when she moved into his studio. She'd just recently turned nineteen. Mr. Victor was forty-three.

I suspected they weren't in a conventional relationship, but I didn't know for sure. Was Sara feeling restless? Was Mr. Victor? I was pretty certain they'd been having sex; how could they live in the same space and not? Sara was young and beautiful, and though Mr. Victor was a lot older, why would she live with him if she wasn't even a little attracted to him? No other guys came by to see her, and Mr. Victor didn't have any lady friends. There was no other explanation.

Does he want me to have sex with Sara?

I knew the winds of change were beginning to blow. Old established values and behavioral guidelines flapped in the breeze like threadbare boxer shorts pinned to a laundry line in the backyard. I knew Kesey and Keruac were *doing it* and writing about it because Mr. Victor had given me *On the Road* to read. Sex and mind-blowing were becoming routine. Flying free was where it was *at*.

I flushed my cigarette and went back to the living room. Thank God Sara's shirt was buttoned.

"Come here, Luke," she said and reached out for an embrace. She was still lying on the futon, and I half fell on top of her as she pulled me down. She kissed me open mouthed, hard and long, forcing me to part my lips. Her tongue moved slowly, stirring up the hormones I'd just tried to suppress. I fought to keep my tongue from joining hers.

"You know I still love you, don't you?" she asked coyly.

"Of course I do." I wanted to sound manly and confident, but my words came out high pitched and awkward. Why was I embarrassed? She had created the situation and made all the moves. She should have been way more uncomfortable than I was.

"You know I still love you too, don't you?" I said weakly.

"Like always?"

"Like always."

I wasn't lying, but as I spoke, I thought about Celia in her wooden-soled sandals and rolled-up blue jeans.

Chapter 30

I picked up the aerosol can and sprayed the final coat of fixative over the mock-up. It was a rough comp of an annual report for United Charities of Chicago.

I loved the sweet smell of fixative. It was used to preserve chalk and charcoal to paper. It had a distinctive aroma that lingered, giving art and design studios a personality all their own. It also gave the artist, and anyone else nearby, a pleasant little high.

Students started showing up for Mr. Victor's session. Then I heard it! The clatter of those wonderful Dr. Scholl's clip-clops that had been playing in my mind for two weeks.

Celia—

"Hello, Celia. Will you be joining us today?" asked Mr. Victor. "We will be happy to have you."

He had no idea how happy that made me.

"Thank you, Mr. Victor. I'm so glad to be here."

Everyone took their seats in their usual places around the work tables. Celia pulled up a stool at the end of one of the tables.

I didn't sit down. By walking around, I could steal glances unnoticed. If I sat with the others, I couldn't observe her without being obvious.

Mr. Victor put a Kool in his mouth, reached in his pants pocket, and pulled out three lighters. One had a Masonic square and compass with a "G" engraved on it. The second displayed a 101st Airborne Screaming Eagles shield. The third was a plain Zippo. He held them up to the group as the unlit Kool dangled from his lip.

"I purchased these at 'Sally's', the Salvation Army Store on North Clark Street. All three are identical Zippo lighters except for their labels, and they are all in similar like-new condition.

"I paid twenty-five cents for one, two dollars and fifty cents for another, and five dollars for the third one. Can anyone guess which ones cost what?"

Toni spoke up. "I'd say ... a quarter for the plain one, two-fifty for the military, and five bucks for the Masonic?"

"Sorry, Toni. You missed all three. Anyone else?"

I thought it would be military, Masonic, and plain, but kept my mouth shut. I didn't want to risk being wrong in front of Celia.

"The Masonic cost twenty-five cents. The plain one was next at two dollars and fifty cents, and the military was five dollars. Anyone care to guess why?"

"The lighter with the military logo is more valuable than the plain one, I guess, and the Masonic has less value," said Marty.

"Why?" asked Mr. Victor. "The devices are identical."

"The Airborne Zippo makes you feel like an American hero when you light a Camel. It's worth the extra money," said Kurt.

"I can see why the military lighter would mean more to someone. My dad had a Zippo with 'The Fighting Seabees' on it. He said it wouldn't even blow out from the prop wash of planes taxiing on the field," said Celia.

Her words belonged to me. She must have said it for my benefit, like a gift. She had to know no one else in the room would understand what she was talking about—

My dad and I stood behind the tall chain-link fence on Cicero Avenue. We watched a huge DC-6 taxi around, lining itself up with the runway. The deep rumble became a roaring hurricane as its engines revved to full takeoff power. The ground shook. My ribs resonated. Four giant fans ripped the air and rocked the silver bird straining against its brakes. Smoke and stinging dirt blew in our faces. The wind stopped our breath—

Celia brought me back to that moment in three short sentences. I wondered if she still had her dad's lighter.

"But do you think the plain Zippo would perform just as well?" asked Mr. Victor.

"Oh, I'm sure it lights just fine. It just doesn't look as cool," she answered.

Right on, Celia!

"The store clerk said the plain Zippo sells for two dollars and fifty cents. Lighters with military insignias have more value because they may have gone through combat situations while in the pocket of their owner. They are worth five dollars."

Celia took out her Newports. All that talk about cigarette lighters must have whetted her want for a smoke. I reached for my Luckies.

I thought about offering her a light but chickened out. She was far enough away that I would have had to get up and walk over. I didn't want to look as stupid as I felt trying to find a way to get close to her.

Mr. Victor lit his Kool and continued.

"The clerk said she hates the Masonic lighters and wishes she could throw them out. She believes the Masons are a secret sect with strange handshakes and ties to Lucifer. The lowest price she is allowed charge for any store item is twenty-five cents. With tax, I paid twenty-seven cents.

"So we see how labels can add or subtract value. The lighter performs a useful function. When we add fiction or romance, it appears special. It can become highly desirable to the right person."

Man, Celia's dad's Seabees Zippo would've been something to see—and have.

Across the room, everyone started lighting up. Clouds of smoke swirled in the air. People instinctively followed the flock, even when it came down to their own bad habits.

"When people apply labels to themselves, they usually add value. When they label someone else, they often degrade or diminish the individuals or groups. Can anyone give us an example?"

Shannon was the most vocal in the group and first to pipe up. Her straight black hair, electric blue eyes, and freckly white skin intensified her strong presence.

"Well, I'm Catholic. I believe my faith is the only true faith. I believe my soul is immortal, and if I live according to the teachings of my church, my soul will go to Heaven when I die."

"Excellent. Thank you, Shannon. So you have labeled yourself a Catholic. What else?"

She thought for a moment and said, "I belong to the Saint Christina Rosary Sodality."

"What about after you graduate?"

"I want to be an architect."

"How about traits, political preferences, nationalities?"

"Well, I'm Irish, and I voted for Kennedy, by the way."

"So we have Shannon—Irish, Democrat, Catholic, Sodality Member, and Architect. Any more?"

"You could add 'Prude'," she said, enjoying her self-deprecating humor. Kurt chortled.

I suspected Shannon might have been a pretty cool chick in spite of her religious hang-ups, but she was no match for Celia.

"I label Marty 'Doofus'," said Kurt. "That should add some value."

"I humbly accept," said Marty, bowing his head. Celia giggled.

"Okay, let us examine the lighters again." Mr. Victor went on. "If we remove their labels, we have three identical lighters.

"To many, Coca-Cola has more value than other colas.

Some people will pay a lot more for a bag with Gucci on it than the same bag without the logo. Labels have always been important to humans." Celia was busy drawing in her sketchbook.

"People have been killing and dying for their labels throughout history. Labels such as Christian, Muslim, Jew, Commie, Yankee, Jap, Kraut, Gook, and the new Vietnamese Slope, are titles that define one's being."

Everyone seemed to get it. No one challenged Mr. Victor with a question or comment.

"As far as the universe is concerned, humans are humans, lighters are lighters, and bags are bags. Even Coca-Cola, the most recognizable and profitable label in the world, is just a soft drink." Then he asked, "Who would like the military and Masonic lighters? I am keeping the plain one."

"I'll take the Screaming Eagles, Mr. Victor!" Kurt was thrilled by the offer.

"Here you are, Kurt. Does anyone want the Masonic lighter?"

There were no takers.

I couldn't stop watching Celia's bare feet play with the rungs on her stool, and wondered why no one else seemed to notice how breathtakingly beautiful they were.

Chapter 31

It was Tuesday and my heart swelled when I heard Celia clip-clop into the studio. She sat in the same spot she'd been the week before, took a sketchbook out of a black canvas bag, and put the bag on the floor. She wore blue jeans and a long-sleeved, pinstriped white blouse. It looked like the top of a nurse's uniform. On her lovely feet were the wooden soled sandals with bone white leather straps.

"Hello, people!" Mr. Victor said. "We will not be drawing Sara today. We are going to do something different." I heard two distinct "awws" from Kurt and Marty.

Sara's denim shirt was buttoned at breast level, but open enough to allow her flat belly to flash just above her jeans. I enjoyed seeing Sara in various states of undress, but with Celia in the room, the only images getting through to my visual cortex were Celia's eyes, lips, hands, feet, nurse's shirt—

Mr. Victor was holding a stack of black baseball caps. He peeled them off one at a time and handed one to each of us.

"So what's with the caps, Mr. Victor?" asked Shannon.

"We will get to that later. Here are some ashtrays." Mr. Victor dropped a few tuna cans onto the worktables.

Everyone ruffled through their pockets and bags. Celia found her Newports and lit one with a paper book match.

"Thanks, Mr. Victor. Does this mean we're all on the team? When are we having our first practice?" Shannon asked with a punky smirk.

"Yes. Go ahead, team. Put them on."

They began adjusting their headbands. The class clowns couldn't resist the opportunity to goof around. Kurt smacked Marty with his cap. Marty made a Jerry Lewis face by crossing his eyes and sticking out his tongue.

I watched Celia as she tried her cap on, took it off, re-adjusted it, and tried it again. Satisfied, she set the cap on the table and tilted her head back, exposing her smooth neck and throat. She raked back her wavy hair with both hands and put on the hat.

"Now please remove your caps and put them on the tables," said Mr. Victor. We all looked at each other with confused faces. Celia took off her cap and set it on the table, freeing her beautiful golden mane.

"I would like all of you to suspend your beliefs. If you are willing to do that, I would like you to acknowledge it by putting the black cap on your head."

"You mean suspend our disbeliefs, don't you Mr. V.?" asked Sara.

"No, Sara. I mean suspend your beliefs. That other way is bad English, even though that phrase has been around for a long time."

"I don't get it, Mr. Victor," said Kurt.

"We all know that man cannot fly. That is not a disbelief. That is a belief. When we go to see a Superman movie, we are not asked to suspend our disbelief. We do not disbelieve that man can fly. We believe that man cannot fly." He dragged on his cigarette.

"Of course, we are not asked to believe that Superman can fly. We simply suspend our belief that man cannot fly for the duration of the movie so we can enjoy the story."

He put on his cap. Everyone except Shannon did the same.

"Shannon, is there something you would like to say?"

"Yes, I would. If by putting this hat on, it means I have to get rid of my beliefs, which include my Catholic faith, I'm definitely not going to do that."

"I did not ask you to get rid of your beliefs. I am asking you to suspend them for the duration of our discussion."

Shannon thought for a moment, then staunchly placed the cap back on her head and said, "Okay. I'll go along with that." Kurt clapped. She flipped him her middle finger.

"What is the significance of the black cap, Mr. Victor?" asked Tad.

"You have probably heard the term 'thinking cap',

Tad. It is simply a contrivance to give you, the wearer, permission to suspend your beliefs," he said. "You can think of it as your artist-philosopher helmet."

"What about the beliefs you're going to talk about, Mr. Victor?" asked Shannon.

"Nothing I say should be taken as a belief. I will only submit ideas for your consideration. I do not believe in beliefs, and I definitely do not wish to encourage others to embrace them," he said.

"I think beliefs regarding faith, social status, political preferences, and educational achievements are exclusionary. They imply superiority. If I call myself a Catholic, I am putting my claim on the only true God. If I am a Capitalist, I think I am better than Socialists, and if I am an American, then I must be superior to all other nationalities." He glanced around the room.

"Those I just mentioned are more than simple beliefs. They represent entire belief systems. Each system is like a house made of bricks. They are difficult to change."

"Why do they need to change?" asked Shannon.

"I will tell you."

Chapter 32

"Art can be used to create fiction. All religious art from the centuries is based on fic—"

Shannon grabbed her cap off her head and smacked it hard on the work table. Wisps of wild hairs slapped her forehead. "There you go bashing my religion, Mr. Victor. What makes you think your ideas are so good, so right that we should drop everything we believe and accept your theories?"

"I am sorry, Shannon," he said. "I did not mean to offend you. My message was lost to my poor choice of words. What I wanted to say is that artists provide visual form to ideas in the way a writer supplies his reader with mental substance and imagery."

It was kind of funny to see Mr. Victor backpedal, attempting to take his foot out of his mouth.

"Now if you will allow me, I will start over."

"Fine," said Shannon, crossing her arms.

"Art can be used to create fiction." He looked back at Shannon. "Would you agree with that statement?"

"I suppose that's acceptable as a generalization."

"Good. If I say that religion is based on beliefs, would you agree with me?"

"It's actually based on faith, Mr. Victor, but if you want to say beliefs, I guess that's okay. I really don't know what the difference is."

"Then would it not follow that religious art is based on beliefs?"

"Sure. Faith, trust, belief—all of those words have similar meanings."

"Artists painted beautiful children and young adults with wings. People believed they were angels," he said.

Shannon's hands were shaking. She broke two matches trying to light her cigarette. Mr. Victor flipped the cover of his Zippo and offered her a light.

"Call me naive, Mr. Victor, but I do, too," she said. "As a matter of fact, or I should say faith, I believe there's an angel watching over me all the time."

Mr. Victor's face softened, and his eyes looked watery. He pulled up a stool and sat closer to his group.

"I used to believe that, too, Shannon."

I was surprised by Mr. Victor's candid admission. I never expected him to share something so deeply personal with the whole class.

"Why did you stop, Mr. Victor?" she asked.

"What happened, Mr. Victor?" asked Sara.

All eyes were on him.

"I was taught the same things you were, Shannon. I

went to Church and took Holy Communion. I was an altar boy. I believed in Heaven and Hell. I loved God, and I believed that He loved me and my family. I talked to Him every night as you do. I always thought He was there for me, my wife, Zita, and my son, Neris. I believed He cared for us and kept us safe. I felt like there were four of us—Zita, Neris, God, and me."

I thought of the DP camp in Landshut. I never knew Mr. Victor had a family. I felt a cold pang in my stomach.

"We lived in Lithuania. When the Communists came, we fled to Dresden in Germany."

Things were beginning to add up. His dark moods, his desire to stay away from everyone at camp. How he had called me his "son" and said "nothing is like you think it is".

"How old was Neris, Mr. Victor?" I asked.

"The same age as you, Luke. He was born in Kaunas two days after your birthday, probably in the same hospital."

The cold in my stomach turned icy.

"On the night of February 13, 1945, Dresden was bombed, burned off the face of the earth by the British. Zita and Neris vanished."

He looked up at the ceiling, then back at us. Tears flooded his eyes.

"I-I was not there ... with them when it happened. I was hiding from the Nazis on a farm outside the city. I should have died with my wife and my son."

Instantly, Shannon ran up and put her arms around Mr. Victor. We all followed and enclosed him in a supportive cluster.

"I'm so sorry, Mr. Victor," said Shannon tearfully. Everyone nodded and mumbled personal condolences. Sara rubbed his back and kissed the top of his head.

"Man, that's horrible," said Kurt.

"You're a good man, Mr. Victor. I'm glad you're still here," said Celia, sniffling.

"Thank you. All of you. I have always felt your love. I love you, too."

He sobbed for a while, then wiped his eyes. Everyone made their way back to their seats.

Celia looked at me.

Shannon put her black cap back on her head.

"Okay, getting back to what I was saying earlier. When you work as artists, you will be creating fiction, especially if you work for an advertising agency.

"You will be asked to paint beautiful people standing beside their beautiful automobile in the driveway of their beautiful ranch house. The man will be handsome, suntanned, and perfectly groomed with straight dark hair neatly parted to one side like Cary Grant. He will have a strong jaw—"

Mr. Victor's voice trailed off and out of my mind. Celia didn't have a strong jaw, but it blended perfectly with her oval face. Her chin wasn't too round or too pointy. It was poetic perfection.

"He will wear a suit matching the automobile's color. He will have broad shoulders and stand about one head taller than his lady. He will be looking down at her while she gazes up at him—"

I couldn't concentrate. I was immersed in the image of Celia gazing up at me with her adoring eyes.

"It is not about making something appear real. A camera can do a better job, but it will not render the image the advertiser wants to create. You, the artists, under the guidance of your Art Directors and Account Managers, will make that happen."

"Can an illustration really be that powerful?" asked Kurt.

"Absolutely. There is meaning in every square inch of an image. Nothing is there by accident. Every detail, color, and shape speaks to the viewer.

"A good artist can do that. They make color nuances that take the eye around so it explores and caresses the image. Shades and shadows balance the composition to give a feeling of stability and security.

"But you will have to work hard to become that good. Only then will you be able to create believable fiction."

I couldn't stop looking at Celia's feet. They looked so happy to be out of their white bobby socks and those hot, heavy Red Cross nursing shoes I imagined she wore while working nights at the hospital.

Summer had arrived and fall would be fast on its heels. Celia would probably replace those cute Dr. Scholl's sandals with socks and shoes. Maybe even boots.

I won't get to see those pretty feet again until next spring.

Chapter 33

"I want us to consider a redesign of an early life form," said Mr. Victor. "I will give you a hint. It is a very early, non-extinct model that we still see in abundance today."

"Man?" asked Marty.

"I thought Adam and Eve were His earliest—oops, I take it back. I think He created animals and then man."

"It is not man, Marty."

"Then how about a dinosaur?" asked Toni.

"I asked for a model that is still here with us."

"There's one!" Kurt pointed at Marty.

The whole group, including Celia, laughed. I didn't think it was funny. Why was she amused by such lowbrow antics? Would she laugh if I acted stupidly?

"Shannon. How much do you weigh? One hundred?"

Mr. Victor called on Shannon often. She was the most talkative and provided good bounce-back. Teachers knew the value of such a student. I remember the priests calling on Stitch, Jr. at Saint Rita. He would always crack up the room and make the teacher look cool to the class.

"Hah! Thanks, Mr. Victor, but I weigh almost a hundred nineteen."

"Does anyone have a calculator? Are there any idiot savants here who can multiply one hundred and nineteen times sixteen times one thousand?"

"One million nine hundred and four thousand," said Tad.

"Without a calculator. I'm impressed!" said Celia.

I wasn't. Any eighth grader could've done that.

"Thank you, Tad. It would take one million nine hundred four thousand of the model I am talking about to make up one Shannon," said Mr. Victor.

Shannon crinkled her face.

"I will give you another hint. It has been around for about two hundred fifty million years, and it is still here in great numbers. It lives and thrives in almost every region of the globe."

"Hey, I know what it is! An amoeba!" shouted Marty.

"You're an amoeba brain!" said Kurt. Celia laughed. Again. Those two clowns had everyone's attention, including Celia's.

Still giggling, she cried out, "I think I've got it! It's a fly!"

"Bingo! Very good, Celia," said Mr. Victor.

He walked to the blackboard and picked up a piece of chalk.

Chapter 34

Mr. Victor drew a horizontal line starting at the left edge of the first of three blackboards. He walked along drawing across all three boards and stopped past the center of the last one. The line was almost twenty-one feet long. Near the end, he drew another line a quarter of an inch long.

"This is a timeline, people. Each inch represents one million years, so the line shows us two hundred fifty million years. That is how long our little friends have been around." Mr. Victor set the chalk back on the narrow ledge of the board.

"The short line is a quarter of an inch long. Can everyone see it?"

Marty squinted through his thick horn-rimmed glasses. He walked to the third board and inspected the chalky speck. "Yep. It's a quarter inch alright."

"The quarter inch represents two hundred fifty thousand years. It is the sum total of our experience on this planet as modern humans," said Mr. Victor. "The fly has lived on this planet one thousand times longer than humans."

"Wow!" Kurt raised his hand with three fingers together and touched his upturned visor cap in Boy Scout fashion. "Makes ya want to salute as they fly by."

"That's the first time I ever heard you talk about respect, Kurt," said Celia.

Kurt punched Marty in the shoulder. "Hear that, Doofus? I got respect," he said, mocking the beloved Dead End Kids. I felt a jealous twinge.

Why is she paying attention to those goofballs? I knew girls liked outgoing boys, even guys who wore glasses. Maybe quiet types like Tad and me were just background for the noisy ones.

Wait a minute—what if Celia starts liking Marty or Kurt?

I couldn't let that happen. I needed to change my classroom behavior, but I didn't know how. Horsing around just wasn't my style.

"Luke, will you turn off the lights, please?"

I stretched back and flipped down the light switch. A Kodak Carousel slide projector had been set up on one of the work tables. As Mr. Victor turned it on, a blinding image appeared on the wall. It was a photograph of a fly magnified to the size of our old 1949 Buick Super.

Kurt fell to his knees under the projected image. "Take me, Master! I will be your faithful servant forever, but please don't eat me! I will escort you to a great dining emporium behind the McDonalds on Broadway—the

McDumpster Room. Your taste buds will be seduced, your appetite satiated, and your tummy filled."

"Can I assist him, Master?" Marty came back at him with a lisping, slobbering, spitting, hunch-backed, bespectacled Boris Karloff impersonation.

Celia laughed.

Why won't they cut that shit out? Why doesn't Mr. Victor establish some behavioral guidelines? Kurt and Marty have all eyes—including Celia's—on them.

I had to get a hold of myself. I was thinking crazy, like a jealous fool.

"That is one scary mother!" said Tad.

I was pretty sure Japanese-Americans used slang to be "hip", but stopped short of using a full swear word out of respect for their culture. Having immigrant parents, the f-word stuck in my throat, too.

"I think he's beautiful," said Celia.

Toni rolled her eyes. I remembered my mother telling me about girls who rolled their eyes. She thought eye-rollers were rude, closed-minded, and unimaginative.

"What the heck have you been smoking? I want some of that," said Toni.

"You don't think so?" asked Celia.

Celia had shown curiosity on almost every subject except politics and history. Once, she brought in what she thought was owl excrement embedded with fur and tiny bone fragments. The group shared her keen interest, everyone except Toni. She thought it was gross garbage.

I started to realize I didn't want Celia to participate in class discussions. I wanted her to sit quietly, draw in her sketchbook, and fiddle with her feet.

The boys hadn't paid much attention to her before, so I felt safe. When she began to speak up, people took notice—and she noticed back. She was making conversations with Marty and Kurt. She hadn't said a word to me. Not once.

I couldn't focus on Mr. Victor. I chain-smoked my Luckies and went through half a pack before mid-day.

Mr. Victor treated the class to four large pizzas and pop for lunch. Celia only ate plain cheese, which was opposite to my preference for the loaded slices.

"Luke, can you turn the lights back on, please?"

I flipped the switch. The giant fly was washed out but still visible. Discussion continued through the munching and masticating.

"Let us talk about the physical features of the fly, and then we will discuss the performance characteristics. We will compare them to our own and see if we find common ground. This is not a monster from outer space. Most of us remember these guys tickling our skin," said Mr. Victor.

"Yeah, they were biting the crap out of us at the beach in Beverly Shores," said Tad.

"Those are not the same, even though they look similar. This one is called *Musca Domestica*, commonly referred to as a housefly. Our friend here does not have the ability to pierce the skin," said Mr. Victor.

"Let us compare sizes. Can anyone guess the length of the fly pictured here?"

"I'd say half an inch?" asked Tad.

"Close. About one-third. What about your length, Tad?" Kurt and Marty snickered.

"I'm five-ten."

"You are seventy inches long. Two hundred ten times longer than our subject. You can run about eight miles per hour, but the fly can only cruise at around five miles per hour. Suppose it was scaled up to the size you see—about two hundred times larger. What would its airspeed be?"

"One thousand miles per hour?"

"Yes. That is what you would think. Faster than a commercial jet. But do not take it to the bank yet. Scale speed is okay for model trains and airplanes, but it would not work here. You cannot magnify one thing and expect everything else to work out."

Celia wasn't drawing. She was smoking and studying the horrifying image. The silky grey hair on its body was the thickness of the radio antenna on a car. Its thousands of body hairs looked like a forest of lethal, tapering spikes.

"The size of the fly has been established by all of its component parts. The parts have been built from smaller parts—cells. The cells were built according to specifications dictated by genes. They were determined by the design and function, and they have been tested millions of trillions of times over the course of evolution. Weaker designs were discarded. Better designs survived." Mr. Victor took a swig of Coca-Cola.

"Flies have adapted to variations in temperature and atmospheric conditions, changes in air composition, and available food sources. They survived catastrophic events like global warming and cooling, meteor strikes, floods and droughts, assaults from predators—reptiles, birds, insects; even attacks from bacteria, viruses, molds and spores—the list goes on."

He took another sip from the pop can, pausing long enough to suggest he was about to wrap it up.

"Flying insects have been among the most successful large life forms on the planet. I say large because compared to all life they are near the large end of the scale. A virus to a housefly is as you are to the city of Chicago.

"But this is not where the story ends. Not by a—how you say it—long shot."

He lit a Kool, took a drag, and exhaled a smoke cloud. As it slowly drifted through the bright rays of the projector, it glowed like cosmic dust from a dying galaxy.

"I would like us all to say hello to one of our oldest living ancestors."

I noted puzzled expressions and wondered: how could we be descended from an insect?

Chapter 35

It was an outdoor affair with long tables set with linens, fine china, silver, and elaborate floral centerpieces. Loud, happy, live-band music blasted out to dancing celebrants in a gaily striped tent with open sides. Further down, people laughed, holding tots on a decorated pony, taking pictures for their family albums.

I traveled from table to table, testing tasty treats—marinated mushrooms, rollmops, cheeses, sausages, liver pate, oysters, anchovies, caviar, and crab legs. My taste buds savored and celebrated. I tried not to gorge. I wanted variety, not quantity.

I sampled prime rib, filet mignon, porterhouse and fine New York beef cuts, ham, lamb, pig, turkey, chicken and duck with small sides of creamy mashed potatoes and flavored gravies.

I drank beer and wine, whiskey and rum. I sipped liquors—Benedictine, Absinthe, and Grand Marnier.

I dabbled in delectable desserts—Napoleon, marzipan, chocolates, tortes, cakes, pies, and ice cream creations. Even Baked Alaska.

From somewhere behind the wet bar, I heard a familiar voice. She beckoned me to a sunny spot on the grass. She faced me and pressed herself into my chest. I pushed gently on top of her and felt her open; letting me in, submerging me deep inside her warm perfection. I felt intense pleasure. I felt loved.

We were lifting. I looked down at the tents and people gently dropping away. I was with Celia, and we were flying.

I thought about the artist, Marc Chagall, and his painting of lovers flying through the sky locked in an embrace. He must have been in love when he painted it.

The wind was gentle. I felt weightless. I was with the two loves of my life—Celia and flying. We watched the world below as we floated above. It was my old world, one I'd left long ago.

I felt myself slipping. Celia tightened her legs around me and pulled me in. We dove down, then shot up and zoomed high over treetops.

Air warmed by the sun rose over buildings and parking lots, lifting us effortlessly. Cool air falling over rivers and lakes made us descend.

We swooped down to the ground where ants and beetles scurried to subterranean cities in the dirt.

We flew over beehives. Droves of diligent workers brought in pollen, spitting it into honey. I felt sad for my flying friends—they gave up the best use of their wings to enslave themselves forever.

Celia and I were free from the toil and trouble of the world. Flying high. Riding the winds.

We moved faster and I felt us separate. I tried to hold on to her but couldn't. She was slipping away. She became smaller and smaller, and then I lost sight of her.

I saw something glowing bright green. It said 2:22. I closed my eyes and tried to find Celia. It didn't work—2:22 changed to 2:23.

I knew I had been with her. Maybe we were flies crashing a gala celebrity wedding. I didn't care. To feel that kind of peace and joy and live in that kind of love—that was enough.

Chapter 36

I couldn't stop thinking about my dream. I'd never flown in a plane or helicopter. Why had it felt so familiar?

Nixon ran to the door long before it opened. He must have heard her close the door of her car parked half a block down the street. She walked in wearing her black philosopher cap. And her Dr. Scholl's. My stomach flipped. God, she looked great! I wondered if she'd had the same dream as mine last night.

Mr. Victor spoke. "Let us pick up where we left off, people. Our assignment was to redesign the housefly. To upgrade it and perhaps make it into something better. Knowing what we know now, who can suggest an improvement?"

"How about a larger brain?" asked Toni.

"To do what with?" Shannon shot back.

"Well ... so it could think more ... maybe?"

"You mean like a bird?" Shannon didn't bother to hide

her annoyance with Toni's ignorance. She had told me once before that she wished Mr. Victor had been more selective when inviting students into his studio. She felt Toni added nothing of value to the group.

"She means like me," said Marty. "I have a bigger brain than a fly. At least I think I do."

"Yeah, you're definitely in bird-brain class," Kurt agreed.

"Okay. Let us suppose that is true," said Mr. Victor, rousing laughter from the group. "I do not mean about Marty. I mean if the fly had a brain similar in size to ... let us say a chicken."

"That would leave Marty at a definite disadvantage," Celia chimed in, getting her own share of laughs.

There she goes exciting those boys again—I can't stand it. Do I have to behave like Marty to get her attention?

"Alright now, what would a larger brain do to the design?" Mr. Victor pursued the idea of a fly having a brain the size of a pea instead of a poppy seed.

"The fly would need a bigger head and some sort of skull to protect it," said Nancy.

"Not necessarily. More than half of the fly's brain is inside its thorax. Of course, to balance the heavier load, you would have to increase the size and weight of its components like the wings, muscles, legs, and sticky pads."

"What are sticky pads?" asked Shannon.

"They are on the feet. They make the fly able to walk on windows and ceilings."

"I didn't know that."

"Most people do not. We really do not know very much about the world we live in. Soon, we will probably know more about the moon than the workings of a housefly. So we would have a fly about the size of a large flying beetle, maybe a Goliath beetle. But what would it do differently?" said Mr. Victor.

"It would not be able to walk on windows or ceilings, and it definitely would not make a good house guest. So how would the larger brain be an improvement?"

"I guess it wouldn't be," said Toni, looking down at her cordovan penny loafers.

"Okay, I am ready to wrap it up. Would it be fair to say that we have been unable to come up with anything to improve the housefly?" asked Mr. Victor.

"Do you think a fly can feel pleasure?" asked Celia. The sound of her voice gave me an immediate rush. Again I wondered if she could have had the same dream. Had we somehow connected with each other while we slept?

"Well, something must feel pretty good for it to seek a mate to have sex with," said Tad.

"I wouldn't know," said Shannon. I was sure she had created her self-made reputation as a prude for attention, and it always worked. Her timing was perfect—everyone laughed.

Celia didn't pick up the thread. But why would she? I had the dream—not Celia.

"Okay, but does a fly really get to have fun, like at a party?" Kurt must have been referring to something deep, like a frat bash with booze, chicks, and the possibility of making out.

"As a matter of fact, yes. Insects are notorious partiers," said Mr. Victor. "They have been consuming alcohol for hundreds of millions of years. Sometimes they get drunk and cannot fly until they sober up. Wasps are known to get rowdy and dangerous around fruit trees loaded with ripe and fallen fruit. Fruit flies originate from fermenting fruit. You could say they are born alcoholics."

That was another tidbit of trivia I never knew. I had always appreciated the busyness of bugs, but I had no idea they were having so much fun.

"Moths can be attracted by painting a mixture of honey and beer on trees. Most insects prefer food mixed with alcohol."

Booze and I went back a long way. I probably drank too much at times, but I didn't see the harm. My most memorable conquests—and some I couldn't remember—happened during parties and holidays, Baptisms, weddings, and funerals where people drank a lot.

When I was bombed, I found all the right things to say. My timing was perfect. Results spoke for themselves—that's how I met Dalia. At a friend's party, she actually left her date sitting alone on a sofa after she asked *me—the shy guy*—to take her home.

"Male flies can find a willing female from a mile away. Females are promiscuous by nature, and some do not even start the fertilization process until they have had multiple male donors."

That was it—the perfect opening for slap-happy actions. Kurt made some pretty convincing pelvic thrusts. Marty wolf-whistled. Sara stuck out her tongue. Shannon mimicked Betty Boop eyes as if she didn't understand. Toni said, "Gross."

"Planet Diptera is party central, folks. The fly and insect kingdoms have been the best kept secret for over two hundred million years!"

"You're not shitting us, are you, Mr. V.?" asked Sara.

"Ask any fly."

Chapter 37

Celia had barely looked at me in days. I thought we had connected, but there hadn't been any follow-up. Why was I waiting for her to make the first move? Why would I expect that? She probably didn't even know I liked her. Even worse, she probably didn't care.

Here I go again—over-thinking everything.

My friends walked right up to new girls and started conversations. They didn't second-guess or worry about saying stupid stuff or miss sleep. The more I tried to think myself into action, the more impossible it became.

My shyness was most obvious with American girls. My mental barrier went up and locked on, rendering me speechless. My crushproof wall of protection was tall and rock hard. Maybe I felt unworthy of their attention.

Class was over. I was about to go home but decided to hang around and grab a smoke in the alley.

"Wanna walk around?"

I couldn't believe my ears. It was Celia! And she was asking to walk with me!

"Sure. I-I have time—" I couldn't think of anything else to say.

"Let's walk around the neighborhood. I love these old buildings. There's nothing like this in Palos Hills. You know, most of them went up in the last ten years, and they're really boring."

"I know. I live in Marquette Park. It's boring there, too. It's nothing like Europe—"

"Oh, you're not from here?" She was walking ahead of me, already up the sidewalk about to cross Laurel. I practically had to run to keep up.

"How much do you want to hear?" I huffed as we cut through someone's yard. I wondered why I'd said such a stupid thing. My dad's old saying "Žodi, gryžk atgal" popped into my head. It meant "word come back". He wanted me to think before I opened my mouth.

"Everything. I want to know what life was like for a normal person."

She sounded interested, but what did she mean by "normal"?

"Well, I could start—"

Celia cut me off mid-sentence. "From the beginning. As far back as you can remember. I want to hear everything."

"Okay. I was born in Lithuania, but I don't—"

"Where's Lithuania?"

"A small country in Eastern Europe behind the Iron Curtain, as they call it—"

"Okay, then what?"

It was a funny conversation. She kept up her quick pace walking in front of me, turning to speak, almost shouting at times.

"I was four when my parents took me and fled to Austria to get away from the Communists when they invaded Lithuania. I only remember bits and pieces before Vienna—" It wasn't a good theme to carry on while sprinting.

"I don't remember anything before I was five," she said. She slowed down to let me catch up.

"My dad took me to the Prater, an amusement park in Vienna. We went on the Riesenrad, a giant Ferris wheel. I could see the whole city from the glass windows in our cabin."

"I'll bet that was fun."

"Oh yeah. After we got off the ride, my dad bought us wieners with mustard. But wait 'til you hear what happened next."

"You begged your dad to go for another ride?"

"Not exactly."

"Umm, you wanted another weiner?"

"Funny. Nope, wrong again. Actually there was a miniature train ride that went through some fake mountains. While we were sitting there eating, all of a sudden smoke started pouring out of the tunnel. The mountains caught fire and started shriveling up in the flames. People were everywhere! Running around, screaming, grabbing their kids. The wind blew fire and smoke over to the Riesenrad. One of the cabins started to smoke and burst into flames. Another one burned right after that."

"Wow! Did anybody die?"

"Probably. The ride was packed. I don't know how anyone could've escaped."

"Oh, man! What did you and your dad do?"

"We were shoved out of the park with the crowd. My dad got us out of there and never brought it up again."

Celia stopped walking. I was grateful for the break.

"That winter, we moved a few times. Our rooms were always cold and only had one small bed for all three of us. There were air raids all the time. Once, when we returned to our pension, there was a deep bomb crater in the courtyard. The building was still standing, but all the windows and doors had been blown out."

"What's a pension?"

"It's what they call a rooming house in Austria," I answered quickly, then went on.

"We went upstairs, and our room was in shambles. The door was gone. Dirt, shattered glass, bed linens, broken pieces of the door were all over the floor. Our suitcases were open, and our stuff was scattered all over the room."

"What did you do then?"

"We picked our things out of the dirt and went looking for another place to stay."

"God! And I thought my childhood was rough!"

I wondered what she meant by "rough".

"In the spring, my parents moved us to a farm in Weixerau—"

"Wikes-a-what?"

"Oh, that's a small village in Southern Bavaria."

"We're still in Europe, right?"

"Oh, yeah. It's bordered by Germany, Czechoslovakia, and Austria."

"Oh, sure! Now I know exactly where it is."

I suddenly realized these names meant absolutely nothing to Celia. "Cute," I said, squinting at the funny face she made. "A farmer was nice enough to take us in. He had cows, pigs, chickens, geese, goats, oxen, a scraggly barn cat, and a couple of really great dogs. He had a fish hatchery full of trout, too. I think he liked my mother. He gave her fish and eggs and called her 'Lahori', which was his own weird version of her real name."

"Neat! You never told me your mother's name."

"Leokadija."

"Pretty."

"Yeah. My dad calls her 'Lia-lia'. Americans say 'La-la'. What's your mother's name?"

"Marcelline. With two l's."

"Sounds exotic."

"Oh, I'm sure she'd love to hear you say that." Her words were upbeat with a slight tone of sarcasm.

"You must've been a happy kid, Luke. It sounds like your parents love you very much."

"Probably too much. My mom embarrasses me all the time. She always kisses and hugs me in front of my friends. Sometimes she even messes with my hair."

"Consider it a gift, Luke. You have no idea how lucky you are. Not everybody is. My mother never loved me.

She made my life a living Hell."

She looked at me, and I must have looked surprised. How could Celia's mother not love her? How could anyone not love her?

Suddenly she tripped. She grabbed my arm to stop herself from falling and let her hand slide down into mine. She steadied herself but didn't let go. My heart was doing handstands.

"Sorry. I should watch where I'm going. These sidewalks are pretty cracked up here—

"Hey! Is your hand wet?"

My face flushed like I'd just stuck my head into a hot oven. I was mortified—Celia had discovered my sweaty hands! I had been living with that shameful secret all my life.

I was trapped like a rat. All I could do was fess up and hope she wouldn't think I was totally uncool.

"Yeah. They've been that way ever since I can remember."

"Mine, too!" she said. "Feel!"

It was an amazing moment. Her hand was soaked. And she wasn't even embarrassed.

"It must be the sign of an artist. You know … we're sensitive, thin-skinned, creative … dreamers," she said.

She wasn't laughing, but I sensed she wanted me to look over at her. As I did, I saw her wistful face with eyes to the sky, fluttering her long eyelashes like the wings of a butterfly. I acknowledged her satire with a knowing smirk.

"Hey! Look at that." She yanked us to a stop in front of an old two-story house. "What kind of siding is that?"

I knew the house. An old woman lived there and had covered the entire building with sheet metal from flattened out cans.

"Tin cans. An old lady did it all herself."

"That is so cool! Looks like a patchwork quilt."

"Yeah, I know. Her house turned into a community project. People brought boxes filled with empty cans and put them in her backyard every day."

"Don't you just love this neighborhood?" She spoke softly and gave my hand a damp squeeze.

"Yeah, for sure." I said. That was the closest I'd ever been to Celia, and it was all thanks to a broken up city sidewalk and my stupid, sweaty hands.

Chapter 38

Northerly Island isn't really an island. It's a small, man-made peninsula along Chicago's lakefront. Adler Planetarium sits on the northern tip, and Meigs Airport occupied the rest of the space, which included a small terminal, control tower, and a single north-south runway.

The island area is one of Chicago's most scenic destinations on Lake Michigan. I went there as often as I could to soak in the sun, enjoy the cool lake breeze, and listen to the cries of seagulls and tinkling pulleys on aluminum sailboat masts.

But the best part of all was watching and hearing the Pipers, Cessnas, Beechcrafts, and Mooneys take off and land on runway 18/36.

"I love this place, Luke."

Celia became obsessed with the lake—and with its moods. She loved it most when the wind blew strong and steady from the north and riled the All-American Great

Lady into a hissy fit of whitecaps, crashing its rocky lake walls, spraying visitors and windshields.

We sat in whichever car offered the best view of the water—my Raven Black Ford Crestline or her Dove Grey Citroën 2CV. Celia's car was no ordinary car, but she was no ordinary girl. To say she was drawn to oddness would be an understatement.

"I fell in love with it on my first drive," said Celia.

"No kidding?"

"Yeah. Pavel lent me his car while he looked for a driveshaft for my old Plymouth."

"Pavel?"

"He's a mechanic who works out of his garage in my neighborhood. He calls himself a 'Russian DP', but I don't really know what that means," she said and laughed.

"Ha, ha. I do. He's an immigrant like me. It means he's a 'Displaced Person' from Russia, Lithuania's next-door neighbor."

"Small world."

"Russia's actually bigger than the entire US continent."

"I should've paid more attention in my geography class—anyway, he called my car his 'dusha'." She said it with partly puckered lips and a half-smile—like the prelude to a kiss.

"That means 'soul' in Russian. And in Lithuanian, too."

"Really? I thought he got it from the French 'deux chevoux', for 2CV. He always cries out 'Moya dusha' when he sees me pull into his driveway."

"He means 'my soul', Celia. And I don't think he's

talking about the car."

She giggled, "I should have known. It's never about the car, is it?"

I chuckled insincerely. "How did you finally end up with it?"

"He wanted a bigger car, so he traded with me for my Plymouth."

She looked at me again with those dreamy eyes. "Pavel said his little dusha would live on as long as he did. He said he'd always take good care of it and wouldn't charge me for labor. Only parts."

Oh, I'm sure he took care of everything in your car, Celia. Please stop saying dusha—

"Nice deal," I said.

"Yeah, I got lucky."

I wanted to change the subject. "Is that your sketchbook?" I asked. "Can I see it?"

A hardbound sketchbook lay face down on the back seat. Celia reached back, picked it up, and handed it to me. It was filled with pages and pages of hand drawn body parts—hands, legs, torsos, faces, eyes, and heads. They reminded me of the Leonardo Da Vinci sketches in the art history books I used to pore over in the art library at Navy Pier.

Most were pencil drawings, but there were a few drawn in ballpoint pen. Celia must have preferred the thin line with every detail clearly defined.

"Who's the model?"

"Mostly Sara. Some Mr. Victor."

"Really? When did he pose for you?"

"Never. It's all from my head."

"What do you mean?"

"It's from memory, from watching him while he does whatever he does."

"Did he undress?"

"No. I never saw him without his clothes. I saw his sleeves rolled up a few times."

"Then how did you know what his body looks like? Those are detailed images."

"I don't know how. It's just the way I imagine everything. I made most of those sketches at home."

"But how do you remember the proportions? Those are really great drawings."

"I don't know how. I just do. I could go home and draw you tonight. As a matter of fact—"

Celia leaned forward and fingered up a few pages. Her hair swept across my arm and smelled like the first flowers of spring—like lilies of the valley.

"—here you are."

"Wow." I smiled big at her rendering of me. It was good. Better than good. It was the best drawing I'd ever seen in my life.

I didn't remember Celia ever drawing me, but there I was. All those times I had thrashed myself, thinking she wasn't paying any attention to me, must have been pure paranoia. Not only had she noticed, she had studied the smallest details. She'd even gotten my droopy eyelids right.

Chapter 39

"You know, my Lithuanian ancestors worshipped trees. I heard there are some who still do."

"That is so cool!" said Celia. "I love trees, too. I'm not sure I worship anything, but If I ever do, it'll be trees."

"I thought you were Catholic."

"My mother is Catholic. She dragged me to church every Sunday, but when I started high school, I quit going. She flipped, but she couldn't force me to go, and I was too old to hit. She said I was going straight to Hell, and she didn't give a Damn."

"So, are you still Catholic?"

"I don't think so. I know I'm crazy, but besides that, I don't know if I'm anything."

Celia traced a line around the steering wheel with her delicate forefinger. She looked at me and said, "What about you, Luke?"

"I used to be Catholic."

"And you're not now?"

"I stopped going to church after I graduated from Rita. I still go with my folks on Easter and Christmas, for their sake, but we never talk about religion."

I didn't want to keep talking about myself. I wanted to know more about Celia.

"Where did your love of trees come from?"

"I always climbed trees when I was a kid. It was so fun. Being up high on a branch away from everything was so ... peaceful. I told our neighbor that he was a jerk for chopping down a great white oak just so he could add on a stupid room addition. And I got Hell from my mother when he tattled on me."

"Wow. How old were you?"

"I think I was nine or ten."

"What about your dad? Didn't he stick up for you?"

"Yep. And he made the big mistake of laughing. That's when my mother unleashed her fury on him."

"Wow."

"Marcelline ruled the roost. My dad was never allowed to contradict her. She told him opinions from a fool didn't count and that he should just keep his stupid mouth shut. She didn't want him to inflict his stupidity on her daughter."

"Man."

"You have no idea."

"What about your friends?"

"I wasn't allowed to have any. I wasn't supposed to go to their houses either, but when my friend, Sally, broke her arm, she asked me to help carry her books home, so I did. Her mom was really nice. She thanked me and asked me to come inside. It was strange and warm. Everyone was happy. They asked me to stay and play, but of course I had to tell them I couldn't."

"Man. What a lonely existence for a little girl."

"Yeah, I guess. When I was young, I spent all my free time playing with my tiny plastic baby dolls. I staged them in bushes, flowers, rocks, sand. After a warm summer rain, I'd put them under the gutter runoff and pretend it was a beautiful waterfall. I created an entire world of fantasy scenes with those dolls. I really loved them. They were my little friends."

She faced me and asked softly, "Are you sure you want to hear about this? It's not exactly the kind of thing guys care much about."

She was calm and lovely and I couldn't resist sneaking a peek at her pretty feet. "It's a perfect subject for this guy. I'm a doll man from way back."

She giggled. "Yes, of course you are."

"No, I'm not kidding. When I was a kid in Germany, I had three plush clown dolls. My mother's German lady friend gave them to her. I made a house and furniture out of cardboard, and I set up stage plays. The dolls were the actors. I even made costumes with my mother's fabric scraps."

"I think I might like you, Luke. But not too much."

My heart quivered and filled with hope. "So, tell me more about your little plastic people."

"There were nine of them. They had badly disjointed arms and legs and homely little faces, but to me, they were precious."

Celia glanced at me, probably to see if I was still listening. She had no idea how closely I studied her soft pink lips, watching them move so perfectly as she formed each word.

"I kept my dolls in a white metal bread box with yellow daisies on the front. I took it with me wherever we went, and I always closed the clasp tight.

"It was the third of July—I remember because we were going to see fireworks the next day—I had put my doll tin on the roof of our car so I could help my mother load groceries. She was in a huge huff as usual, yelling at me to hurry up. As we were pulling out, I reached over to where my dolls should have been on the back seat, but they weren't there. They were still on the roof. I was horrified. I begged her to turn back, but Marcelline refused."

"Are you serious?" I couldn't believe any mother could be so cruel. "How could she not have turned back? Didn't she know what those dolls meant to you?"

"Oh, yeah. She knew. It was another chance for her to beat me down and punish me, to take out her hatred on me. You've never known a mother like her, Luke. Believe me."

She was right. The women in my world were kind and loving. They protected their children no matter what.

"What did she say when she heard you crying?"

"She didn't say anything. She screamed at the top of her lungs. 'I paid a lot of money for those stupid dolls! Now you, with your goddamn lackadaisical attitude, lost them! You're just like your goddamn father! He couldn't find his own head if it wasn't stuck to his stupid neck! Stop that crying! I can't think straight with all your sniveling. I never should have had you. Your father *had* to have a baby ... *I* never wanted you."

Tears filled Celia's eyes. Sadness filled me. I had no experience with anything like that. How could a child have grown up in such Hell and still be as sweet as Celia?

"And she never went back to look for your dolls? You never saw them again?"

"No. I watched my pretty bread box get smaller and smaller until it finally disappeared. Then she pulled over and stopped. I hoped, and waited, for her to make a U-turn. Instead, she took a Kleenex out of her purse and wiped off her big thick glasses. They were probably covered with her spit from yelling at me. She drove off and kept going. I knew then I'd never see my little buddies again. And I never did."

I fought back tears. I'd never heard such a miserable story. I wanted to wrap my arms around her, to hold her, to kiss her. I wanted to say something meaningful, but what could I have said or done to ease the pain of a lifetime of abuse, especially when it had come from her own mother.

"I feel so bad for you, Celia. Nobody deserves to be treated like that. How do you keep up such a brave face?"

She looked up and said, "I didn't know things weren't supposed to be that way."

Chapter 40

"What kind of work do you do for Mr. Victor, Luke?"

We sat in Celia's car. I preferred hers over mine because it was filled with her presence: lilies of the valley with a dash of Newport tobacco mint.

The 2CV was compact inside. It had a slippery bench seat which allowed our bodies to touch permissibly and often. Seat belts were an optional feature in automobiles. Thank God her car didn't have any.

I loved being her passenger. Her hip slid into mine when she turned left. Her arm brushed mine when she shifted gears. Her leg bumped my knee when we stopped. Her cute feet were in plain sight working the pedals on the floor.

There was no legitimate excuse to sit close together in my Ford. The seat was too wide to innocently close the gap between us. I remember Celia crashing into me only once when I made a sharp, tire squealing, ninety-degree hard right veering over to an exit ramp on Lake Shore Drive.

"I don't think he had any one job in mind when he asked me to work for him, but he's had me do everything imaginable."

"Like what?"

"Well, I learned all kinds of things—plumbing, electrical work, carpentry, furniture making, graphic design—"

"Oh, you built furniture, too? My dad did lots of work like that on our Oak Lawn house."

"Cool. What did your dad do professionally?"

"He was the Art Director for Argonne Laboratories. You know, they do particle research and all kinds of nuclear stuff. They built part of the first atomic bomb there."

"What did Argonne need from the art department?"

"He did all of their artwork and preparation for print."

"Was he a graphic designer?" I wondered if he had worked in the field I was aspiring to.

"He called himself a graphic artist and he really loved cartooning. He invented some adorable characters. One was 'Lemme Atom'. It was a cheerful little atomic go-getter type person, you know—with orbiting electrons around its fat little body.

"It eventually became the official logo for Argonne. They used it on letterheads, newsletters, signs, even bathrooms. My dad made a 'Lucy Atom' for women. She was either Lemme's wife or girlfriend, like Minnie is to Mickey. I don't think anyone really knew if they were married or just ... pals." Celia snickered.

"You know, I always wondered if my comic book heroes were married. I knew Donald Duck had nephews, but no kids."

She laughed, her front teeth twinkling in the sunlight. "I think I might like you, Luke. A little." She squinted and held up her hand, pinching her thumb and forefinger close together as though she were trying to measure an imperceptible gap between the two. I couldn't see a space, but it was a huge leap forward in our relationship.

"All my dad's coworkers loved him. He was talented and very kind. And humble. If anyone needed help, he was there to lend a hand. He made art posters for church bazaars and bingo nights. Women asked him to design their wedding invitations and draw cartoon characters for their kids' birthday party decorations. He even wrote weekly articles for the local newspaper which he illustrated with his cartoons."

It was obvious she really loved her dad. More proof was her cherished little neck pendant: the pewter PBY flying happily over the world's most inspiring terrain.

"He must have been a super good guy. What about his flying?"

"Oh, he said he lost his taste for flying after he came home from the war. Along with his taste for rice." She laughed, but I didn't get it.

"I thought he flew combat missions in the PBY."

"He did. Mostly reconnaissance, supply runs, and search and rescue at sea. He was so brave." Her face glowed with pride.

"Once, he rescued a downed Navy pilot out of the water near a Japanese held island. He landed his 'Cat', you know, nicknamed from the 'Catalina Flying Boat'—"

"I know, I'm looking at one," I said, thrilled to have something smart to say and an excuse to peek at Celia's chest. She smiled.

"Did he tell you any more about that time, Celia?"

"Yeah. He was spotted by the enemy when they were pulling the guy on board. Bullets were hitting the water all around them as he started his take-off run. Luckily, the bad guys only had rifles. He wouldn't have made it back if they'd had bigger weapons."

"That's fantastic. Really cool. But—I feel stupid for asking—why didn't he like rice?" I cringed, worried she'd think I was the dumbest guy in town.

"Oh, no Luke. I should've explained. My dad hated rice because of all the bodies on the beaches. That's what the Seabees saw when they first landed. Our troops left the enemy corpses for the Construction Battalion. They had the heavy equipment to dig huge holes for mass burials."

"I still don't—"

"The bodies were putrefied, rotting, crawling with maggots, and ... you can imagine ... stinking to high Heaven. He said they looked like they were covered with white rice."

She said it matter-of-factly, but her face didn't match that sentiment.

"I get it. Your dad suffered from shell shock. The sight of rice triggered his mind to relive the horror."

"Yep. Even my cruel mother never kept rice in the house after my dad came home from the war."

We both reached toward the ashtray and accidentally touched hands. I wasn't sure, but it seemed like she waited a whole extra second before pulling her hand away from mine.

Chapter 41

"What my dad really wanted was to work as an artist for Walt Disney."

"Why didn't he?"

"It meant moving to California, but my mother quickly put an end to that dream." Celia sounded disappointed.

"What's wrong with California?"

"Somewhere she heard California was the 'Land of Fruits and Nuts'. There was no way in Hell Marcelline would move to a state full of 'Goddamn homosexuals and crazy people'."

"Didn't your father try to reach some kind of compromise with your mother? You know, talk about it like a family?"

"He wasn't a coward, Luke. And he wasn't afraid of my mother. He just wanted to keep peace in our family. He knew it would have harmed me a lot more to see and hear them fighting and screaming at each other. She saw it as his weakness, but I always knew it was his strength that allowed him to take her abuse without protest. He let her think that she won—when in reality he was the champion. I have the greatest love and respect for him. I know he did it for me."

"Wow."

"Then he died."

"Oh, I'm so sorry, Celia."

"He had a heart condition and refused treatment. I never even knew about it, but I remember him telling me once: 'Sam, I just want to live long enough to see you graduate high school.' Maybe he thought I wouldn't need him any more. I was a sophomore when he died. He didn't make it to my graduation."

"That is so sad. I can't imagine how you must have felt. I don't know what I would have done if either of my parents had died."

"It was really bad, Luke."

"Wait. He called you Sam?"

"Yep, that was his nickname for me. He never called me Celia. Well, unless he was mad at me."

"You said your dad refused treatment. Wasn't that sort of like suicide? I mean, it sounds like maybe he could have had surgery or something—"

"Hmm. I never thought about it like that. Maybe. Yeah, you could be right, Luke."

I hoped I was wrong. I'd heard somewhere that suicide ran in families. I felt bad for bringing it up. I needed another subject change—I felt awkward.

"Want a Newport?" she asked, glancing up. I didn't think I'd ever get used to looking into her eyes. They transformed my reality, especially when she shared something really deep with me.

"Sure." She flipped back the box top flap with her delicate fingers. When they moved, they drew lines in space—but not jagged, ugly lines. They formed curves that flowed, twined, and danced. They were lines made by the fingers of an artist.

She put two cigarettes between her parted lips. She took the paper matchbook, and with one fluid motion of her wrist, folded back the cover, pulled out a match, and swiped it on the striking strip. Her wrist rolled as she held the burning flame.

I watched the twin cigarettes catch fire as she inhaled the minty smoke. She placed the filter tip between my lips. I breathed in the cooling menthol, the flavor of Celia.

"I don't want to like you too much, Luke."

"Uhh—"

"Because then I would hate you." She looked at my befuddled face.

"Someday maybe I'll explain."

"Thanks," I said, wondering what she meant.

"Any time."

We sat quiet, smoking, watching the sun fade down. The darkened skyline began to twinkle as the city lights came up.

Chapter 42

Whoever engineered the design of the front bench seat in my Ford must have had making out in mind. It was upholstered in soft, pleated, easy-clean white vinyl. It was a smooth move to glide over to my lovely passenger and get busy.

No matter how hot things got, I kept a watchful eye open for cops. When a police vehicle approached, there was just a nick of time to peel off, zip up, and slip back behind the wheel while she sat up, tugged her skirt down, crossed her arms over her blouse, and assumed an innocent pose.

Dalia and I had been dating for over a year, and despite our youthful hormones, sex had become somewhat routine. We usually skipped the preliminaries and got right down to business.

From the length and depth of our relationship, we'd earned certain rights and privileges. Dalia didn't have to feel like one of those wild American girls the bad boys talked about—a girl who would let a guy slide into home base on the third date.

We had declared our love for each other when I'd given her my Saint Rita High School graduation ring to wear as a sign of our commitment. She wound red angora yarn around the skinny part of the base until the ring fit the third finger on her right hand.

I picked up Dalia after dinner and drove to Marquette Park. Cars with couples lined the curbs as usual, but I saw from a distance that my favorite spot directly under the street lamp was vacant. It was the perfect petting place because the car was bathed in strong light, making the interior even darker and harder to see into. I don't think the other kids knew that trick: my spot was always available.

We flicked our cigarettes out of the open window vents, and she slid into the far corner of the front seat. She kicked off her shoes and stretched her leg out over the seat.

I slid into the deep warmth of her thighs. I moved my arm up her back under her blouse. My fingers released the familiar bra hooks. My free hand snuck in and cupped her breast as it had countless times before. She let out a soft sigh like she always did. We kissed and I tasted Wrigley's mint, like I had so many times before.

But something was different.

Strange thoughts invaded my brain while my hand fondled Dalia's softness. I wondered what Celia's breasts felt like. They looked smaller than Dalia's—maybe they were firmer?

Two and two weren't adding up. Instead of feeding my ardor, thoughts of Celia quickly cooled my lust for Dalia. Nothing felt right.

"What's wrong, Lukai?"

"I don't know. Maybe I'm catching a cold or something. You want a cigarette?" I withdrew my hands and returned to my side of the seat.

"Yeah ... sure."

She sounded disappointed, but seemed to accept that sometimes things happened in old, time-honored relationships. She put her leg down on the floor and reached behind her back with both hands to refasten her bra.

I thought I should tell her but hesitated. I wasn't ready to admit that I'd met someone—and that she'd barbecued my brain and marinated my mind.

I felt like I was cheating. But on whom, I wasn't sure. I thought I was being unfaithful to both girls. I was betraying Celia with my body and Dalia with my mind.

I suspected my new confusion was here to stay, and would probably get worse. I wasn't looking forward to my next date. I had to end it with Dalia.

Chapter 43

"I want to talk with you both," said Mr. Victor.

Sara and I had been working in the studio when he came in and walked to the blackboards. I got up from my drawing table and sat in one of the Herman Miller buckets, swiveling around to face Mr. Victor. Sara plopped into another one and threw a leg over the side.

He picked a new piece of chalk and drew an equilateral triangle. Near the left-hand corner, he printed the word SOURCE. On the right, he wrote SYSTEM, and at the apex, EXPRESSION.

"This is an ideogram of an Expression. I have been talking to you about this concept, and I want to show you how I see it all coming together. By discussing it with you first, I can work the bugs out of the idea before I present it to the group on Thursday."

We both said, "Cool," and Sara asked, "Are all Expressions triangular in shape? Is that how we'd see them?"

"No. The triangle is only a visual aid for the concept. It is like a figure of speech. Like a diagram of an idea."

"Is that the most basic configuration of an Expression?" I asked.

"Yes. It can be a single cell or an entire body made up of trillions of cells, each one built according to a blueprint—the genetic code. Every cell is made up of smaller parts, and each of those is made of molecules, atoms, electrons, protons and neutrons. It is practically endless, impossible for our human brains to fully comprehend."

As Mr. Victor elaborated, he made notes, lines, and arrows on the board. Soon, a tangled hairball swallowed up his original triangle.

Sara and I looked at each other, unsure where Mr. Victor was headed.

"Cells die regularly in the living body. Many are replaced by new living cells," he said.

"What if an Expression loses the Source?" asked Sara.

"It cannot. The Source is everywhere. The Source cannot die. Neither can the System. Perhaps I should not say cannot. There is no cannot in the universe. If the Source or System died, it would be the end of everything."

"Couldn't what you call 'Source' be another word for God?" I asked.

"Of course it can. Words are just words."

"And a cigar is just a smoke," said Sara, casually swinging her dangling leg. Mr. Victor chuckled.

"I have no problem calling the Source God. Actually, that does not conflict with what we are discussing. We are talking about physical reality. It is not in the realm of the metaphysical or spiritual. The Source is named, but not explained."

"Can it be spiritual?" asked Sara.

"If you mean can it be an unexplained force in the universe—yes. Boundless in space and time? Okay. Invisible? Fine. Creator of Heaven and Earth? Well, that is where we are entering into areas subject to beliefs, desires, emotions, and individual interpretations. It is a messy sandbox full of sticky sand. I choose to leave it alone and leave it at that."

He lit a cigarette and asked, "Okay, what do you think so far?"

"I'm confused," I said. "You've been talking about cells and atoms and molecules having a Source, a System, and an Expression. But a body is also composed of a Source, System, and Expression. So a body is a collection of Expressions, but a collection of Expressions will not necessarily makeup a body."

"Yes, you are right, Luke. It is confusing. Sara, how do you see it?"

"I'm with Luke. How about eliminating the particles from the conversation? We know they exist, but we don't have to acknowledge them when we talk about Expressions as bodies."

"Yes, that is okay," said Mr. Victor. He erased the mess on the board. "Simpler is better." He drew a new triangle.

"Let us start with a triangle with each corner representing a component. Two of the components are infinite and invisible. They are the Source and the System."

He wrote the words near the bottom of each corner.

"The third component is the Expression. It is the part visible to the eye, and it is temporary. It has a beginning and an end." He wrote Expression at the top and drew a circle inside the triangle.

"The circle represents a hole. It is open and allows energy—the Source and the System, the power of the universe—to pass through it. This is a simplified graphic representation of an Expression. But it also represents all living things."

"I think I understand now," I said, "Except for one thing. If we're all made up of solid matter, how are we open? How can anything penetrate us?"

"That is just it, Luke! We are not solid! In fact, there may be no such thing as solid in the cosmos. All matter is made of elemental particles—molecules, atoms, electrons, protons, and neutrons. Scientists are talking about even smaller particles existing within those particles.

"They are all empty space! Electrical charges spinning around at incomprehensible speeds. They are saying matter is ninety-nine-point-nine plus an endless number of nines percent empty space, which means empty space by any practical measure."

"So if we accept that all matter is empty space within empty space, then we are all just holes in the universe," I said.

"Yes, Luke. Exactly!" said Mr. Victor. "We are HOLES in the Universe."

Chapter 44

After his HOLE in the Universe presentation, Mr. Victor asked us to pull down all the studio window shades except the one facing Laurel Street. He wanted that one left half way open. It was a bright and sunny Thursday in Old Town, and we were sitting in semi-darkness.

He walked around and handed us each a sheet of black construction paper and a sheet of regular white typewriter paper. Then he passed out some ordinary sewing pins like the kind my mother kept in her pincushion.

"Okay, people. Look toward the window and block out the light with the black paper. What do you see?"

"I see people in my peripheral vision," said Kurt.

"I want you to focus on nothing," said Mr. Victor.

"Okay. I see nothing," Kurt obliged.

"Good. Now with the pin, poke a hole near the center of the black paper and hold it up again to block out the light. What do you see?"

"A tiny, bright light," said Shannon. "When I move the paper closer to my eye, I see the whole window."

"Good. Now everyone take your white paper and hold it about a foot back from the pinhole. You will see a faint image on the white paper. By adjusting the distance, you can focus the image. Now what do you see?"

"The window and the street outside, but everything is upside down. You're going to introduce us to the pinhole camera, aren't you?" asked Celia.

"Actually, I am not going to talk about pinhole cameras. I am going to talk about us," he said.

"You can all see that the light coming through the little hole carries all of the imagery from outside this building. Only a tiny part of that light hits the black paper, and an even tinier part passes through the pinhole. If we go outside, the light of the sun and all of the surrounding reflected lights will be transmitted in perfect order through the little opening. An image of the universe will pass through the tiny pinhole."

"But we wouldn't be able to see the image any more because the bright light outdoors would wash out the light showing through the pinhole," said Celia.

"That is absolutely true," said Mr. Victor. "But seen or unseen, the light would still be there. Yes?"

"Yes, of course."

"Now let us imagine the light is the life energy of the universe. Imagine it is the Source and the System."

Everyone squinted while twisting and turning the papers in their hands.

"Now cover the pinhole completely. No hole—no

light. Did the light go out? Of course not. Only one pinhole was closed." He studied his students' faces.

"What if we are all pinholes?" asked Mr. Victor.

He walked over to the window and opened the shade. Sunlight flooded in.

"I would like you to chew on that before our next class. I will see you all next week."

I glanced at Celia and her eyes met mine. It was another melting moment. The sun beamed in and sparked the green amber. Her eyes shimmered like watercolored crystals. I wanted to see inside and uncover the secrets hiding behind those wondrous windows.

"Have you ever prayed for something you wanted really bad, and then had your prayers answered, Luke?"

"Hmm." I thought for a moment. "I do remember one time—"

"Tell me about it."

"I was flunking my analytic geometry class two semesters ago. It was bad—I was already on probation because I had low grades in rhetoric and chemistry. Blowing analyt would have meant I'd have to leave Navy Pier and go to Wilson for a year to pull up my average. Then I'd have to petition to get back into the Pier."

"So you prayed."

"Yep. I didn't really believe in it any more, but I decided to give it a shot anyway."

"How did you do it?"

Wow. I can't believe she's really interested.

"I snuck into Nativity and gave it my all."

"You snuck in? And prayed to God?"

"Everybody—God, Jesus, Mary, Saint Anthony."
"Who's Saint Anthony?"
"He's the saint my dad is named after."
"Your dad's name is Anthony?"
"Actually, it's Antanas, but Americans call him Tony."
"Cool! So I take it you passed the course."
"With a 'D'. But at least I was able to hang in there for another semester."
"So your prayers were answered."
"Well ... I guess. If I was a believer—"
"Luke, I wanna go there! It's still early. Can we swing by on our way home?"

Oh my God! Celia wants to visit my old church—

"Yeah, let's go! Follow me in your car."

Chapter 45

My hands were sweating and slipping on the steering wheel. Seeing Celia's little grey bug in my rear view mirror filled me with nervous anticipation.

I had to pull over and wait for her on Western Boulevard when she got caught by a changing traffic light. Some angry motorists glared at me as they leaned on their horns and flew around my car.

This was my regular route home from Mr. Victor's, but the ride had never felt like this before. I didn't even smoke, and I forgot to turn on the radio.

I pulled into the church's empty parking lot. Celia parked next to me.

It was the new Nativity, built after I had graduated from Saint Rita High School. It was a mix of stone, blond brick, and Italian Renaissance Modern with Lithuanian motifs. Inside was Italian marble, terrazzo, white oak, and fake gold. The windows were stained glass created by a

Lithuanian artist.

Our jewelry store is less than a half block away. I can see it from here. If my folks knew I was here—

"Can we go in, Luke?"

"Sure."

We walked up the stone steps to the three pairs of double doors, each one with a cross-shaped window. The middle doors were always unlocked during the day. It was Tuesday afternoon, too late for a funeral and too early for an evening novena or Rosary prayer session. I was sure the place was empty and opened the door for Celia.

I followed her up the left side aisle toward the altar. She stopped at the second row of pews. She sat down on the glossy varnished oak bench and slid to the right to make room for me.

Sunlight streamed through colorful leaded glass artwork illuminating Jesus, Mary, angels, and saints against backgrounds of sunny and stormy skies, pastoral scenes, and famous Lithuanian churches. Celia was glowing, bathed in glorious colors.

What a heavenly sight!

She reached forward and pulled down the padded kneeler. She knelt down and rested her arms on the back of the bench in front of us. She clasped her hands together.

Is she praying?

I knelt down next to her, leaned forward in prayer position, and peeked at her face. Her eyes were closed and she was still.

God, she's so beautiful!

A nun came out of the sacristy door behind the altar and headed down the aisle toward us. It was Sister Francetta, my second grade teacher. She recognized me and smiled as she walked past. I smiled back.

Sister, if you only knew who I'm worshipping—

I smelled incense, probably from a funeral mass earlier. The priest would have walked around the casket with a brass hanging incense burner anointing the spirit of the deceased.

I wondered what was going on in Celia's mind. Maybe she was praying for her dad.

Sister Francetta was gone. A couple of old 'babushkas' were huddled together in the back pews exchanging whispers. I didn't know them, but they probably knew me. The old biddies knew everything that went on in the neighborhood. I hoped I wouldn't have to explain to my mom what I was doing in church—

I stand at the altar. Father Zak is next to me holding a book. We turn and look down the wide center aisle. A white linen runner is sprinkled with flower petals—poppies and bright blue cornflowers. Big bouquets of flowers are attached to the ends of the pews.

I see friends, neighbors, and faraway family I haven't seen in a long time. I see my mom and dad. Everyone is smiling.

The huge pipe organ belts out with tremendous power. The faces turn toward the back of the church.

Celia steps into the center aisle. Mr. Victor is beside her in a black suit. She holds onto his arm and they walk together slowly. The pipes are roaring.

She is dressed in a white satin wedding gown with a lacy flowing train. Her eyes are on me. Only me. She smiles. She looks like an angel. My angel.

They gently step up to the altar. Celia never takes her eyes off mine. She lets go of Mr. Victor and he joins Stan, Duck, and Droopy, my groomsmen. Celia's bridesmaids are on her left—Sara, Shannon, and two girls I don't know.

Father Zak motions to Celia and she takes her place next to me. My head is buzzing. Father Zak is saying words, but I can't hear them. I don't care what he's saying. I nod and say—

"Luke?" Celia whispered softly.

"I do ... I mean, are you okay?"

"It's so beautiful here. So peaceful. I don't want to leave, but we probably should."

"Yeah. I know."

I followed her to the exit and pushed open the heavy door. It was warm and sunny outside. I saw my old school behind the playground parking lot. A couple of kids were chasing around, kicking a can, making noise. Some sparrows hopped on the asphalt pecking at a piece of white bread, probably a leftover from someone's lunch box.

"Thanks for bringing me here, Luke. It's a lovely place. Did you have any extraordinary visions? Say any special prayers?"

"Yep. Did you?"

"I'll never tell."

Thank God she can't read my mind.

"I'll tell if you'll tell—"

"I'm sorry, Luke. I hate to run, but I have to go home

and get ready for my night shift at Christ Hospital."

"Aww ... okay, Celia. I'll see you at Mr. Victor's Thursday?"

"Yep. I'll see you then. Bye, Luke."

I was sorry she had to leave, but it was probably a good thing. I was pretty sure I would have said or done something stupid if left in her company for much longer.

She drove off and turned south on California Avenue. I leaned against my car and lit up a Lucky.

Chapter 46

I tried to stay focused on my work, but I was glad when Thursday finally arrived.

Mr. Victor carried in two buckets filled with small plastic multicolored blocks and set them on the workbench.

"You are probably familiar with these."

"Legos," said Kurt.

"Yes. Everybody help yourselves. Take three or four handfuls. You can have more as you need them. Do not worry about colors. See what you can make with them."

The students scooped up the blocks and brought them to their worktables. They played around for a few minutes, then began to build objects.

Kurt created a long form with wheels on the end. He said it was a flying penis for Dick Spacy. Marty constructed a tank. Celia built a large spider using red, green, and blue bricks. Tad tried to see how far he could get without having two blocks of the same color touching. Sara assembled a Jesus to annoy Shannon who was building a residence on stilts.

"All of your creations are being constructed from the same kind of blocks."

I was at my drafting table across the room. Playing with Legos looked like a fun exercise, but I couldn't participate. I had to finish and deliver a graphics job for David Levin, Mr. Victor's client.

"The blocks are designed as a modular system. This one is quite limited as you will see when you try to build something simple like a wheel. But even with limitations, you can achieve considerable variety." He walked to the front of the room.

"The object you will construct can be called an Expression. You—the builder—are the intelligent Source. The method in which the blocks combine is determined by the System. Your assignment is to create. Limit your vision to something achievable in twenty or thirty minutes. I will be back by then."

He left the room.

When he returned, he surveyed their works. Kurt performed aerobatics with his space banana, attacking Marty who tried to shoot it down with his tank. Sara pretended to walk her Jesus on water, further irritating Shannon.

It was obvious the Legos were much better suited for mechanical expressions. Considerable leaps of imagination were needed to see them as Jesus, the penis, or even as Celia's spider.

"When you are finished, pass your Expression to the person on your right."

Sara got the space penis, Tad got the tank, Celia received Tad's color experiment, and Kurt ended up with Celia's spider. Shannon accepted Jesus and gave Sara an evil "I'll get you for this" look.

Marty examined Shannon's house on the water and cried out, "Help me! I'm sinking!" He mocked the motion of a residence being swallowed up by a lake when its footings collapsed.

Carrying the bucket, Mr. Victor walked around and poured extra piles of Legos onto each workstation.

"Alright. Now I would like you to study what is in front of you and replicate it exactly. Take your time and make a perfect copy."

Celia had a little trouble with Tad's color creation. She had to remove some blocks to see what color was behind them, and then put them back as they were.

In less than fifteen minutes, everyone had a cloned copy. Sara was the only one who took a few creative liberties. She made the tip of her space penis red.

"I thought it would be an improvement. Isn't that what evolution is all about?" asked Sara. Everyone laughed.

I hated to leave, but I had to wrap it up and get to Mr. Levin's office. At least I was able to see Celia's Lego construction, which was really cool, but I wondered why she chose to make a spider.

When I returned a little over an hour later, Mr. Victor was ending his session.

"... exactly," he said. "Now, everyone take apart your Expressions and put the Legos back into the buckets."

There was an immediate change of mood in the room. The students were hesitant to dismantle their creations. I'd noticed a similar apprehension before when Mr. Victor had gathered up their drawings and threw them into a fiber drum to be disposed of with the trash. It appeared the creators were reluctant to destroy their creations even when they had no apparent value.

"You should never fall in love with your creations," he said. "Your drawings are a process—a journey—not the destination. When you save a sketch, you are pausing on your passage. You might get stuck.

"It is tempting to stop and admire your progress rather than pushing to new ground, but if you do so, you are in danger of becoming stale and obsolete at the outset of your trip. You will cease to be creators and artists. You will become imitators, even when copying your own work."

Celia slowly dismantled the copy of her spider and returned the blocks to the bucket. When she picked up the original spider, she hesitated and turned to Mr. Victor.

"Can I take him home? I'll replace the Legos. I grew kind of fond of him. His name is Edgar."

Mr. Victor answered gently, "Celia, you are missing the point of the exercise—"

"Pleeeeeeze, Mr. Victor?" Celia scrunched her eyebrows and posed a pouty bottom lip.

It was pretty clear to me that everyone thought she was clowning around. They hadn't detected the anguish in her voice—but I had—and it was painful to watch. I desperately hoped he'd let her keep him.

"Well ... alright, Celia. I cannot turn down such a heartfelt request. Keep Edgar. And there is no need to replace the blocks. We have lots of them."

I was relieved he gave in to her plea. Maybe he'd seen something in her eyes like I had—something unexplained.

"What you have demonstrated today is one—when given an intelligent Source along with building blocks, which are designed to work within the System, you can generate thousands of different possibilities. Each possibility is an Expression.

"Two—you have shown your ability to replicate. That is how nature and the human body work. Each cell generates an identical copy of itself before splitting into two cells, then four, then eight, and so on. It is reproduction taken to its most basic form.

"Three—Sara added a mutation. The next copy will be a penis with a red tip. If the red-tipped version proves more attractive and beats the plain one by out-reproducing, it will become the prevailing design. In time, the mono-colored penis will be extinct."

Most of the group laughed and clapped their hands. There was nothing like penis talk to uplift the spirits. A big hooray went out to the two-toned penis. Sara stood up and took a bow.

I noticed Celia hadn't joined into the playful penis hoopla. She looked detached, drawing intensely in her sketchbook. Edgar sat on her workbench.

"Okay, okay. Now I would like to share an observation with all of you. I have noticed that all of your creations have been ordinary. I have not seen any radical departures from what is familiar. I would like to suggest that is exactly how nature works. Little steps at each time. Drastic leaps do not survive. Ordinary kills the extraordinary every time."

The room quieted. I wondered if anyone else in the class felt like an uninspired imitator. I know I did. Were we all killers of creativity?

"When we see the enormous variety of life all around, we must realize that it all mutated from a single source. Little changes that happened along the way managed to survive and reproduce. Whatever branched off over time became what it is today."

"How do you account for humans evolving from a fly, Mr. V.?" asked Sara. "That seems like a pretty drastic leap."

"Many little steps over a long, long time."

"But flies are still here and so are we. I don't understand."

"Only some of them went on to evolve—slowly. Until finally they became the human race, Sara. The rest remained as they were—flies. There are still many originals, and likely it will stay that way for a long time. At least that is my hope."

I looked at Celia and remembered my dream.

Chapter 47

"Mr. Victor, I've never heard you use the term 'Intelligent Source' before. Do you believe in God?" asked Shannon.

He sat on a stool near Shannon's table and lit a cigarette.

"I said Intelligent Source and you said God. If they are one and the same, my answer is yes. But before I go on, I want to say that I do not like using the word 'believe'."

"What word would you like to use?"

"No single word. I cannot believe in something I do not understand. My brain is much too small."

"What do you mean?"

"I cannot describe the Intelligent Source. My Lithuanian ancestors worshipped 'Dievas'. Some thought it was formless. Others thought it had substance, but it was invisible. Only much later, Dievas began to proliferate and manifest into a variety of visible forms like Perkūnas, the god of lightning and thunder."

Celia wasn't drawing. Her attention was on Mr. Victor.

"Lithuanians attached high moral qualities to their gods such as modesty, chastity, and fairness. Dievaites were minor goddesses who represented dawn, fate, luck, the sun, the moon, and the more important heavenly bodies."

Celia looked intrigued.

"Many centuries later, Dievas began to assume human characteristics, probably imported by religions brought by marauding armies. People began defining God in a way they could understand. Artists made images and people began to accept them as reality."

Mr. Victor tapped his ashes into Shannon's ash can.

"God the Father was a kindly, robust, older gentleman. The Holy Ghost was a white bird. Angels were humans with white swan wings. Devils were part human and part animal. And Jesus was a tall, handsome man who was born of a virgin mother, and said he was the son of God."

He dragged on his cigarette and observed his listeners' faces.

"Because people saw what God looked like, they did not have to fear Him any more. He was portrayed as someone who spoke Lithuanian, knew everyone personally, and would easily forgive them for anything they had done wrong. The sinners only needed to say a few prayers—forgiveness was instant."

He paused to tamp out his cigarette.

Shannon seemed to be the only one visibly disturbed by Mr. Victor's words. That, or the smoldering fumes of his dying cigarette were stinging her eyes.

"People were comfortable worshipping a God they could relate to. They started thinking small. And the smaller they thought, the more content they became—until they thought they knew it all."

I expected Shannon to speak up, but she was silent.

"I prefer to think of God as ever present, everlasting, and limitless. I find any attempt to describe God, even by calling Him God, takes me back to where all of the organized religions are today. They are much too confining."

"So you really don't have a definition for God, do you, Mr. Victor?" asked Shannon.

"My definition is no definition. Do you have a definition, Shannon?"

"You know where I stand, Mr. Victor. My understanding of God comes from the teachings of the Catholic Church."

"Some of my best friends are Catholics. You in particular. Some of my best friends are atheists. And me? I am neither, and I am all of the above. I am a believer in nothing and accepter of everything."

"If you were to believe in something, Mr. Victor, what would it be?" asked Shannon.

"I would be you, Shannon. I would believe in you," he answered.

"Are you making fun of me, Mr. Victor?" she asked.

"Absolutely not. I want you to keep Jesus in your heart, and if you can and when you can, I would like you to go even farther."

"What do you mean go farther?"

"Like you, I was taught to believe in God. Like you, I was happy with my beliefs. I was taught that God and I had a close and personal relationship. Of course I believed it. I wanted it to be that way. Who would not?

"My beliefs were shattered in Dresden. That is when I stopped believing in God. But later—years later—I realized that it had been my own fault."

"What do you mean?"

"My belief was founded on my own selfish desires. If I was good, God would be good in return. And the more selfishly I thought, the smaller my vision of God became. I personalized my God. I made him into my friend whom I loved and who loved me back. I made God into what I wanted Him to be."

He paced slowly around the room.

"After I lost everything, I felt betrayed and abandoned. I was angry at God, and I turned my anger at myself for having been so naive. I thought I had been a fool for believing in such a fairy tale. Then, to restore my own credibility and to ease my own pain, I decided that God did not exist."

"But that isn't how you feel today. You said—"

"Yes. Today I do not believe in a personal one-on-one God. I think my idea of a Source that gives life to all Expressions in the universe is a much more appropriate model."

"But you said the Source doesn't care about the Expressions. That means your God doesn't care about humanity," said Shannon.

"'Care' is a word that expresses a small idea. 'Humanity' is another small idea. 'Believe' is a small idea. People who use those words do not understand what they are saying. They are words human brains made up to express their own selfish needs. Our brains are much too limited to understand the needs of the universe."

"It's a nice story, but as always, I'm not buying it. No offense, Mr. Victor."

"That is fine. You do not offend me, Shannon. I am not selling the story," he said, smiling.

Shannon smiled back, then asked, "Why do you teach us, Mr. Victor? You don't charge tuition. You spend your own money on the building and utilities. You buy us drawing paper and supplies. You give us your time. You teach us skills to turn us into better artists. Sometimes you propose ideas which leave us with more questions than answers. Why do you do it?"

Mr. Victor stopped pacing and spoke directly to Shannon.

"I want to equip you with tools to fix the world. You are the only ones who can. You are the artists with the vision. You are the hope for the future of our world.

"In the past, artists used their skills to further the aims and serve the needs of others. You can go forward to craft reality founded on your own ideas."

He paused to look at everyone before making his point.

"I want you to take yourselves as far as your brains will allow, and then—I want you to push further."

Chapter 48

"How can we push our brains to do more than they can?" asked Celia. "How can anything do more than it can?"

I was thrilled to hear her speak. I hoped a broader discussion would open up and I'd get a chance to throw in my two cents.

"It needs a couple of helpers," said Mr. Victor.

"Let me give you an example. I made up a little story to illustrate the idea. It is very simple—like a children's book."

"Sometimes children's books tackle the deepest mysteries," said Celia.

"Yes they do, Celia. I have learned more from children's books than from many college textbooks. I especially like Theodor Geisel's books."

"Doctor Seuss!" she cried out. "He's my all-time favorite."

I vaguely remembered the cover of *The Cat in the Hat*

but didn't want to spotlight my ignorance. I hadn't read any Dr. Seuss books.

"Ahh, yes. Now, let me introduce you to my three characters," he said. Celia lit up a Newport.

"The main character is the brain. Let us give him a name. Let us call him Reason. I picture him like a fat little boy. He is curious, but he can be quite lazy. He would like to be strong and run around. He has the energy, but he lacks the initiative."

People laughed. Celia was smiling. A fat kid named Reason was funny and a likeable protagonist.

"The second character is a little girl named Love." I looked at Celia. She was focused on Mr. Victor and still smiling.

"Love is exactly what the word says. She loves everything in the universe. You can picture her happy, innocent, running around, picking flowers, giving them away. She touches everything with love. Love is the only emotion she is capable of having.

"The third character is Passion. She is a girl who is hungry for adventure. She is athletic, loves to run, jump, climb, explore. She has a lot of energy and is always moving. She is never satisfied to sit around and do nothing."

My mind saw young Celia as Passion and myself as a taller, thinner Reason.

"So you have Reason, Love, and Passion," he said.

"All right. Imagine Reason is home sitting on the sofa eating snacks and watching television. He sees and hears personalities saying and doing things he would like to say and do while performing feats that defy gravity and daring. Reason is pretending he is the one jumping off rooftops and speeding cars."

Celia giggled.

"The doorbell rings. Love and Passion are at the door. They ask Reason to come out and play with them. Reason is bored, so he agrees."

Mr. Victor stopped and lit up a Kool.

I had noticed a pattern to Mr. Victor's delivery. He never rushed through his stories. When he wanted something to sink in, he'd light a cigarette or walk to another part of the studio to give pause in his speech. Sometimes he left the group for five or ten minutes so they could discuss among themselves what he had proposed.

"'This is how we play together,' Passion explained to Reason. 'Love will tell you what she loves, and you will have to love it, too. If you do not, she will go home. I will do fun things you have not done before. If you do not do them, I will not play with you any more either. Do you still want to play with us, Reason?'"

Mr. Victor's story was a huge hit. We couldn't wait to hear more.

"The three friends agreed and went off together. They loved the trees. They loved the pigeons. They loved the ants. They loved an old lady and helped carry her bags."

To fortify his story, Mr. Victor added his own animations using body movements and coordinating facial expressions.

"They ran through a meadow. They picked wildflowers

and climbed an apple tree. They did somersaults down a hill and took turns jumping across a ravine.

When Reason got home, he realized he had more energy, confidence, tolerance, love, and understanding than ever before. He could not wait to go out with Love and Passion again."

Celia grinned big. "I love your story, Mr. Victor. But how does it fit in with your HOLE in the Universe theory?"

"I am glad you asked, Celia," he said. "Your brain, or the fat kid named Reason, is what creates the idea of you. Love and Passion are emotions. When you are open to emotions, you allow them to flow through your mind, to energize you, stimulate your thoughts, and animate your feelings. The energy of the universe flows through you like a river. You are alive, and your HOLE in the Universe is open."

We were all uplifted by Mr. Victor's story—Celia was still smiling. I knew she had reason and passion in her, but I wasn't so sure about love. She'd said some strange things about it that made no sense. I didn't understand how she thought she could like a boy so much—and then hate him.

Chapter 49

I bought two hot dogs and two orders of French fries from a vendor near the Planetarium. We walked slowly along the pier at our favorite of all places—the boat slips on Northerly Island.

We found a perfect spot to sit on the concrete apron bordering the marina. We dangled our legs and unwrapped our food.

Celia saw something in the water. It was a white body with gold and black markings—a koi fish. He poked his head out of the water and stared at us. She immediately named him Felix.

It didn't take us long to realize Felix was in serious trouble. Koi are not native to Lake Michigan. He must have been displaced from someone's garden pond—one full of white water lilies and a fountain with a peeing cherub. No doubt Felix's owner drove for miles keeping him alive in an ice chest just to dump him into the marina.

Koi are trained to be fed by hand. Their food floats on top of the water, and they depend on humans to feed them. Felix had probably been waiting between the boats for someone to show up with dinner for who knows how long.

We tossed him bits of our bread and fries. He grabbed each one as soon as it hit the water. He ate an entire hot dog bun and a half bag of fries in minutes.

We didn't want to leave him. We hoped he would disappear when we walked away, but Celia turned back and there he was, watching and waiting. She gave me a pathetic look of helpless exasperation and anger.

"How can someone do this? He was part of a family! Would they do that to their kids or their dog—pack them up, drive them to an unknown place, and let them wander around suffering, slowly starving to death?"

Celia threw another fry in the water.

"So now what? What will happen when other people come by? There'll be crowds here this weekend. Will they feed him?"

I shared her despair, but felt powerless to help her or Felix.

"What if someone throws a baited hook into the water? People fish Lake Michigan all the time. Sure, the sign says 'No Fishing in the Marina', but who's going to stop some mean kids from teasing him? Or worse? He's so friendly. He'll just swim right up to them and—"

She dropped to her knees on the concrete and started to cry. I knelt down next to her, but she waved me off with her hand and told me to go home. She said she'd be fine.

I couldn't leave her. Not like that. I wracked my brain for something to do, but I came up empty.

Watching her tears flow freely broke my heart. I decided to do something I hadn't done before—I wrapped my arms around her.

She didn't resist. Her golden hair brushed my face softly as I held her tight. I wanted so much to kiss her to make the hurt go away, but I was afraid she might misunderstand my intentions.

What if she started liking me too much? And then—what if she hated me?

Chapter 50

Mr. Victor sat on a stool with both feet on the rung. He held a tuna can in one hand and a lit cigarette with the other. He blew out a blue smoke cloud and watched it hang in the stillness of the studio.

"Many people believe that after they die, they will leave their human form and continue to exist as a new being, like a spirit or soul. They believe there is a place called Heaven where the good souls go. Some people worry that their soul will end up in Hell if they do not play their cards right."

He flicked his ashes into the can.

"Others believe they will return in the form of another human or animal or plant. And there are some who believe there is no such thing as an afterlife." His gaze lingered briefly on each attentive face.

"I think we have always been here and will always

remain here on this planet, Earth. But not as *us* or *we* because there is no such thing as *us* or *we*."

Mr. Victor blew another smoke puff. It hung near the first one, which had almost disappeared. It looked like a departed spirit trying to catch up with its own essence. I wondered if he was doing that intentionally.

"This may surprise you, but I think there *is* a Heaven and a Hell."

Mr. Victor often expressed unconventional ideas, so we were not as surprised as we were interested to hear what he had to say.

"Heaven exists, people, but not in Heaven. Hell exists also, but not in Hell. Heaven and Hell are right here on Earth. They are both man-made. And they are both temporary."

He crushed out his last burning embers in the tuna can and stood up.

"First, I would like you to put on your philosopher caps." Everyone donned their caps.

"And now, I would like to present to you—Heaven and Hell." He started to pace.

"Heaven is where the little child thrives in the loving arms of its mother and father. Hell is where the little child wilts and dies, unwanted and unloved. Heaven is where animals dwelled before man came. Hell is where they are today—"

"I feel sorry for you for thinking that way, Mr. Victor," said Shannon. "It's a lonely existence without God in your life. I agree with part of what you're saying. Love for children and animals are good things. But what about love for God? Why leave Him out?" Shannon looked annoyed but kept her cap on.

"I am not leaving him out, Shannon. Please bear with me." He stopped pacing and addressed the room.

"I offer this to you as Plan B. It is not meant to replace your existing life plan, if you have one. It is a fallback plan in case what you imagined and hoped and believed does not turn out like you thought it would. You will not experience the moment of truth after you die. In your new form, you will have no memory of your former life."

He looked like he was collecting himself, winding up to deliver a fastball.

"I want you to have your moment of truth right now while you still can. I want you to GET THE HELL OUT!"

That was the first time we'd heard Mr. Victor raise his voice. It was somewhat unnerving.

Sara spoke up. "Do you want us to leave?"

"Of course not, Sara. I want to impress an idea into your brains so you do not forget it. I want you to fix our earth by getting rid of the Hell—by getting the HELL OUT."

Mr. Victor spoke loudly and with authority. He was in full control of himself.

"Plan B is very simple. If you do not want to be the next starving child, stop hunger. If you do not want to stand crammed inside a dirty pen until you are slaughtered, stop eating animals. Stop using leather. Stop wearing fur. Stop animal testing. Stop killing and torturing. Stop hurting children. Stop hurting each other."

"That sounds great Mr. V., but I think it's easier said than done," said Sara.

"You are absolutely right, Sara. People do not want to give up anything."

He looked at Sara. She was holding Orphan Annie on her lap. Nixon was lying at her feet.

"Some people have a good life. For a while. I am temporarily among those fortunate few.

"I think most people believe that when they die, all of this will be left behind and they will never have to experience it again. They do not think they can be thrown back into their own messes again after they leave planet Earth. They do not realize that they are not going anywhere. Anywhere else. They will remain here, in one form—and another—and another—and another—for better and for worse."

He paused.

"Dying will not give anyone a Get Out of Hell Free card. Cleaning it all up while we are still alive, while we have the means and the brains to do it, is the only way. It is the only hope."

"Wow! That's some heavy shit, Mr. V.," said Sara.

"Yes. It is."

Chapter 51

"What do you call Hell, Mr. Victor?" asked Toni.

"I will give you my short definition," he answered.

"Hell is the experience of pain, both physical and non-physical. Emotional pain can be as real as physical pain. Every animal with a brain—large or small—has the ability to experience pain."

"What about Heaven?" asked Celia.

"Heaven is the other end of the scale—the pleasure end. When pleasure outweighs pain, the animal is in Heaven."

Celia nodded her head. Toni sat still, chewing on an eraser.

"It is a question of balance," he said. "One end of the scale is pain. The other end is pleasure. The trick is to dwell in the middle where there are no extremes. Not too much pleasure or pain."

"Why not try to have pleasure all the time and stay in

the Heaven end, Mr. Victor?" I asked.

"Good question, Luke. Imagine yourself on a balance beam. The more you favor one side, the more you will need to move back to the other side to rebalance."

"Why would anyone want to go back to the Hell side at all?" asked Tad.

"They would not. The universe will jerk them back, and sometimes it may make a pretty drastic adjustment."

"You mean like going from riches to rags?" asked Sara.

"Exactly. Rags to riches, riches to rags. It swings both ways. Often quite unpredictably. Who can think of another example?"

"Drugs and booze," I said.

"Excellent, Luke," said Mr. Victor. "They are both drugs. Now, let me ask everyone: what is their appeal? What is the purpose of drugs?"

"They help you get laid," said Kurt.

The room went up for grabs. Celia was cracking up.

Damn. Maybe I shouldn't have said that—I set him up for that great punch line.

When the commotion died down, Mr. Victor went on. "People drink and take drugs to feel pleasure. And to relieve pain. I do it myself. I am sure everyone in this room has done it, too."

"Not me," said Shannon flatly, invoking laughter from the group. I envied her courage to say what wasn't even popular. I didn't think I'd ever be that brave.

"So now I have decided I like drugs—how they make me feel, how they seem to make my troubles go away. They put me into a pleasure state—into a Heavenly state.

I feel wonderful. I want to use drugs all the time now. I want to live in a perpetual state of pleasure."

He walked to the far end of the studio.

"But what have I done to my balance beam?"

"It wants to correct itself?" asked Sara.

"Exactly. I will soon discover I have damaged my body and my brain. I have lost friends and loved ones. I destroyed my career. I lost any focus I ever had in life."

He took a step toward the class and continued. "By shifting myself out of the middle and staying over in Heaven, I have actually caused myself to be thrown backward into a self-made Hell."

"Wouldn't it be impossible to get rid of the Hell, Mr. Victor?" asked Celia.

"It would not be so hard if everyone realized there is no *I* or *we* or *them* or *me*. We are all Expressions of life. Every action and every inaction affects all of us in the immediate and long term. We made Hell. We can unmake it."

"What if Hell lives in our brain? How can we get rid of it then?" asked Celia.

"Do you mean if it is incurable, like a cancer in the brain?"

"Yes."

"I do not know, Celia. Sometimes the only cure for cancer of the body is death. I would suppose death is also a cure for a brain that has Hell residing in it."

"I'm afraid you may be right."

Chapter 52

"Does anyone know the Our Father?" asked Mr. Victor.

"I do," said Shannon.

"Ahh, good. I would like you to write it on the board. If you do not mind."

She went to the blackboard and wrote:

Our Father, Who art in Heaven
Hallowed be Thy Name;
Thy kingdom come,
Thy will be done,
On earth as it is in Heaven.
Give us this day our daily bread,
And forgive us our trespasses,
As we forgive those who trespass against us;
And lead us not into temptation,
But deliver us from evil. Amen.

"Thank you, Shannon," he said. "I do not doubt that you have said that prayer frequently. I have also said those words in Lithuanian. They have been repeated millions of times each day for over a thousand years in most countries, cultures, and languages all over the world. But I do not think they have benefited life on our planet."

Shannon didn't look happy. He'd just sucker punched one of the most sacred tenets of Christianity.

"Those words have helped create and maintain attitudes that have persisted throughout history. They have generated a culture of complacency."

"What do you mean by complacency, Mr. Victor?" asked Tad.

"Complacency. Accountability. It is about people not wanting to take responsibility for their own actions. People have been taught to have blind faith that God will handle everything on earth and in Heaven. They have been instructed to believe that God will feed them, forgive them for poor behavior—even when they commit mass murder."

I wondered if he was referring to Churchill when he ordered the firebombing of civilians in Dresden that killed Mr. Victor's family. But then I thought of Hitler and the Holocaust. Stalin plundering the Baltics. Roosevelt burning Tokyo. Truman destroying Hiroshima and Nagasaki with atomic bombs. And—

"When you put it that way, it makes me wonder why so many people keep believing in God," said Sara.

"It is because they want to. You have heard people say

over and over: 'It is God's will.' It is convenient to blame God for all the bad in the world. And because God is, by definition, blameless, then everybody is off the hook."

"But didn't God give us religion, Mr. Victor?" asked Toni.

"I do not think so. I think people gave us religion." He walked to the board.

"I want to submit this for your consideration. It is not religion, and I do not intend for it to become religion. The world does not need more religion. It is not a set of beliefs. The world does not need more beliefs."

Mr. Victor picked up a piece of chalk and said, "Make sure your philosopher helmets are on tight."

He started a new column to the right of Shannon's Our Father prayer. It read:

I am a HOLE in the Universe.
Expression born of Source and System.
I will be open to the flow
And tread lightly on the earth
Taking as little as I am able
And returning as much as I can.
I will stay free of beliefs that
Confine and confuse.
I will stay suspended and curious.

"That is some ultra-heavy shit, Mr. V.," said Sara.

"Thank you, Sara. I am assuming you mean that as a compliment."

"That is genius, Mr. Victor," said Celia.

Marty and Kurt clapped. Tad was deep in thought. Toni looked vacant. Nancy was digging through her purse. Nixon was sleeping by Sara's feet.

"Okay! That does it for me. You're all so hip and I'm just a square. But I'm out of here, man!"

Shannon threw down her black cap and stormed out of the studio. Sara ran after her saying, "I'll talk to her."

"She will be back," said Mr. Victor calmly.

"I will now conclude our HOLE in the Universe discussions. I will continue our drawing sessions and see you all next week. But please—keep your caps on."

Chapter 53

I wasn't in the habit of sharing intimate details with my friends. If I had, they may have told me I was out of my mind. Why would I give up a sure thing like Dalia for a girl I had some kind of fantasy love for?

My friends would've been right. That's why I didn't mention it.

I was expecting a big dramatic, tearful scene. Maybe something like: Dalia whips my high school ring at me sobbing, "How can you do this to me, Luke? What about all your promises? I gave you my virginity! You're a selfish jerk! I hate you!"

Instead, true to Dalia's kind, mature nature, I got: "Okay then. I was already thinking about breaking up with you, too. Things just haven't been the same lately. We can still be friends if you want."

She didn't offer to give my ring back, and I decided not to ask for it. It was a small price to pay for being let off the hook so easily.

"Sure," I said with as much droopy-eyed sincerity as I could muster. "And thank you for being so cool about this, Dalia. We had some fun, didn't we?"

Maybe I'd pushed it a little, but Dalia came through. "Yeah, we did. I know it's none of my business, Luke, but have you started up with someone else?"

"No. I haven't. I swear." I was consumed by Celia, but we'd never gone out on a date, so it wasn't a lie.

"Well, I'm sure you'll get plenty of offers when you start school downstate."

"All I'm thinking about is school, Dalia."

That was the lie.

Chapter 54

"Can you help me move our seat, Luke?"

With all four doors wide open, the 2CV resembled a June beetle with wing confusion. We flopped the seat down into its near-flat reclining position and laid back.

Celia wore pink shorts and a white cotton blouse. She slipped off her Dr. Scholl's sandals and let them drop on the car's floor. In one smooth move, she raised both legs to rest her bare feet on the steering wheel.

She lit two Newports and handed me one.

"Thanks."

"Any time."

The warm breeze fanned our smoke out of the car while we relaxed in cozy comfort, enjoying the sun and lake wind from the marina. Celia reached for her black philosopher's cap on the back seat and put it on.

"So ... what do you think about Mr. Victor ending his HOLE discussions, Luke?"

"I wanted to hear more. His ideas were really interesting. When I asked him why he was stopping, he said he had nothing more to say. He didn't want to repeat himself and sound 'dogmatic'."

She looked so damn cute in that cap. I felt inspired and did my best Mr. Victor impression. "Dogma is for religion, Luke, and I do not want to create another one of those."

She smiled and said, "That's pretty good—"

She interrupted herself and went on, "Okay, when we build with Legos, we're making Expressions. We're the Source of the Lego creation, we use the Lego building block System, and the final construction is the Expression."

"Yeah, that's what I got out of it, too."

"He said not to fall in love with our constructions. That means the Source or creator of the Expression shouldn't fall in love with their creation," she said.

"I think he was trying to say that all constructions are temporary. That makes sense when you think of cells, molecules, and atoms. Supposedly matter can't be changed or destroyed—it can only be rearranged. That's what the physics books say," I said.

I could almost picture the wheels turning in her mind.

"He alluded to the Source as being intelligent. When Shannon nailed him on it, he said he believed in God. That means he thinks the Source is God," said Celia.

She mini-punched my shoulder with her little fist. "What do you think, Luke?"

"I think when he says 'Source', he means God—but I

see what you're getting at," I said, thrilled by her sudden physical contact—a major move in the advancement of our relationship.

I went on, "We're the Expressions, the journey for the Source, not the destination. The Source doesn't care about the Expression. It will just recycle our parts after we die. Basically, we'll all end up back in the bucket."

"Yep. In the bucket. All back together again."

"Yep," I said. *Together again. With you.*

Celia's feet stroked the smooth, painted steering wheel. Her toes gripped it as if she were driving. She slid them along, following its curve, then let her toes spread out. I had a hard time keeping my mind on pleasant conversation.

"I know one thing for sure, Luke. I should've been tossed back in the bucket as soon as my first Legos clicked together. I shouldn't have been finished. I shouldn't have been born. The Source never loved me, and it never will."

She blew out a smoke ring. Before it fully formed, the breeze tore it apart and carried its remains out of the open sunroof. The sun kissed her neck and reflected off pools in her green amber eyes. Whiffs of lilies of the valley mixed with mentholated Newport tobacco and balmy air.

"Yeah, right. You're super unlovable, Celia," I added, risking a badly humored quip, wishing I hadn't said it as soon as I did.

"I'm totally serious, Luke. You don't know me very well. I'm completely nuts. I try to hide it as much as I can. That's why I like to study other people. I want to be able to imitate them so they're not on to me. So they'll think I'm one of them. You know—if it walks like a duck, quacks like a duck, swims like a duck—it's probably a duck."

I loved her offbeat humor. I loved her reference to walking like a duck, and the funny face she made after saying it. I loved her beautiful eyes. I loved how her blond hair shimmered in the sunlight. I loved her feet, and I loved her fast-paced walk. I loved the way she smoked. I loved to watch her drive her car with those silly, bug-eyed headlights. I loved how she chewed her food—

Celia's car didn't have a factory-installed radio, but she kept a small Motorola transistor radio on the storage shelf under the dashboard. She turned it on. The Everly Brothers were singing *Dream*, their top hit single. Celia's minty smoke washed over me. The words were so perfect. So real in that moment. I started singing along in a whispery voice.

Celia smiled and put her hand on mine. My heart couldn't take it any more.

"I love you, Celia!"

I blurted it out so fast, the words just flew out of my mouth.

She jerked her hand back as if she'd been burned.

"I hate you, Luke."

She stared at my face. There was no need to explain my shock, embarrassment, regret—my confused expression showed it all.

"Just trying to balance my universe, Luke. I told you I didn't want to like you too much. I'm trying to tell *me* that I don't like you."

She held her sad and pretty stare and patted my hand gently. "Don't take it to heart, Luke. I didn't say it to hurt you. It's for my own stupid brain. You want a hot dog?"

"Sure. Sounds good."

She left her sandals in the car and locked the wings of her little flying bug. I watched her bare feet maneuver around scattered stones and gravel on the warm asphalt. Her toes sank into the cool grass beyond the parking lot. We walked to the aluminum-sided concession stand near the entrance to the Planetarium and bought two hot dogs and two orders of fries. We both knew what we'd do next.

We headed toward the water's edge. Celia threw a piece of her hot dog bun into the dark water. I did the same. The bread bits drifted into a corner between two cement walls and stopped beside a floating Styrofoam cup.

It was dusk. Trees cast long shadows over the marina. The sun was setting over the Chicago skyline and slid behind the treetops. Everything was in deep shadow except the control tower in the east. It was bathed in orange and gold, and its windows reflected the setting sun like a slowly dimming red searchlight.

Felix wasn't there. We hadn't seen him in over three weeks. We called off the search.

"I'm not hungry," she said.

"Me neither."

"Let's go back to Mr. Victor's. Nixon will love these."

Chapter 55

In a gangway between two storefronts, the skinny black kid took a small twenty-two out of a briefcase.

"Bigger," she said.

He produced a twenty-five caliber.

"Got something bigger?" she asked.

"Okay, little lady. How about this thirty-two automatic? Like James Bond. You know—Double Oh Seven?"

"Will it blow someone's brains out?"

"Brains—whatever. It don't matter what kinda shit they got in there. It'll all go flyin' out for sure. Guaranteed. Forty bucks, blondie."

She held the pistol and examined it closely. "Is it loaded?" she asked.

"No, ma'am. That comes after we close the deal."

"Twenty bucks. Loaded."

"You drive a hard bargain, ma'am, but this is your

lucky day! It just so happens I need to reduce my inventory. Gimme twenty-five and you got a deal."

The kid pulled out the magazine and loaded seven cartridges. He slid the magazine back into the handle.

"What kind of bullets are those?"

"Hollow points. Guaranteed to stop 'em dead in their tracks with the first shot. They're the best there is."

"What other kinds are there?"

"The old ball type—full metal jacket. They don't flatten out when they hit somethin'. Not so good for stoppin' power. Usually go right through without losin' their shape."

"Even through the head?"

The kid's eyes shifted from left to right. Her words didn't match her sweet young Barbie girl image.

"Yep. The hollow point might rattle around inside, but the FMJ will fly out the other side for sure."

"I want those."

"You got it, goldie." The customer was always right, and the sale was almost final, so why ask questions? His job was to sell, and he'd done it well. She handed him two tens and a five dollar bill.

Celia watched the kid reload the magazine with the copper-jacketed, round-tipped ammo.

"Don't put the clip in 'til you wanna use it. Some folks keep it loaded with the safety on—this little doohickey right here. They get all mixed up—is it on or off? Bam! Shit! Too late! That's how people get killed. You don't want none of that, little lady. Want this gift wrapped?" He started to put the gun into a tan paper sack.

Celia smiled and said, "No. I'll take it as it is."

She took a pink chiffon scarf out of her mail-carrier bag, wrapped it around the gun and ammo clip, and then shoved the whole pretty bundle into her bag.

"How about a stereophonic phonograph for your Ricky Nelson records? Gold watch? Genuine diamond necklace?"

"No, thanks. Can I have a receipt?"

"Not with the deep discount I just gave you, ma'am. I can't even pay Uncle Sam outta that."

"Okay. Just thought I'd ask."

"No problem, Miss Barbie Doll. No problem at all. Now, how about a white fur jacket? Look damn fine with your blond hair."

"Nope."

"Okay. Come back again. And tell your friends about me. Just ask anybody around here for Marv. They'll know how to find me. Oh, and don't try to register it with the cops or none of that bullshit. They'll want a bill of sale and all kinds of personal information. You don't need none of that, sweetness."

"Thanks, Marv."

"No problem. And be careful. That ain't no toy."

Chapter 56

"Is that a gun in your bag or are you just happy to see me?"

I had noticed a strange lumpy shape inside a canvas bag on the back seat of Celia's car and decided to be clever. It was a worn out cliche at best, and it didn't even apply—girls don't have problems like that. I felt like an idiot as soon as I'd said it.

"Yes. To both." She laughed, but it sounded more obligatory than sincere. She'd probably heard the expression before and was just being kind, trying to rescue me from my own humiliation.

I felt my face flush with heat. I knew that once it started, there was no way to stop from turning beet red. I leaned out the door and pretended to observe something interesting—like her tires.

When I thought my skin had cooled down slightly, I readjusted into my seat and peeked sideways at Celia. She looked like she hadn't noticed, but I was sure my dopey comment would fester forever.

"You don't have to be kind, Celia. What I said was dumb. Why don't you just tell me I'm a jerk?"

"Okay. You're a stupid moron, Luke. Do you feel better now?"

I wondered if she'd seen my magenta face and was just being nice because she pitied me.

"Yeah. I feel better. Thanks." My lungs were filled with pressurized air. I exhaled big and felt lighter.

I loved that she called me a stupid moron. That was another milestone toward closeness. You wouldn't call just anyone a stupid moron unless you were comfortable with them. And you'd never say that unless you liked them. You wouldn't punch someone other than a friend in the shoulder or in the guts. Only a true friend deserved a painful knuckle sandwich.

"Any time."

She pulled a pistol out of her canvas bag and handed it to me.

Holy shit! What the—

I thought it was just a bunch of girly odds and ends like pens, tissue, makeup, cigarettes—

I cautiously took it from her hand and was immediately impressed by the fine artistry of the weapon. I inspected the engraving: Carl Walther Waffenfabrik Ulm/Du. Modell PPK Cal.7.65mm.

"It's one of James Bond's favorites," she said.

"Why—"

"A girl needs protection in today's world."

"Are you joking?"

"No joke. I drive through some tough neighborhoods on my way to school. My friend was robbed by a kid with a baseball bat. Luckily for her, he didn't use it."

It was only the second time I'd held a real gun. My first was in seventh grade, when my friend Geno brought his dad's pistol into the boy's bathroom at Nativity.

Celia's gun was cool and heavy in my hand. I felt an odd rush knowing I held the power to snuff out a life. The lightest touch on the trigger would send anyone, big or small, from there to eternity.

It was somewhat unsettling and reminded me of the sensation I'd had when I'd been near a window in a skyscraper. My muscles had pulled hard in the back of my legs. They were so tight they hurt trying to back me away from the danger.

I assumed my leg cramps were caused by my fear of heights, but maybe it was from fear of my own brain. Maybe my body didn't trust my brain. What if it decided to do something momentarily insane—like jump out of the window?

I felt a strong need to manage my brain with strict discipline—to allow it to think only straight and level.

"Is it loaded?"

"Yes, but if you try to pull the trigger, it won't shoot. You have to chamber the first round by racking back the slide before it'll fire."

I was relieved to know the gun wasn't about to go off in my hand, but still surprised at my own reaction.

"Okay—"

I fondled the deadly device. It was truly beautiful

and nestled into my hand perfectly. The metal was finely polished and felt as smooth as my freshly Turtle Waxed black Ford Crestline. The patina was a rich blue-black that glistened in the sunlight and morphed to jet black in the shade.

"Where'd you get it?"

"Maxwell Street."

That didn't surprise me. Maxwell Street was the place to shop. Stores offered a huge variety of items at prices that couldn't be beat if you knew how to haggle.

In the open air outside, merchandise lined the streets for even better bargains. The street sellers used trucks, car trunks, and suitcases as their storefronts. All sales were cash only with no returns, guarantees, or receipts. They offered great deals on appliances, clothing, shoes, jewelry, furs, TV's, and stereos—

And guns.

Chapter 57

The summer sun was bright as a little grey rain-stuffed cloud floated over Northerly Island, just long enough to drop a warm, teasing sprinkle. By the time Celia and I finished our smokes, the last few drops had already dried on my windshield.

Celia crushed out her cigarette butt in the ashtray. I flicked mine out the window and got a good-natured "tsk, tsk" for littering.

"You looked upset last Thursday after you saw Sara's 'Think' paintings. Did something happen between you two?" I asked.

"Oh, no. Not at all. It's nothing like that. Actually ... well, this might sound kind of odd to you, but ... bathrooms aren't the best topic for me."

"Oh? What do you mean?"

"I love participating in Mr. Victor's sessions and seeing everyone. But—"

She was fidgeting and looked away.

"If Sara exhibits any more of her bathroom art, it'll be Sayonara for me, Luke."

Sara had created portraits featuring famous people sitting on toilets. Included in the prestigious lineup were President Kennedy, Einstein, Elvis, and Marilyn Monroe. Mr. Victor had also posed for the cause. Celebrants were positioned on commodes in similar fashion to Rodin's *Thinker*—elbow on knee, chin resting on clenched hand. Sara was inspired after seeing the original sculpture at the Musée Rodin when she'd visited Paris with her family. She named her series: *Think*.

Celia's comment was strange—I wondered if I should delve deeper.

"What do you mean?" I asked.

"Are you sure you want to hear this?"

"Well, yeah. I'm sure."

She rested her bare feet on the dashboard. Her shorts hiked up and exposed an extra eight inches of leg. I loved watching her leg muscles work under her smooth skin. She was constantly moving. Her toes wiggled my glove compartment latch as she talked.

"His name was Richard. We dated for over a year. He was a really good guy. We were very close."

All of a sudden, I wasn't sure I wanted to know any more.

"His family was Italian and Roman Catholic, and he really wanted to save himself for marriage. He was so handsome. We always parked somewhere—in the woods or on a side street away from the city lights. We came really close to consummating our relationship. We did almost everything else."

I would have broken out in an ugly jealous rash if there had been such a thing. I was torn in half by what she said. Hearing about her and Richard making out was tough to take. Knowing they actually hadn't done the deed offered some relief. I tried to maintain my composure so she wouldn't know I was jealous as Hell.

Celia looked into my eyes and took a drag on her Newport. She must have sensed my discomfort because her lips curved into a wry little smile.

"Things were moving along nicely. Richard suggested we take a few days off and drive down to Missouri to visit my mother. He'd never met her and was curious about Marcelline."

There was Celia, sitting in my car, barefoot, her shapely legs balanced elegantly against my dashboard. Our windows were rolled down. Strands of her golden hair floated on the wind as she described in far too much detail her sordid love affair.

"I never knew what to expect from my mother. I thought she might throw us out as soon as she saw us, but she didn't. She ordered pizza and shocked me by inviting us to spend the night. She said motels were expensive, especially in Branson. There was no need to throw away hard earned cash."

Her toes caressed the shiny surface of my dash. I pictured those lovely legs in my bed as they rested idly on top of my sheets—

Light golden hairs thinned toward the top of her inner

thighs, her skin pale and yielding. My hand moved slowly over her silky smoothness. Suddenly, a man's body appeared between us: Richard!

I felt nauseous. I had wrecked my own fantasy by letting him in and pushing myself out. Why did I do that? And why was I even thinking like that when Celia was finally sharing an intimate story with me?

"Richard was all flattery and manners. He told her she had such a smart and beautiful daughter, and oh ... she must be so proud. It was embarrassing. I had to kick him in the shins two or three times under the dinner table to get him to cut the crap and shut up."

"What did your mother say?"

"She ate it all up."

"So ... where did you end up sleeping?"

Damn! Why did I ask that? What the Hell is wrong with me?

"I slept on the living room sofa, and Richard slept on the floor right next to it."

Phew! My nausea was subsiding. At least they hadn't shared the same sleeping space—like a bed—but I still felt jealous.

"Marcelline brought us pillows and blankets and went to bed early, so Richard and I set ourselves up for the night. He hugged and kissed me good night, and naturally, we did a little more on the floor—not much. My mother's hearing was out of this world from growing up blind, so nothing too fancy happened and we went to sleep."

Gag! Again.

I wanted to stop her from going on, but I also needed to know everything.

Celia sat up and slid her feet into her sandals. She looked like she was about to leave, but she turned to face me and spoke in a tense voice.

"That's when it started. I woke up when I heard the floor creak. Richard was in the bathroom. I saw the light under the door, and then I heard the sound. I heard his stream as it hit the water—hard. It was so loud. It rang in my head and went on and on. Forever. I thought it would never stop."

She was rigid. Her face was close to mine, her eyes staring, piercing straight through me.

"I wanted him to die right then and there, Luke. I didn't want him to walk out of that bathroom alive. I hated him like I never hated anyone before."

The watery green amber had transformed to acid lime; her eyes looked like nothing I'd ever seen before. If looks could deliver death rays, Richard would have been long dead. Her dilated pupils promised a cold grave as black as the hole in the barrel of her Walther PPK.

I was stunned by her words and mesmerized by her crazy frozen stare.

"Then what happened?"

"It was over. I hated him so much, I didn't even let him drive me home. I took a Greyhound bus back to Chicago and never saw him again."

I was glad she hated him, but her story was ominous. She was so lovely and smart, but in that moment she scared the Hell out of me.

Celia's story was hard to believe, and yet she told it as though it were factual; as though Richard had actually done something horribly wrong to her. It was as real in her mind as I was, sitting there listening to every word.

"You mean this happened to you from one time? One visit to the bathroom?"

"He went twice, Luke. The first time I wanted him dead. The second time, I knew it was over for good."

As she said it, tears filled her eyes. Tears of hurt and hate. She wasn't exaggerating about wanting him dead. It was written in her tears. She didn't even look like Celia any more. I wondered if she looked like Marcelline.

"What happened after you went home?"

"He kept calling and crying and writing and sending cards and letters and flowers. His mother and sister called. He talked about killing himself. He said if he couldn't be with me, he didn't want to live. This went on for months." She stared deep into me again. "But I didn't care."

"Did you ever tell him why you left him?"

"No. I never did. The first time he called, I answered the phone. I told him I'd changed my mind—that I didn't want to see him any more. I didn't give him a reason. He asked why over and over again, but I didn't tell him. Don't people change their minds about people, Luke?"

"Well, yeah … they do, but usually they give an explanation or some kind of an excuse. I think."

"And sometimes they don't. Right?"

She looked angry. Maybe she wondered why I was asking; why I didn't know that it was a clear-cut matter. The man had committed a terrible crime. Celia's reactions were completely appropriate.

"True. Sometimes they don't," I said, struggling, hoping to say the right thing. It was the strangest story I'd ever heard.

I was getting worried. What the Hell would happen to us? Would there ever be an us? I barely believed it myself, but I wasn't jealous of Richard any more. Not at all. Celia had taken a meat cleaver, opened his chest, spread his ribs, torn his heart out with her adorable little hands, and flushed it down the toilet. Was there anything worse I could have wished on poor Richard?

"You said you and Richard went together for over a year. Was that the first time he went to the bathroom when you were around?"

"No, but he never made it obvious while we were on a date. In fact, I never even thought about it. The first time I ever *heard* him go to the bathroom was in my mother's house. I can still hear it right now, right in my head—exactly as it happened that night. It's a sound that never stops. It makes me sick to this day to be reminded."

I wondered if there had been others besides Richard, but I didn't want to ask. I wasn't sure I wanted to know. I knew I was in real danger of losing Celia, and with one wrong move or comment, I could easily be her next casualty.

I hesitated before asking my next question.

"What ... what happens when other guys go to the bathroom?"

"Nothing. If I don't care about them, then I don't care what they do."

Her words of warning flashed back to me: *I don't want to like you too much, Luke, because then I'll have to hate you.*

I had mixed feelings about Celia's wild disclosure. On the positive side, our conversation meant we had reached a deep level of intimacy in our relationship. I was certain she'd never shared such dark secrets with anyone. Not even Richard.

The other side spelled huge trouble. I hadn't given much thought about sharing a future with her, but—in the most remote regions of my mind—maybe.

I knew I was teetering dangerously close to a mine field. But I had no choice. I had to keep going.

Chapter 58

Celia and I had agreed to bring our swimsuits and meet at Northerly.

I stood by my car hoping to keep the parking spot next to me open. Luckily, no one drove in, and I didn't have to get into an argument with some motorist insisting he had to park there. She was about twenty minutes late. I was relieved to see her little grey bug pull into the lot.

She stepped out in cut-off jeans and a white T-shirt. Her hair was up in a ponytail under a red bandana with large white polka dots. On her feet were the clip-clops. God, she looked great!

"Did you bring your suit, Luke?"

"Uh-huh. I'm wearing it."

"Oh. Silly me for not noticing."

"It's under my jeans. Where's yours?"

"Under mine."

I took off my gym shoes, peeled off my white T-shirt,

and unzipped my jeans. She kicked off her sandals, pulled off her T-shirt, and opened the top button of her jeans. She stood that way for a few seconds, fussing with some stray hairs that had fallen from her bandana. It was just long enough for me to imprint the partially stripped down Celia into my brain.

She pulled her zipper down the rest of the way, and we took off our jeans at the same time. We both put on our sunglasses.

She wore a two-piece bathing suit, but it was by no means a bikini. It was maroon which, until that moment, had been one of my least liked colors. Her PBY pendant bounced along the edge of her suit and back to her chest every time she moved—maroon was fast becoming my favorite color.

With her hair up, I saw the graceful nape of her neck. The folded fabric of her bandana covered the tops of her ears and held her sunglasses in place. She looked sexy, but efficient—like a beautified Rosie the Riveter.

She opened the passenger door of her car, leaned in, and stuffed her street clothes into a colorful beach bag. From that angle, I saw that she was thinner than she looked in clothing. Her back had a strong V-shape, which tapered down to a narrow waist and small, but feminine, hips. Her legs were amazing.

I tossed my shorts and shirt on the front seat of my car and held my Luckies, Zippo, and car keys in my hand.

She laughed. "I see you're well equipped. Here. Put your stuff in my bag." She mumbled something loud enough for me to hear: "Just like a guy."

"How would you know?" I asked, trying to be funny but was suddenly afraid her answer might be that she'd learned it from Richard.

"Oh, I've seen a lot of Lucy and Desi on TV, Luke. He's never ready for anything. It's always up to Lucy to think of everything." She laughed as she spoke, tucking last-minute necessities into her bag.

My sunglasses were dark—they allowed me to watch Celia without her knowing—I thought. I hoped she was watching me, too, behind her own blackened shades.

"Okay, I'm ready. Which way are we going?" she asked.

"Let's cut through here."

Her skin was light pastels. It was soft and healthy and hadn't been damaged by hours of harsh sun and Coppertoned weathering like the other brown-baked bodies strewn over Chicago's lakefront. I wanted to touch her.

I let her walk ahead of me. Her muscles were well-toned, flexing gently with each step. Her shoulders were straight, and her bubble butt was stellar.

We reached the end of the beach past the public swimming area where there was an expanse of unclaimed space. Celia spread out the blanket, and I helped her straighten it on the sand.

She sat down first, and I sat next to her, but not too close. Nothing is more embarrassing than plopping down too close to someone and watching them squirm away.

Celia didn't move—she allowed the distance I chose. We both lay back. I turned on my side, and propped on one elbow to face her. I watched her breathe, her suit top lifting from her skin with each breath. The PBY idled rhythmically.

I studied the fine body hairs on her flat belly. Her suit covered her belly button, but I envisioned it to be pretty, like everything else on her. She even had a beauty mark over one rib, slightly to the left side about two inches below her top. It was similar to one Marilyn Monroe had near her upper lip.

I really wasn't undressing Celia with my eyes, imagining her breasts bursting free from the confinement of her bathing suit, lines impressed into her soft white skin from the seams in the fabric of her tight bra. Or loving her soft pink nipples hiding just under her suit top. Or tasting the dewy drops of her sweet sweat as my lips kissed them.

Well, not too much.

The sun was hot. A single glistening drop trickled slowly down her belly. It came from under the bottom of her suit top. It must have been born between her sweet, sweltering breasts. I watched her closely while trying to keep my craving in check, but my hormones had ideas of their own. I felt that familiar tickling, rising sensation in my groin.

I turned to lie on my stomach and let myself push into the blanket, indenting the sand. I hoped my quiet delight would go on uninterrupted—

Celia's feet started moving, toying with the strap on her canvas bag. With her toes, she pulled her bag up toward her hand, grabbed it, and sat up. She took out her cigarettes and 7-UP matches.

"Want one?"

I never smoked my Luckies when I was with Celia. She'd offered me a Newport on one of our first outings, and I'd taken it. From then on, it became our thing to do. I'd already gone through a lot of her smokes, and made a mental note to buy her a carton soon.

"Sure," I said. "Use my lighter."

She took my Zippo and inspected it like she'd never seen it before. She flipped it open and tried to roll the little spark wheel with her index finger. It didn't work.

"Here. You do it," she said, handing me the lighter. She put two cigarettes in her mouth and leaned toward me. I reached up and lit them both. She took one out of her mouth and placed it between my lips.

I didn't care for menthol cigarettes, but I loved to smoke Celia's. I always imagined she left a little of herself on the filter even though she never wore lipstick.

"Thanks."

"Any time."

Chapter 59

"How do you imagine a perfect god, Luke?"

"You mean assuming I believe in God?"

"No. I want to know your very own idea of God. You don't have to believe He exists or not, but if He did, I want you to describe your idea of what He might be."

"He?"

"Okay, He doesn't have to be male. But that's what everyone says, right? I don't think I've heard anyone refer to *He/She* or *Him/Her* before."

"Hmm. Maybe. I know for sure we're not supposed to say *It* when referring to God—"

"Okay, okay. Just call God *Him*."

"You're not—"

"I should be mad, Luke. But it's not your fault. It's always been a male-dominant society. You're just the evolved product of countless generations."

I laughed. She was always on her toes, always wearing

her own brand of thinking cap.

"Now describe your God to me."

"Okay," I said, drinking in her gorgeousness. I knew right then that if God was made in the most perfect imagery, *She* would be Celia.

"God would be all powerful, all knowing, and able to manage all life on all planets in the universe."

"Good start. Is God a *He* or *She*?"

"Hmm. I'm leaning toward *She*—"

"Well, I like that idea, but are you sure you're not trying to pull my leg, Luke?" I turned my attention to her divine limbs, my sneaky stare safely concealed behind my shades.

"Umm, as much as I'd love to—" I snickered a little wickedly. She giggled.

"No, really. I'm thinking about all the wars and crap—"

"Do you think if a woman had been running the show, there wouldn't have been any wars?" she asked.

"Oh man, that's heavy ... not necessarily."

"Well, I can think of something to fight about right now."

"Ha-ha. I'm sure you can."

I realized I might have sounded like a smart ass, but if she'd caught my sarcasm, she didn't mention it.

"What about eating animals and all the cruelty that goes along with that? What about riding them and using them to do hard work like pulling wagons when we can use machinery? What about killing them for their furs and skin when we can wear man-made fabrics?"

She wasn't smiling any more. She had opened a subject that was obviously troublesome. I agreed with her, but I had never even thought about giving up my carnivorous habits.

"Do you eat meat, Celia?"

"You know I do, Luke. You and I have hot dogs together all the time."

"So, why—"

"Mr. Victor brought up a bunch of great ideas to improve our world and get rid of the Hell, as he put it," she said. "He also said we're going to stay here on this planet after we're dead, meaning the next time around we'll show up in another form. How would you like to be a pig or a cow on your way to the slaughterhouse, about to become the main course at a Fourth of July cookout?"

I couldn't see her eyes behind her sunglasses, but I felt like she was staring, or maybe glaring, at me pretty intensely.

"I'm going to do it, Luke—stop eating meat, I mean. I know it's not a big thing if one person does it, but if everyone does, pretty soon—like Mr. Victor said—we'll start getting rid of the Hell. Animals will live happily in peace—in their own little Heaven on Earth," she said.

I knew one thing for sure. If there was a God, I wanted to thank *Her* for bringing me Celia.

I loved Celia's enthusiasm for her new cause, but then I pictured all those Easter hams dripping with pineapple slices and red cherries, Thanksgiving turkeys smothered in gravy, rare roast beef swimming it its own decadent juices—all on white linen tablecloths—

Oh man.

I could smell the aroma of those delicious White Castle hamburgers stuffed in white bags on the front seat of my car while my best friends, Stan, Droopy, Duck, and I took turns swigging from a pint of Seagram's Seven. I could see the wet snowflakes falling, sticking, melting, sliding down the outside of the steamed up windshield as we ate, drank, smoked and joked—

"Sure! Let's do it, Celia! I can give up meat!"

"Cool! So as of—let's start right away! Tomorrow! No more meat! Right?"

"It's a deal. Let's shake on it," I said, hoping I'd get another chance to feel her sweaty little palm in mine. She reached out with her right hand, and I held onto it as long as I could. God! I wanted to hold it forever, but she let go.

"Back to God, Luke."

I thought about the most desirable image to apply to my version of God, and again, Celia's face popped into my mind. Celia would smile down on everyone, be prayed to, be worshipped, be loved by all—

Crap!

I couldn't stand the idea of sharing her with the entire universe. I wanted her all for myself.

"Well, let's see. *She* should be boundless in time and space, ever present, there for everyone, everywhere. There would be no hate, and no animals eating other animals. People would be vegetarians and love each other. There'd be no fighting or killing or trying to out-do each other. Diseases wouldn't exist. We'd all just die of natural causes—when we decided it was time. And then—we'd just go to sleep."

She took off her sunglasses and leaned in close.

"Oh—and we'd all stay soapy and clean forever," I whispered.

Celia smiled sweetly and said, "I could really love your God, Luke. What would *She* look like?"

"My mother."

Chapter 60

We smoked our cigarettes down to their filters and sank them into the sand. I gave her a little "tsk, tsk" payback for her earlier reprimand to me for littering. She smirked and stretched out on her stomach. The blanket was hotter in spots where the sun had baked into it, and I wondered if Celia felt the changes on her body as much as I did.

She bent her legs up and let her feet play with each other, cleaning off sand grains. Her feet were luminous and inviting against the azure blue water of Lake Michigan. I thought of the Statue of Liberty in New York Harbor welcoming my parents and me to the New World. It had been a truly inspirational sight.

But, not nearly as stirring as Celia's feet. I saw them rising up out of the water, beckoning me, luring me with their splendor. Her feet were the gateposts to Heaven.

I decided that when I was successful in my design career, I would have her foot modeled in thin shell concrete and erected out in the lake. I remembered an exhibit of the work of Felix Candela, a renowned Spanish-Mexican architect who'd created fantastic buildings using thin shell concrete.

Celia's foot could be fabricated using the same type of technology. My living quarters would be inside. On the sole side facing east over the lake, tall windows and balconies would provide breathless views of the water. Extending off Celia's ankle, a boat dock and a landing pad for my helicopter would be ready and waiting for use—

She lifts one lovely leg, then the other, into my chopper, and off we fly to my hideaway—Lake Foot House. We make love all night long in the cabin cruiser anchored nearby, pitching and swaying with the rhythm of the waves that lap the rich red mahogany hull. We watch dawn's golden hue paint the quieting water. We're naked, holding hands, walking slowly together on the concrete dock platform, passing through the foyer, beyond the white Steinway concert grand piano. The glistening white Italian marble floor is cool from the night air. With one touch of a button, white linen curtains glide soundlessly over glass windows, hiding the day. We fall, consumed and spent, into the billows of my huge white feather bed—

Celia lowered her legs and fell asleep on her side facing away from me. I sat up and wondered if she was really sleeping. My right hand was flat on the blanket close to hers. I inched it over, barely nudging the edge of her pinky finger.

She didn't move. I took a chance and carefully placed my pinky over hers. I felt an instant shiver down my spine. What if she wasn't sleeping? What would she think of me sneaking a pinky feel?

I pulled my hand away fast.

I thought of her story about Richard. Could she have made it all up? God had warned Adam and Eve about the damning dangers of disobedience; Leonardo Da Vinci had once spread a false rumor about having a poisoned tree in his orchard to scare away would-be thieves.

But why would Celia have contrived such a bizarre story? Maybe she was afraid of affection and wanted to keep us apart—or—maybe she was telling the truth.

I fell back on the blanket and closed my eyes. The sun felt good and hot on my skin. I wanted to relax, but I couldn't stop thinking—

Celia and I had reached a deep level of intimacy with our brains. We dove into theories and shared our feelings. I understood her aching over separation—over the loss of her dad, her dolls, Felix, and even Lego Edgar.

From what I could tell, it seemed like Celia longed for love, but didn't understand what it was. Her mother had never loved her, so she didn't know how it felt. She knew from watching others that it was supposed to be warm and wonderful, but she couldn't feel it with her heart. Her father had seemed to care, but maybe somehow his affection had been hijacked by her mother's abusiveness. Celia had abstracted an emotion she couldn't feel.

But what about us? I felt like Celia had some sort of barrier in place, but it wasn't like a wall that some people had to protect themselves from hurt. Hers was more like an invisible magnetic field that didn't attract or repel—it deflected.

It wasn't complicated with other girls. Physical attraction was the first thing to announce itself. Either it was there or it wasn't. If it was, you both knew it and proceeded accordingly. If it wasn't, you walked away.

I imagined Celia may have wanted me in that way, too, but if she did, for some reason she needed to resist. I respected her feelings and didn't want to risk hurting her even if it meant keeping my mind, hands, and body to myself.

I don't know why I found her strangeness so attractive. My friends weren't like that. They preferred ordinary girls to have ordinary sex with to make ordinary families and lead ordinary lives. they wanted their lives to be like Doris Day movies—like what I'd had with Dalia.

Maybe Celia had made up an elaborate story about herself because she was looking for someone who wasn't ordinary. Maybe it was a filter she'd invented, like a shield to protect herself from the common, conventional man.

Had my own peculiarities drawn her to me? Did I possess curious qualities? Some of my friends seemed to think so.

Maybe that was why she dumped Richard. Maybe she had realized that with him, she would never get anything but ordinary, middle-of-the-road average. Maybe she had been all too willing to use the bathroom excuse.

Celia was still sleeping, so I decided to go watch the planes take off and land. There was a south wind blowing. The pilots were using the north end of the runway to warm up their engines and perform instrument checks. I grabbed my Luckies and my Zippo and started walking.

I was almost in front of the two white concrete buildings that had toilets and showers for men and women. I decided it was a good time to pee, then I wouldn't have to go when I was back with Celia. She'd never even know I'd gone there.

I ducked into the first facility marked with a big blue and white sign: MEN.

Chapter 61

The bathroom was empty.

Three white urinals were mounted on a white concrete block wall. Bright blue deodorant cakes gave off a strong chemical odor. I watched the yellow liquid flow over the white porcelain, swirl around the urinal cake, and disappear down the drain. I felt odd and wondered what Celia would think if she knew what I was doing.

Oh man. How would she feel if she knew I was peeing here? Would she want me to die? There isn't much sound—I can hardly hear it myself, so she wouldn't hear it even if she was right outside the door. If Richard had peed quietly down the side of the bowl, would she still have hated him?

What the Hell was I thinking? I wasn't doing anything wrong, nothing I hadn't done a zillion times before. Maybe she was just testing me in some creative girly way.

I remembered her eyes, her face, her anger as she told the tale. I did believe it. All of it. Her hatred for Richard was the real thing.

I flipped up my sunglasses and stared at myself in the wall mirror over the sink. I lit up a Lucky. The guy in the mirror didn't look flaky—sun-streaked blonde hair, blue eyes, nice tan, good shoulders. I wondered what James Dean would have thought in my place.

If Celia had been acting, her performance was award-winning. Her delivery had left a deep impression in my mind. I had a feeling I would always think of Celia every time I used the bathroom.

Suddenly the room felt like a dangerous place. I wanted to get the Hell out of there.

I walked on the grass toward the cyclone fence near the end of the runway. I paused to watch a Piper Apache twin-engine take off. As it lifted, it's wings flashed in the bright sunlight. I promised myself that one day I'd learn to fly and buy an airplane.

I started back toward the beach. In the distance, I saw Celia lying on her side facing me. She was reading and smoking. As I came near, she dog-eared a page and closed the book. It was *The Snake Pit* by Mary Jane Ward.

Celia had often said her brain was broken, even referring to herself as nuts. Maybe there were clues to her mind in that novel.

I should check out that book.

"Where'd you go?"

"I went to see some airplanes."

Her mood had changed. I couldn't see her eyes through her sunglasses, but her mouth was tight and her body was stiff. She picked up her cigarettes and the book and shoved them into her bag.

"I want to go," she said.

I didn't understand her sudden transformation, but I was always reading too much into everything, especially when it concerned Celia. Maybe she'd had a sudden girl emergency—

"Here, let me give you a hand." I picked up the blanket and shook off the sand. She took it from me, picked up her beach bag, pulled out my car keys, and handed them to me.

"I'll walk you to your car," I said.

She didn't say a word all the way back to the parking lot. When she reached her car, she didn't put her tee-shirt and shorts on over her suit. She opened the door, threw her bag on the front seat, got in, started the car, and said "Bye."

I thought of the beach bathroom. I'd done something that would have freaked the Hell out of her—if I were Richard.

What a crazy story.

But I couldn't get it out of my mind. I watched her little grey car fly out of the lot. All of my Lake Foot House fantasies flew away with it.

Chapter 62

Celia was distant during class on the following Tuesday, but she agreed to meet me at the lake after my going away party. I was leaving for Champaign-Urbana the next morning. I'd be back in two years with a Bachelor of Arts in Industrial Design degree.

"Hey, listen up, everybody," said Sara. "I made these for you, and because Luke is leaving tomorrow, I decided to give them to you today."

Sara handed each one of us a silver triangle. It measured inch and three quarters on each side. There was a three-eighths inch round hole near the center. A jump ring was threaded through a smaller hole in one corner.

"This is my own design of Mr. Victor's HOLE in the Universe. You can wear it as a pendant or pin, or sew it into your underpants for all I care," Sara said, laughing at her own joke.

I remembered the small silver medal of the Virgin

Mary my dad kept in our jewelry store's safe. He said his mother had sewn it into the lining of his coat before we left Lithuania. I often wondered if that was what had kept us safe through the war.

"Why isn't the hole in the middle of the triangle, Sara?"

"Because that would be boring as Hell, Luke." She looked at me with mock exasperation.

"I thought maybe the drill was walking on you," I said, trying to rescue my credibility.

"Yeah, right. Like I've never heard of a center punch."

"Really cool, Sara. What's it made of?" asked Kurt.

"Silver. I got it from a jewelry supply store."

"Really neat," said Shannon. "But I think I'd burn in Hell forever if I were caught dead wearing it around my neck." She dropped the pendant into her purse.

I belonged to the Illinois Air National Guard and always wore my ball neck chain and dog tags. I added the silver HOLE in the Universe pendant to my chain. It dangled next to two stainless steel tags that read:

NORKUS

LUKAS

232 87 9179 AF IL ANG

O POS CATHOLIC

Celia unfastened the chain that held her PBY, slid the HOLE pendant on, and put it back around her neck.

Sara disappeared and came back shortly carrying two hot cookie sheets loaded with baked creations. Mr. Victor brought in two six packs of Coca Cola.

I made my way around the room. I hugged Mr. Victor, Kurt, Marty, and Tad. I kissed Nixon, and patted

Orphan Annie. I hugged and kissed all the girls except Celia. I was saving our goodbyes for the lake.

It had been raining all day. The marina was filled with boats, but the parking lot was almost empty. We parked next to each other, and Celia got into my car. She wore a grey Illini sweatshirt, faded blue jeans, and red canvas shoes. I marveled at how cute her little feet looked even in that silly old lady gardening footwear.

I was relieved when she took out two Newports and lit them. Maybe everything was going to be all right after all. But my hopes were dashed instantly. She didn't say "any time" after I thanked her.

I noticed a white gauze dressing pad peeking out from under the sleeve of her left arm.

"What happened to your arm?"

"Oh, it's nothing. I scraped it on something when I was trying to get my pen out from under the seat."

She sounded like she was lying, but it was my last day with her, so I let it go.

I rolled down my window. The lake air was humid and smelled fresh from the rain.

"So, Luke. Where are you going to live at school? I mean, are you going to be in a dorm?"

Her jaw was clenched as she spoke.

"I'll be leasing a room in a house close to the campus."

"Oh, are there going to be other boys there, too? Do you know them?"

"Yep. Eight or so Lithuanian guys like me. I know most of them from Marquette Park."

"What about Dalia? Is she going? Will she be living with you?"

"No, Dalia's not a student. And she wouldn't be living with me even if she was. We broke up, remember?"

Her tone was tense and I felt weird. She'd never quizzed me before about my comings, goings, or doings, but I was about to leave, and I'd be gone for a very long time. Of course she was curious.

"Well, that's what you said. I mean about breaking up."

"Don't you believe I broke up with her? I did. I'm not lying—if that's what you're thinking."

Damn. I don't want to get into a fight now, of all times, but this is pissing me off. She's interrogating me.

I felt my face get rigid like hers. I didn't like being falsely accused. I crushed out my cigarette in the ashtray. Celia did the same.

"Sure, Luke. I believe you. Are you going to be drinking beer with your new college buddies? And coffee? And wine? What about pot? Are you going to drop acid like everyone else does, too?"

"Umm … I hadn't really thought about any of that, Celia—"

"You're going to be peeing a lot. I mean if you're going to be drinking a lot, Luke."

What the Hell? She said peeing was only an issue if she cared about someone.

Is she falling in love with me?

Chapter 63

She slid away and shrank into the corner of her seat. Her body was trembling, and her lips were pale. The greenish-grey light of the rainy day made her look ghostly and small. I moved next to her and wrapped my arms around her.

"Celia, what's wrong? Oh man—"

She was shaking violently.

"Please ... tell me what's going on," I said, not sure what to say.

I held her tighter, and she didn't pull away. She started to cry, but her arms stayed stiff and cold at her sides. Her tears bled into my shirt.

"I d-don't ... w-want you to ... g-g-o." Celia's teeth were chattering uncontrollably.

I didn't know what to do. Celia hadn't expressed any emotions to me other than light-hearted friendship, at least not that I'd recognized. I had no idea she liked me more than just a friend. Why had she waited until the very last minute to show it—when I had no choice but to leave?

I held her with firm pressure. Her jaw shuddered into my shoulder as she cried.

I tried to think of calming words like telling her my school was only a three or four hour car ride away. I'd be back often. We could see each other soon and make plans for her to move down to southern Illinois close to my school. Sure, we'd miss our outings on the lake—terribly. But we'd make new good times.

Then I remembered her separation issues. She couldn't even take Lego Edgar apart. And, what about the peeing stuff? I wouldn't be anywhere near her—not even in the same city—when I had to use a bathroom.

But we hadn't been physically intimate, so it shouldn't matter.

Should it?

A few minutes passed, and she began to relax. She hadn't stopped shaking completely, but she was able to talk without the jaw tremors.

"Luke, I can't—"

"Celia, really ... I think your idea of college life is bigger in your mind than it is for real. It's a tough school. A lot of kids struggle with their classes. I doubt most of them party. The ones who do flunk out right away. My parents would kill me if I did that," I said tenderly.

She pushed me off and sat up straight. I edged away and gave her some space.

"You're lying, Luke," she said in a calmer tone.

"You're covering up for yourself and your friends. That's what guys do. You all stick together. You'll probably tell them about this insane girl up north—how she's messed up and worried about crazy stuff that doesn't matter. You'll all be drinking beer and peeing outside on trees and in people's yards. You'll have contests together—to see who can pee longest and farthest."

I watched her make words that formed sentences and couldn't believe she sounded so logical. She wasn't yelling or screaming or crying. She was composed and in total control of her words. She believed everything she was saying.

"Celia, I—"

"You're a liar, Luke. Don't bother to deny it. You lied to my face at the beach. You said you went to watch the planes, but I saw you go into the bathroom. You thought I was sleeping, didn't you? Well, I wasn't. And I saw you."

Her words were ice daggers.

"Celia—"

"I want to give you and your buddies something to talk about, something to toast."

She groped for the door handle behind her back.

Chapter 64

I lunged fast and yanked her hand away from the door.

"Let me go, Luke! I'm not a coward! Let me go and then you can all laugh and drink and make fun of poor psycho Celia!"

I held her tight against my chest, hoping the madness would pass. She resisted, squirming like a child, but I held firm. She tried to kick out her legs and push me away. I clasped my hands together and embraced her, using my will and as little force as possible to stop her from opening the door. I didn't want to hurt her. I wanted to crush the crazy out of her.

"I hate you, Luke! You know what you did! You thought you got away with it! Let me go!"

"No, I'm not letting you go until you calm down!"

She fought to escape my hold calling me a liar and a betrayer, but I outweighed her by seventy pounds. She couldn't break free. I was at war with a demon—something alien—something dangerous that had invaded and taken over my Celia.

She stopped struggling and sank into my arms, crying softly. I kissed the top of her head. Her baby fine blond hair tickled my lips and nose. Her head was warm, and the faint scent of lilies of the valley reminded me that she was still my Celia.

I felt like we were churning in a sea of black water. If I had loosened my hold, she would have slipped away and drowned. I gripped her for dear life—her dear life. The waves washed over me, and I tasted the salt of my own tears.

It was drizzling and dark over the lake. The car windows were steamed up. Clear tracks of condensation ran down the glass.

She stopped crying and lifted her head slowly. Her eyes were swollen. The parking lot lights shined through the rainy windshield and cast eerie patterns over her face. She smiled weakly. "I'll be alright, Luke. I can drive myself home."

I didn't want to pry myself away from her. Not then. Not ever. But I did. I wondered if I should ask for her gun. But I didn't. She might have felt betrayed, or like I didn't trust her, or that I was lying again.

Then she did something I had only imagined in my wildest, sweetest thoughts. She wrapped her arms around me and kissed me. It was passionate—like in my dreams—the softest lips I'd ever kissed.

I held that kiss for as long as she let me.

When I finally let her go, she picked up her bag,

opened the door, and said, "Bye, Luke."

"Bye, Celia," I choked out.

She closed the door and everything became a blur. Tears flooded my eyes. I heard her tiny, scooter-sized engine start up, and she drove away.

Celia was gone—but her kiss lingered on my lips. I knew I would never forget it.

Chapter 65
Champaign-Urbana, Illinois, August 1961

Seven Eighteen Green was an old two-story frame house near campus, a short walk to the quad at the center of the original campus. At the northwest corner of the quad was the Alma Mater: the university's own version of the Statue of Liberty, welcoming all seekers of sheepskins and knowledge to her warm and ample bosom.

The house had a living room, a big kitchen, three bathrooms, and eight or ten rooms leased out to Lithuanian students.

The leases were passed along from friends or friends of friends, which worked out well for the owner. They hadn't had a vacancy in years. The Lithuanians were a respectable minority. New applicants came pre-approved by the former leaseholder. I was lucky to know a girl whose brother was about to graduate. She'd arranged for me to take over his lease.

There was no co-op student housing on campus. Girls

visited on the sneak, but rarely spent the night. There were loads of stories of wild happenings, but I thought they were made of the same stuff as myths: imaginations running wild.

There were two refrigerators in the kitchen. We kept our perishable food items in one. The other had a sign securely taped on the front:

ABSOLUTELY NO FOOD ALLOWED
BEER WINE HARD LIQUOR ONLY

Seven Eighteen Green meant freedom—a first time experience. I'd be living away from my parents.

I could smoke in my room and leave cigarettes out in plain view. I could stay up all night and sleep all day if I wanted to. I could throw my clothes anywhere—on the floor or a table or bookshelf or windowsill. I could shove them under the bed and let them stink up the place if I wanted to.

For the first time in my life, I could keep booze in my room. I could even ask a girl to visit. But I wouldn't want to—unless it was Celia—and I knew that couldn't happen. At least not right away.

Chapter 66

I missed Celia.

Terribly.

Three weeks had passed since our sad farewell. I realized that in all the time we'd known each other, our only connection had been through Mr. Victor's studio. I didn't have her address or phone number. We had only met up on Tuesdays or Thursdays after class. Just once, we'd arranged to meet at Northerly on a Saturday, but after that things hadn't gone so well.

In spite of my new freedom, I had been having some very strange thoughts. I was in constant conflict every time I went into a bathroom. It was as if Celia had cast a spell over me, and not in a good way. I remembered her horror and suffering in my car, and pictured her having a terrible reaction whenever I had to use a restroom. I could almost count the times I peed in those three weeks.

My friends and I didn't do what Celia had predicted.

We drank and played cards, but we didn't have any peeing contests. I remembered how she had looked and acted on that drizzly evening, and I felt all wrong inside—like I was betraying her every few hours of every day just by doing what was natural and necessary.

I wanted to sneak in and out of bathrooms fast to hide what I was doing *from me*. I'd even gone so far as to estimate the number of times I'd gone to pee. An average of five times a day multiplied by twenty-one days—plus twenty or thirty extra trips due to beer consumption—put me at well over a hundred and thirty times that I'd betrayed Celia.

Betrayed? Have I gone fucking crazy?

Maybe, but I loved Celia. What was wrong with a little crazy anyway? I had learned in my sociology class that Freud thought everyone was nuts when they were in love.

I lit up a Lucky. I remembered a time when I was tempted to switch to smoking her brand, but gave up the idea as soon as I tried one. Puffing on a Newport without Celia was the saddest smoke I'd ever had.

Chapter 67
September 18, 1961

Seven Eighteen Green had a single mailbox set up outside the front door. All residents were responsible for finding their own mail.

I sorted through the pile on the coffee table in the front room. A pale grey envelope caught my eye. It was addressed to me and had "Svarbi Žinia" written on it. That meant "Important Notice".

It was from Mr. Victor.

Chapter 68

I started to read—

Oh my God. Oh, God! No. Please, NO! PLEASE! She's DEAD!

I knew this was going to happen—after that night! No, I didn't. This isn't even fucking true. Somebody's fucking around playing a really bad prank on me. Maybe it's Marty. Or Kurt. They're sick shits. Maybe it's Sara—maybe she's jealous—

This can't be true. God, please. God, please, no, no, no. Please, please—

I ran to my room and slammed the door. I dropped to my knees. I slid on my belly and stretched out my arms, my hands clawing at the linoleum. I cried out loud, rolling around, twisting like a worm on a fish hook.

"Dear God, don't let this be true!"

I begged to the room, to God the Father, to anything listening.

Sounds came from my mouth, but they were bizarre—long, anguished animal wails. I felt surreal and desperate. My own noise was confirmation. It had really happened. Celia *WAS* dead.

"Jesus! I'm here! Remember me? You used to sit on my bed in Weixerau and listen to me. Please, please, *please* tell me this isn't true. Give me a sign—anything! Show me she's not dead—"

I cried and cried and heard sounds I'd never heard before. They were coming from me—sick and shrill.

"Celia, if you're there—please help me now."

I pulled the sheet off the bed and scrubbed my face hard.

I remembered my mother's scented handkerchiefs; how she'd wiped away my tears and fears and made everything all right again.

Who's going to make anything all right now?

The letter was lying inches away. I skipped over the part I'd already read. I couldn't bear to see those words again.

After Mr. Victor had announced Celia's suicide, the group formed a circle and held hands. Kurt made an Edgar Lego spider just like Celia's original. Marty wrote a poem. Toni made a card. Shannon put a rosary and a note in an envelope for Celia. Sara baked cookies. Everyone wrote goodbyes in the white lining of Celia's black philosopher cap.

Mr. Victor finished by saying there would be no wake or funeral for Celia.

I refolded the letter, put it back in its envelope, and

pushed it down into my back pocket. I left the musty room. I was suffocating.

I walked around town aimlessly. Celia and I had never been there together. Not one sidewalk square had been stepped on by her pretty feet. No tree had been touched by her curious fingers, testing the texture of its bark. There was no cozy diner booth where we had smoked, snacked, and gazed into each other's souls. No sacred space, place, or object held the tiniest remnant of Celia's life or spirit.

I had never thought of Celia as my connection to the universe, or that she had been my anchor—until she was gone. I was cast adrift on a still and glassy surface blending seamlessly into grey nothingness.

Alone.

I sat down on a bench in a little park and studied the letter. Mr. Victor said it was suicide but left out the details.

I knew the details. She had blown her broken brain apart with her Walther PPK, James Bond's favorite sidearm.

I felt her first and last kiss. I remembered the taste. Salty tears on baby-soft lips. I felt her warm breath from her sweet mouth. That was all I'd ever have of Celia—

I'll never see her again.

My stomach was in ruins. Sharp, metallic saliva flooded my mouth. I put my head down between my knees and began to retch.

I could have stopped her.
She begged me not to go.

I didn't listen.
I killed her!
I killed that sad, abused girl!
No. I didn't. How can it be my fault?
I didn't even understand what she was talking about.
That weird peeing stuff?
She never even told me she liked me—
I didn't know it would bother her when I did that.
Not really.
No, I definitely didn't know.
This isn't my fault!

Go get drunk, man. Stinkin' fuckin' ugly drunk. Just chill out. Forget it. It's over. Repeat after me: It's not my fault. It's not my fault. It's not my fucking fault!
    IT'S
    NOT
    MY
    FUCKING,
    FUCKING
    FAULT!

Chapter 69

I couldn't go back to Seven Eighteen. I didn't want to be around people, and I didn't want them to see me. I wanted to stay away until everybody went to bed and then sneak in unnoticed.

West Side Story was playing at the Cinema on Main Street. I'd heard it was a modern adaptation of Romeo and Juliet.

I needed tragedy. The deeper and darker, the better. Maybe the world's saddest love story would be a welcome visitor to my vacant soul.

I felt disconnected. I was in an unfamiliar town sitting like a ghost, watching a movie about a white boy in love with a Puerto Rican gang leader's sister. It looked like Maria was going to kill herself after Tony died in her arms. She had saved the last bullet for herself. She had the gun—

Yes! Do it!

I edged up in my seat waiting for the big payoff.
She dropped the gun.

Aww! What—fucking—shit.

The movie was a total letdown. Romeo died, but Juliet lived—by her own choosing. Where was the love?

If Shakespeare had written that kind of crappy cop-out ending to his play, nobody would have heard of Romeo and Juliet.

Hollywood, you really fucked this one up! What were you trying to do? Pacify us? So we can go home feeling good?

Well, I sure as shit don't feel good! Officer Krupke—West Side Story—fuck you!

I walked back to the house and got into my car. University Liquors was off-campus near the train station. I turned west on University Avenue and was blinded by the setting sun. It sat like a giant red stoplight centered inches above the street.

I yanked the visor down as far as it would go, but it still didn't keep the sun out of my eyes. I drove slowly, hunched forward over the steering wheel peering through the horizontal glass slit above the dashboard.

I was already twenty-one so I could use my real driver's license to buy the hard stuff.

But that was the second item on my shopping list.

Chapter 70

Leonard's Pawn Shop was on the right side of the street. I pulled up to the front of the store and parked. I had met Leonard Greenman the week before when I had run out of cash. He still had my stereo, and I owed him fifteen dollars, but I had some time left on my loan.

Leonard was fortyish, short, slight, handsome, nattily dressed, and looked a lot like Ed Sullivan. He was standing in front of the counter talking with a customer. He sounded agitated.

"I could be in the window stark naked pulling on my putz, Hyman, and they would still walk by and never even look in."

Leonard disappeared, returned with a handful of cash, and handed it to the customer who left immediately.

"That was my younger brother, Hyman. He owns the clothing store next door. He still thinks I'm his bank.

"What do you have in mind, young man? Guitar, TV?

How about a nice electric hot plate for your dorm room? I remember you. You brought me a stereo. Are you here to redeem or pay on your account?"

"Luke Norkus, Leonard. I want to know if you have any guns for sale."

"Shotguns? Are you going hunting for pheasants? Some students buy them from me at the beginning of the season. I charge them thirty dollars and they pawn them back to me later for fifteen. But they never come back. You could say I'm in the shotgun rental business," said Leonard with a wormy chuckle.

"I need a handgun."

Leonard bent down, then gave me a quizzical look as he straightened back up. His jet black hair glistened with moving blue highlights like Superman's from the comic books. He probably used a hair tonic like Brylcreem to slick it down.

"It's for my parents in Chicago. Our jewelry store was robbed a month ago. I'd feel better if they had a gun. I know my dad would feel safer having it. You know what I mean."

Actually I wasn't lying. Two men had walked right into the store and robbed my dad. One man kept his hand in his coat pocket and led my dad to the safe behind the partition at the back of the store. The other guy stood guard by the front door. They only wanted cash. We would've been ruined if they had taken our jewelry.

Leonard wore a dark blue pin-striped suit with a solid white pocket square. He folded his arms exposing a gold Omega Seamaster wristwatch on a very hairy wrist. On his ring finger was a gaudy Las Vegas style diamond ring.

"A lot of people come through my door. Some are students like you with big ideas about bright futures. Then there are the local drunks who want a few bucks to buy some relief in a bottle. They leave their high school graduation rings and their fathers' gold watches and pay me after I cash their Social Security checks."

He scratched his chin and rubbed the stubble of his five-o'clock shadow.

"Then there are the single mothers short on rent money. Sometimes they come in with nothing to pawn. I lend them the cash, and I don't charge them interest. Some never come back to pay me, but I don't mind. It makes me feel kinda better about myself. You know what I mean, Luke?"

I really didn't know what he meant, but I didn't ask.

"Some folks walk in like they've got a noose around their neck, like they're looking for a few more inches of rope. I give them cash—they give me their power tools, their mothers' silver, their wives' engagement diamonds, their wedding bands. I never see them again. I have a store full of unredeemed items."

Leonard finally stopped blabbing and led me into a private office behind the back wall. He opened a desk drawer and showed me a few semi-automatics and a blue .38 caliber Smith & Wesson.

"I recommend the revolver for your dad, Luke. Pistols are unreliable for self-defense. That's why cops don't use them. They jam and let you down when your life depends on them—when you need them most."

Where was I when Celia needed me most?

He charged me thirty dollars for the Smith & Wesson. He picked out six .38 caliber cartridges from a shoebox filled with everything from tiny .22 caliber to large 12 gauge red paper Remington shotgun shells. He sealed the bullets in an envelope, wrapped the gun in newspaper, and put it all into a Safeway shopping bag.

"I can't give you a receipt, Luke, but if you want to return it for any reason, I'll stand by it. You have my word."

I believed him.

"Don't load it 'til you give it to your dad. If the cops stop you with a loaded gun, you'll be in deep kimchi."

"Thanks, Leonard."

Chapter 71

I drove past the Art and Design building on Peabody Street and turned south on Fourth Avenue. A building of nightmarish proportions loomed up on the right. It was the new Illini Assembly Hall, still under construction.

Ahead on the left was an open parking lot next to a cemetery. The burial ground was a popular place to eat, study, or nap between classes. Kids loved to make out in the soft, perfectly maintained grass, discretely shielded from prying eyes by a tombstone. I pulled in and parked.

The lot lights illuminated the empty front seat where Celia had struggled and cried in my arms. No one had been there since—

Oh, man—the ashtray—

I opened the glove compartment and found a clear sandwich bag. I pulled out the ashtray and poured the contents into the bag. Celia's Newport filter tips were mixed in with the ashes. I couldn't tell which ones were hers because she never wore lipstick. I only knew they were in there—together with mine.

I lay down across the seat and held the precious packet to my face. I kissed it and said good night to Celia.

It was eleven fifteen when I awoke. I sat up and put the ashes in the pocket of my yellow windbreaker. I got out of the car and walked into the graveyard.

A quarter moon was shining and the air was cool. A thin ground fog veiled the thick grass carpet. I spotted a flat tombstone tilted at a good angle for a backrest. It was under an ancient weeping willow whose branches formed a stringed curtain that gently enclosed the grave. I parted the willows, slipped through the leafy space, and sat down, leaning back against the cold gravestone. I felt my pocket and started to choke on my tears.

Why did she do this?

She had so much to live for. She was talented, gorgeous, and smart. Millions had lost their loved ones—like Mr. Victor. Billions were less fortunate than Celia. Yet they'd decided to keep on living, trying, coping, and hoping.

Did she really kill herself because of me?

Under the faint moon's light, rows upon rows of dark shapes marked final resting places, standing like silent sentinels beside their owners.

Would Marcelline put up a stone for Celia?

Oh, who gives a crap about a stupid stone anyway—

I took out a Lucky and lit up. I watched my smoke rise and disappear into the foliage.

They say souls rise when they leave the body. I

wondered where Celia was. If she was anywhere, she must be far away.

Unless she's coming back for me!

But why the fuck would she? I didn't listen to her when she begged me to stay. Sure as shit she wouldn't want me now. She probably hates my guts.

And I don't blame her.

Wait—maybe she isn't dead. Maybe Mr. Victor got the story all wrong. Maybe someone told him she attempted suicide. His English isn't perfect. Maybe he misunderstood. Maybe she's in some hospital recuperating right now!

Romeo thought Juliet was dead, and she was just sleeping—

My dad had always advised me against making rash decisions. I had no change for a pay phone, but it was too late at night to call Mr. Victor anyway.

Luke!

Stop fucking with yourself.

Celia's dead.

Chapter 72

I drove back to Seven Eighteen. On my way to the stairs, I passed a reading resident, but I doubt he'd noticed me.

The linoleum flooring in my room had a muted brown and green geometric pattern. The walls were painted robin's egg blue. In the corner was a steel-framed single bed. On the floor next to it was a dented aluminum ashtray—probably stolen from the school cafeteria. On the wall, I had mounted two wall shelves to hold books, record albums, and my stereo. An empty space on the lower shelf awaited the return of the amplifier, turntable, and speakers from Leonard's.

A kitchen table with chrome legs and a grey Formica top edged in stainless steel stood next to a window. Under the table was a yellow vinyl-cushioned kitchen chair. A brown paper bag served as a trash container. On the ceiling was a round pink glass light fixture with silhouettes of nine dead flies and a moth resting in peace inside the glass globe.

The room reminded me of Van Gogh's bedroom in Arles, the subject of a number of his paintings, and possibly where he'd contemplated his suicide.

The difference between my room and Van Gogh's was that his was a lot more cheerful.

On the table, I arranged a clean jelly jar, the quart of cheap vodka I'd bought at the liquor store, the ashtray, a pack of Luckies, my Zippo lighter, Mr. Victor's letter, and the Smith & Wesson. Next to the weapon I laid the packet of Celia's ashes.

I lit a Lucky and sat down at the table. I tore open Leonard's envelope and poured out the bullets, forming a barrier with my left hand to stop them from rolling off the table. They clicked and clattered as they hit the hard surface.

I lined up the little soldiers in standing formation on the smooth tabletop. The two tallest stood on the left, the others fell in to the right in descending order. It was a rag-tag group of two flat-heads, three hollow-points, and one shorter copperhead.

Let's see ... who's in charge here? The copperhead was shiny and looked a lot smarter than the taller, dull-witted flat heads and hollow-heads.

Copperhead it is.

Time for practice. But first—a drink.

I filled the jelly jar with the booze, took a long sip, and picked up the revolver. I wasn't familiar with handguns, but I could tell it was old and hadn't received the best care. The bluing was faded and worn, and there was rust around some of the screw heads. I released the cylinder and gave it a spin. It didn't make the clicking sounds like I'd heard in the movies.

Another Hollywood letdown. In every cowboy movie I had seen since my early days in Landshut, the spinning cylinder always clicked. The sharp, ratcheting sound was the prelude to the drama. It summoned the senses to the ensuing danger like the rattle of a Diamondback snake.

I snapped the cylinder back into the weapon and cocked the hammer.

Time for dry fire. But first—another drink.

Dry fire was what the Training Instructors called it when we practiced shooting with an unloaded rifle in training for my Illinois Air National Guard unit.

I closed my left eye and searched the room for targets. Light switch on the wall. Books on the wall shelf.

Aha! Analytic Geometry!

I lined up the sights on the spine and squeezed the trigger. There was a heavy click and the book disintegrated. Enemy number one—gone. Another textbook: *The Lonely Crowd* by David Riesman—pass.

Another sip. The vodka went down smooth and easy. My throat was already anesthetized from gulping the eighty-proof liquor.

I aimed at the ceiling light. Click! The room rained pink glass and dried insects.

I looked out the window, aimed at the moon, cocked back the hammer—click! The man in the moon somersaulted and disappeared beyond the trees.

Someone walked out of the house across the street.

I drew a bead. Click! Headline in the morning papers—
INSANE SNIPER KILLS UNIVERSITY STUDENT.

Nah! I don't hate humanity—present company excluded.

Hey, ASSHOLE! Put it up to your head—I'll bet you don't have the guts—

I pressed the muzzle into my right temple and pulled the trigger. CLICK! The sound was amplified traveling through my skull.

Yeah, you're a real big, brave man—with your empty gun—you fucking chicken!

Don't call me chicken—

I released the latch on the cylinder and let it flop out. I dropped the Copperhead into one of the holes, spun the cylinder, and flicked it shut.

Well then, there now ... where are you, soldier?

My vision was getting wonky from the booze. I thought I saw the bullet near the top of the cylinder on the left.

Or was it on the right?

Where the fuck is it?

I lit up another Lucky and pondered the smoke clouds.

What would James Dean do?

I fondled the weapon.

More vodka.

More clouds.

More Luckies.

Wait.

Am I supposed to leave a note?

My little brother, Algytis, was gone—dead by the

time I was four months old. His death had nearly killed my mother, but she still had my father and me to take care of and keep safe through the war and all the bombings.

She never gave up. She had to go on for me—
But her love for me had saved her, too—
So, how would she feel if I decided—
AWW—FUCK! This would kill my mom and dad.
But I wouldn't feel a thing. Not one fucking thing. I'd be out of my pain.
But they'd live in it every day for the rest of their lives—
If they wanted to live at all—
They might even think it was their fault—
But what about my Celia? Could she be waiting for me? Somewhere?
Maybe I'm just shit-faced drunk—
If I go to sleep, maybe I'll wake up and find out none of this ever happened—

I staggered to my feet, turned off the light, and fell on the bed. Everything was spinning. For a moment—

Chapter 73

"Pagauk mane, Lukai, ir aš būsiu tavo, amžinai!" Celia called to me. "Catch me, Luke, and I'll be yours forever!"

She was naked, running through a field of tall red poppies. I had never imagined such beauty. I ran behind her, watching her blond hair blaze like golden flames from an Olympic torch. Her eyes flashed emerald fire when she glanced back at me.

I looked down and realized I was naked, too. The grass was lush under my feet. She dove into a pond, and I followed her into the clear water. She swam gracefully, sending underwater rainbows out from her body like colored neon lights.

She emerged on the other side and flopped down on her back. I watched the sun's rays twinkle along the outline of her perfect body. Her hair was wet and curling. Sparkling diamonds rolled off her eyebrows and lashes, dropping lightly onto the blades of grass below. Her breasts rose and fell gently as she breathed in fresh air. Her skin was taut and cool from the light breeze.

I followed her flat stomach down past her belly button to a light layer of golden curls. Her legs had dried silky smooth, and her feet were lovely.

I let my arm drop into the water and picked up a snail. I placed it on her belly. It sat for a second before making a move. Celia giggled as it traveled slowly to the top of her hip bone. It almost toppled before I rescued it and returned it to its home under the water.

Celia put two cigarettes in her mouth.

"Nori parūkyt?" She offered me a smoke.

"Taip. Ar turi su kuom uždekt?" I answered yes, and asked if she had something to light them with.

"Taip."

Celia had a gun in her right hand. She drew the muzzle to the cigarettes and pulled the trigger. A small flame shot out and lit both. She put one in my mouth.

"Ačiū," I thanked her.

"Bele kada," she answered, which meant "any time".

We lay on our backs under the dark blue sky and watched our smoke swirl above us. There was a crescent moon in the east; the sun was still high in the west. Bright stars twinkled in between. A tall man dressed in a white robe stood beyond a stand of poppies; an aura of golden light outlined his silhouette. He was smiling and familiar. I sat up and looked at Celia.

She put the muzzle to her chest between her breasts. I heard a click. A small red dot appeared on her skin where she'd clicked the pistol. She laughed and handed me the gun.

"Dabar tu." Now you, she said. I held the gun to my breastbone, imitating Celia. I pulled the trigger and heard the click. I looked down and watched a red dot like Celia's form on my chest. A warm and pleasant feeling washed through me.

I looked up. The man in white was gone.

Celia laid back and opened her arms, inviting me to come closer. I faced her and balanced my body over hers, slipping my hands behind the small of her back. I lined up our red dots and pressed my chest into hers.

She wrapped her arms and legs around me and pulled me in tight. I felt a rushing stream gush through my body. I felt our blood mixing, our hearts beating hard and fast together. I wanted to stay that way forever.

Forever didn't last long.

She began to fade away. Her face became my pillow.

I sprang up from the bed drenched with sweat.

AM I DEAD?

I searched my chest with my hands—feeling for the hole—the mortal wound that killed me.

No hole!

I tripped over some clothes and stumbled toward the door. I flipped on the light and looked down at myself.

Nothing. No blood. No hole. Where's the gun?

There it is! On the table.

FIVE! There's only five bullets!

I counted and recounted. Five to the right. Five to the left. I was afraid to touch the weapon.

Was it fired?

I moved carefully, stalking toward the muzzle end—squinting—desperately wanting to see the shiny head in one of the holes—like squeezing for the last card in a big poker hand—the one that would take the pot.

There it is!

The Copperhead was still in the cylinder.

All present and accounted for.

It had all been a dream, but what had it meant? Was Celia calling me?

"It is all about your brain," Mr. Victor used to say. He might have theorized that I had invented the dream; it was my subconscious at work. I was feeling guilty about Celia's death, so my brain made up a way of balancing the scales, making things right again. Romeo would join his Juliet, and they would be together again— eternally happy.

I sat at the table and smoked. The moon was gone. The sky was brightening up behind houses and treetops. The nightmare sweat had dried on my skin and I felt groggy. I finished my smoke and went back to bed.

I was deep in the cellar with the praying man as sirens screamed outside. He turned and glared at me, eyes glowing like electric cigarette lighter coils. He raised his arm and pointed a gun at my head. He was Mr. Victor.

A beautiful face appeared and blocked him.

"Nebijok pupuliuk, aš tave myliu ir tave apsaugosiu."

It was my mother. She told me to have no fear because she loved me. She would protect me.

The man jumped from one side of her to the other trying to get around her. The gun appeared and disappeared from behind her face as she turned me away and out of his reach. He tried repeatedly, like a crazed rabid dog, to outflank her and get to me.

My mother's face was as calm as a deep mountain lake on a windless day. She shielded me without one ripple of fear, just like she always did. When I awoke, I understood.

Celia wanted me to die—

But my mother wanted me to live.

My mother was saving me.

Again.

Chapter 74

I didn't go back to my classes. I went to see Dean Fitzsimmons in the College of Art and Architecture. I told him what happened, and he helped me withdraw without penalty. He sent a note to Admissions and Records requesting a full refund of my tuition along with permission to maintain my student status still entitled to all free services. He also scheduled an appointment for me with Dr. Rosen.

He had a desk in the Student Services building, and he didn't look old enough to be a graduate student, much less a PhD. He was handsome with long, dark, straight hair. He asked me a few questions, and said he would like to see me the following day in his office off-campus. He scribbled out a note and handed it to me. It said:

512 South Poplar Street, Urbana
Wed 9/20 10 AM

Chapter 75

Poplar Street was narrow. Weeds grew out of dirt-filled cracks in the old pavement. Both sides of the street were lined with timeworn trees, some touching each other with long limbs and fingers, forming a leafy canopy overhead. Sunlit, grassy gaps were interrupted by low, flat stumps—remnants of those departed.

I was surprised his office was a private residence; an old two-story frame on a street of old two-story frames. The house looked similar to Seven Eighteen Green with faded peeling paint on wood clapboard siding. A beat-up white VW Beetle with a dark blue passenger door and matching front fender was parked on the pebbly, grass-covered remains of a side driveway.

A little old lady walking her little white dog was about to pass me on the sidewalk. She was bent down low taking small steps, trying to avoid cracks in the ancient cement. She strained to lift her head and smiled while shuffling past. Her dog ignored me.

I muttered, "Good morning," but I doubt she'd heard me.

I climbed three steps up to a wide wooden porch and stopped in front of the screen door. I rang the doorbell.

Dr. Rosen was barefoot wearing an orange Fighting Illini tee-shirt and faded blue jeans.

"C'mon in, Luke."

"Hello, Dr. Rosen."

I stepped inside and he offered me a Kent. I took it out of courtesy even though I preferred my own brand. I pulled out my Zippo and offered a light. The smell of antiquity and old varnished wood mixed with the rich aroma of freshly lit tobacco.

Dr. Rosen didn't fit the profile my brain had conjured up for a shrink. He looked more like a student than a professional, but it was comforting. He didn't speak, which gave me a chance to get acclimated to the atmosphere.

With its collection of non-matching furniture, sofas at odd angles, bookshelves made of bricks supporting planks loaded with a haphazard array of books, records, and a stereo—his office could have been mistaken for a student's residence.

A low table sat next to one of the sofas. It was laden with textbooks, one closed on a notebook with a yellow pencil wedged in the spiral binding. A spoon stuck out of an open Chinese food carton, and two aluminum ashtrays overflowed with ashes and filter tips. A floor lamp with an orange cardboard shade printed with Red Ryder and

Little Beaver graphics stood by the table. Maybe it was a fond leftover from Dr. Rosen's boyhood room.

He handed me an ashy tuna can, and motioned for me to sit. I noticed an art print with ratty edges thumb-tacked to the wall—*Flying Lovers in the Red Sky* by Marc Chagall. How odd. Seeing the painting and holding the familiar ashtray made me feel sad, as if a ghost from another lifetime was welcoming me into the room.

"I'm not going to fix you, Luke," said Dr. Rosen. He plopped down on the other sectional and threw his leg over the side.

What a strange thing to say to a new patient.

"People see a doctor for a broken arm. The doctor lines up the bones and makes a cast to support them. Their bones heal and they say, 'Oh what a wonderful doctor. He fixed my arm so well. It's good as new, and he said the bone will be even stronger than it was before it broke.'"

He dragged on his filter tipped Kent, and exhaled through his mouth and nose.

"The doctor fixed nothing, Luke. The patients fixed it all. Their bodies fixed themselves. The doctor just made sure they wouldn't injure themselves further.

"I'm not going to work on your brain or your pain. You'll do that yourself. It'll take a little time, and I'll give you a few pointers to help you get started. But your brain will fix itself, and you'll be in charge. Do you want to be fixed, Luke?"

"I ... I'm not really sure, Doc."

I felt nauseous.

What right do I have asking for help, trying to fix myself? No one helped Celia. She died alone. She cried to me, asking—no, begging for my help. I just left her. I took off and never looked back. Now here I am sitting in this shrink's office trying to make myself feel better. I'm an asshole. I don't deserve to live.

Dr. Rosen pointed to an open door. "Bathroom's in there, Luke."

I ran in and dropped to my knees in front of the porcelain commode. The seat was up, and I stared at the reflection in the water below. A long string of saliva stretched down from my parted lips. The face stared back with its open, drooling mouth. *It* looked like a gargoyle ready to vomit its venom all over *me*.

I spat and the image vanished. The wave of sickness passed. I stood up and looked in the mirror over the sink. I saw the face of a betrayer.

I guessed the doctor was going to try to convince me that I was just an innocent young man who got trapped in a very unfortunate circumstance. Or something similarly psychologically believable. What else could he do? Say that I was an asshole, and that I really didn't deserve to live?

I returned to my seat in the living room. "I'm sorry, Doctor. I didn't want to barf on your furniture. I'm okay now."

"Try to relax, Luke. And call me Bob. Forget the doctor crap."

He sat up, put both feet on the floor, folded his hands, and rested them between his knees. He looked straight at me and went on.

"Okay. You're here because your girlfriend killed herself, and you feel like it's your fault."

"She wasn't my girlfriend, Bob. She was a really good friend—"

"So, as I understand it then, you didn't fuck her—right, Luke? That would be the requirement for a real girlfriend. Celia was a good friend, but not a girlfriend—because a girlfriend is a friend you fuck."

Did I hear right? What the Hell did this guy just say? I want to kill you, you fucking bastard! Are you even a doctor, you arrogant prick?

My blood was hot pressurized steam in a racing locomotive. My head pounded—

"I can see you're pissed off, Luke. That's good. Now we're getting somewhere."

What the Hell is this fucker talking about?

I shook from the adrenaline rush.

"I don't want you to like me, Luke. If you do, you'll look to me for answers—but the answers are inside you. I'm the guy who's going to shove you into the pool. You're the guy who's going to swim."

A big, long haired, black and white cat strolled into the room and began to rub on Dr. Rosen's leg. "I'll be back in a minute, Luke. Sigmund wants his tuna."

I had never thrown a punch in my life. I'd had dreams where I was so mad at someone, I tried to hit them. But my arms didn't move—they were paralyzed. That's how I felt sitting in Dr. Rosen's office. I wanted my body to move, to get up and clobber that clown. But I couldn't move. I wanted to shout, but nothing came out.

I didn't have a short fuse like some of my friends. I thought I was slow-witted. By the time I had worked myself up for a good comeback, the window of opportunity had slammed shut. The moment was gone.

Or maybe I was just a coward.

I had hoped my sweaty hands and armpits would have dried up by the time I got to high school, but that didn't happen. I still had to rub my palms on my pants and blow on them before shaking anyone's hand. I was a slow-witted coward with sweaty armpits and soggy hands.

Celia had clammy little hands. Tears flooded my eyes.

Doctor Rosen came back into the room. "Do you like to drink, Luke? Do you get drunk often?"

I'd started drinking when I was thirteen, but I lived with my parents so how much could a kid drink without getting caught by his folks?

Why is he asking me about my drinking? That's not why I'm here! Drinking is my business, and I have no problem with it! I'm here about Celia, not my fucking drinking, you asshole!

"Not more than once a week," I answered.

"As your doctor, I'm ordering you to not drink," he said, and scribbled a note on a prescription pad. It read:

Cry as much and as often as needed—
Next visit Mon 9/25 10 AM
NO ALCOHOL

Chapter 76

No alcohol—doctor's orders. Who the Hell does he think he is? Why am I going back to this jerk?

Dr. Rosen looked even younger with his face shaved clean. He wore dress pants and a long-sleeved, starched white shirt tucked under his waistband. He had a gold Lord Elgin watch with a black leather watchband on his wrist, and a pair of black horn-rimmed glasses peeked out of his shirt pocket. An untied tie hung over his crispy shirt, and I smelled fresh aftershave.

"Meeting in the Chancellor's office at eleven, Luke. It's going to be about budget cuts, so I must play the part. They'll be looking for heads to chop, and I'm not going to stick my neck out. I want them to think I'm one of them. You know, if it looks like a duck—"

Those were Celia's words!

"You love Celia, Luke. I want you to stop running away and pretending you're not responsible for her suicide."

This guy is FUCKED up. What's he trying to do? Get me to kill myself?

"You're in love with Celia, Luke. You could have prevented her death."

Oh my God!

I ran to the bathroom and heaved my guts up into the toilet. Hunched over the sink, I splashed cold water on my face. I held my hands under the faucet and felt the current between my fingers. I remembered the creek and the snails at Weixerau, when life was beautiful and full of wonders.

How did everything get so ugly? Am I in the Hell Mr. Victor always talked about?

I didn't tell the doctor about my night with Smith & Wesson and Mr. Green Label, and I decided not to mention Saturday night when I'd downed another quart of vodka.

The bottle was full, and the house was empty. All residents had gone away for the weekend. I smoked my Luckies and drank vodka from the jelly glass. I drew an ugly face on a piece of typing paper and taped it to a wall in my room. I picked up a heavy salad knife I'd borrowed from the kitchen and threw it at the face. It bounced off the hard plaster wall, but after a few tries I got the hang of knife-throwing. I made it stick every time—right through the eyeball—into the brain.

I started to stir midday Sunday. I was in bed, nauseous with a nasty migraine headache. The empty vodka bottle was on the floor. A patch of wall plaster was missing, exposing the framing and wooden lath of the hundred-year old structure. The knife and shredded marker sketch lay in the debris. There was a burn hole in the bed sheet, and a charred space on the mattress the size of a large pizza. The room smelled like smoldering cotton and booze.

I'd read about the bums on West Madison Street in the Chicago newspapers. Mattress fires were the norm in flophouses. Firefighters routinely carried burned corpses out of water-soaked rooms. Those people were winos and drug addicts—the human garbage of life. Nothing like me.

"You're in denial, Luke," said Dr. Rosen.

"If you keep hiding from it—from the real reason Celia died—maybe one day you'll be able to gloss over it for good and remove it from the foreground of your memory.

"You'll invent stories. You'll tell yourself you never loved her, and she never loved you. If she had, she wouldn't have hurt you like this.

"You'll paste each new fairy-tale on top of the last one like movie posters on a billboard until the real truth can't show through any more. Over time, you won't even remember exactly what happened.

"But the cover won't last forever. One day the facade will crumble and fall away. You might be an old man when it does, and you may realize then that you've lived your entire life in the shadow of a lie."

This fucker really loves to hear himself talk.

"Soldiers who manage to survive—many come back as war heroes. They're honored in hometown parades as proud defenders of our freedom. They've killed the enemy and protected our families and our way of life. So why aren't they happy? Why do so many veterans turn to alcohol and drugs?"

I'm sure you're going to tell me.

"Vets commit suicide more than any other statistically monitored group. They think the psychological trauma caused by battlefield events produces severe negative and long-lasting consequences. But that's not necessarily what leads to the suicides."

"So, what causes the suicides?" I asked.

"I think it's all about guilt. Guilt they never admitted or confronted. Guilt they never grieved over."

"But what do *they* have to feel guilty about?"

"About coming back alive."

"I don't get it. Why wouldn't they be happy about that?"

"It's about coming home when some of their buddies didn't. So many of those guys saw their best friends blown up right next to them. They think they should have done something to protect their friends. They think if they hadn't been so focused on their own safety, maybe they could have prevented their deaths."

"But that wasn't their fault! Their friends didn't make it, but they did. It's sad, but it wasn't their fault!"

"That's exactly what they keep telling themselves, Luke. And—that's why they never heal. That's why they never get over their pain."

"So, what's the vet supposed to do?"

"First, he has to stop denying what really happened.

He has to stop rationalizing, justifying, telling himself he had no choice. He has to assume responsibility for his friend's death."

"But it really wasn't—"

"That's how the mind works, Luke. He has to stop it from squirming around in denial. Each horrible, painful thought needs to live and be acknowledged. He has to take ownership. Then he has to grieve."

Dr. Rosen looked straight into my eyes.

"I want you to take all of the blame for Celia's death, Luke. I want you to cry every time you think about her, and I don't want you to tell yourself you're worthless—because that would be a lie. I don't want you to tell yourself you should die—because that would be a lie. You need to stop lying to yourself, Luke."

Tears filled my eyes. Suddenly, I didn't hate Dr. Rosen any more.

"I love Celia, Doc."

"I know you do, Luke. I knew it from the first time I talked to you in the Services Building. Now I gotta go. See me next week."

He handed me a note.

I couldn't read it through my tears.

Chapter 77

I needed to see Mr. Victor. I needed answers.
How did he find out about Celia's death?
Did he see her before she died?
Did she ask about me?

It was a three-hour drive to Chicago, and another forty-five minutes to Old Town. Route 45 was a tortuous two-lane road full of stop signs and sharp turns every couple of miles.

I chain-smoked, flying through tiny speed-trap towns dotted along the route. It was two in the afternoon when I pulled up in front of the Laurel Street Studio. The iconic red door was unlocked, which meant Mr. Victor was probably inside.

Nixon sprang at me the second I cracked open the door. He cried and woofed when I knelt down to greet him. He licked my face so hard he bloodied my lip. I didn't mind. I had missed him, too.

Sara heard the commotion and flew down the stairs. She grabbed me and we both broke into tears, hugging and kissing each other. She took my hand and led me upstairs where Mr. Victor was waiting. We hugged and kissed each other tearfully.

Sara went into the kitchen and came out with two mugs of coffee—one with milk—and a platter of some sort of home baked pastry bars.

I sat on the futon next to Mr. Victor. Sara and Nixon plopped down on the floor.

He said he wasn't giving private classes any more; he wanted to spend more time working on his own art. He said he was being recognized in the art field for his collage work. His friend, Richard Gray, had a gallery on Michigan Avenue, and was buying and hoarding his art—gambling on his future potential.

Mr. Victor looked smaller than I remembered. I looked into his sunken eyes. His enthusiasm—the energy he'd always projected filling me, the students, and the space—had been extinguished.

Only a few weeks earlier, the corner of Laurel and Ash had been the sole focus of my existence. It was where I'd learned my skills and dreamed my biggest dreams.

And then there was that day—that one crazy day—when my eyes first locked on to Celia. I knew in that moment that my life, as incredible as it had already been, would never be the same again.

Chapter 78

Mr. Victor stood up. "Come with me, Luke. I want to show you something."

He brought me into his private study and turned on the overhead light. Sara went out on the roof with Nixon.

Leaning against the wall was what looked like a painting mounted on a stretcher frame. He picked it up and handed it to me.

"This is part of what Celia left, Luke."

Hearing her name chilled me.

She never told me she painted. Maybe she started it and never finished—

The painting was nothing unique: just a yellow sky with a few floating clouds.

"Look here, Luke." Mr. Victor pointed to a small round hole in the canvas near the lower right-hand corner. "This is a bullet hole."

I ran my hand through my hair. A queasy sensation

was filling my stomach.

"The hole was made by the same bullet that killed her."

"What? I-I don't understand. She shot the painting and then shot herself?"

I felt faint. My arms and hands were numb.

"No, Luke. She shot herself, and the bullet went through the painting."

"I still don't … w-was it an accident?"

"Luke," said Mr. Victor, resting his hand gently on my arm, "The police think it was not an accident. They think she propped the painting against a box, covered it with a piece of cardboard, sat down, leaned her head against the cardboard, put the gun in her mouth, and pulled the trigger."

What the Hell? She never even told me she painted!

Mr. Victor opened a cardboard storage box and removed a large manila portfolio. Inside was a stack of sketchbooks and folders full of typed papers.

Celia's sketchbooks!

I flipped through what looked like a strange architectural project. Then I read her handwritten letter—

She had dedicated her project to Mr. Victor!

And there wasn't a single mention of me!

I felt sick. And mad. And stupid. I'd been fooled. Like I was by Emma—the girl who'd promised me her everlasting love in May, and sent me a photo of her slutty self sprawled across the hood of some new guy's convertible the following August.

No! THIS is a THOUSAND times worse!

It was worse than walking in on the love of my life

having sex with another man—giving him her body. But Celia hadn't given Mr. Victor her body—

She gave him her LIFE!

Tears gushed down my face, and I had trouble choking my guts down, keeping them from spewing out of my throat.

Celia betrayed me.

No! She fucking tricked me!

How could she have done this? She must have had this all planned out long before our last meeting at Northerly. She already had the gun—she didn't buy it for protection. She probably had the painting, too.

She was lying to me all along!

How could she have faked all those tears?

I would have sent my soul to Hell for her. I would've carved my heart out and put it into her lovely little hands if she'd wanted me to.

I didn't care that she was dead. Or that she begged me not to leave. In fact, I was relieved. I didn't even care if I *had* killed her!

Mr. Victor reached out and put his arm around me. I didn't do it consciously, but my body turned itself, causing his arm to fall away from my shoulder.

"My parents are expecting me for dinner. Say goodbye to Sara and Nixon for me. I have to go."

"I understand, Luke. I will see you soon?"

No, you don't.

And no, you won't!

Chapter 79

Let me out of this fucking place, man!

The stairs went on forever. I ran out of the building and slammed the red door behind me. All I could hear in my head was, *"GET—THE—HELL—OUT!"*

I was glad my parents didn't know I was in town. I had lied to make a quick exit, and made a hasty plan to head straight back to Route 45, and then non-stop to Seven Eighteen Green.

I jumped in my car, turned the key, threw it into first, stomped on the gas, and popped the clutch. The tires screeched, spinning and smoking on the cobblestones.

I pushed in the cigarette lighter and stuck a Lucky in my mouth. When the lighter popped, I touched the bright red spiral to the cigarette and inhaled my first breath of freedom.

The glass packs and dual exhausts belted out a dramatic duet under a viaduct on North Avenue. The roaring staccato amplified as it bounced off the concrete tunnel walls. I threw it into first gear doing forty-five. I let off the gas and the engine over-sped, releasing a series of ear-splitting backfires from the twin chrome tailpipes. Behind me, cars were showered with blue-flame fireworks.

I turned on the radio. Loud. *Bye, Bye, Love*—the Everly Brothers!

Fuck that shit!

I pushed another button. Eddie Cochran was doing *Summertime Blues.*

That's more like it!

I ripped down North and turned south on Cicero Avenue. After a half an hour of tire-squealing starts and stops, I realized there was no need to rush.

By the time I crossed Eighty-Seventh Street in Oak Lawn, I was hungry. I hadn't eaten in days, and I hadn't had meat in more than a month because of my deal with Celia.

Fuck that!

I spotted a Dog n Suds drive-in restaurant on the right. I parked and walked in. The dining room was empty. A young waitress came over, slapped her order pad on my table, and bent down to write.

"What'll ya have?"

She leaned in and balanced her weight on her elbows, her face almost touching mine.

"I'll have a pair of—"

She giggled.

"—cheeseburgers. Make that a double cheeseburger and a large fry. And a medium root beer."

She took forever to write out my order. She cracked her gum with her mouth open. If she'd ever worn lipstick, it was long gone—probably chewed off with her gum. She burst a bubble in my face and giggled. I smelled warm cherries.

She couldn't have been much older than sixteen. She wasn't bad looking with strawberry blonde hair done up neatly in two rubber-banded pigtails. Her hands and fingers were covered with ballpoint pen drawings of hearts and flowers. Her nails were trimmed short, but not ratty like a nail-biter's.

"It comes in a glass mug, is that okay?"

"Sure," I replied.

Her face flushed the longer she wiggled and giggled and wrote. She straightened up and walked back to the kitchen, swiveling her hips just enough to hold my attention.

I lit a Lucky and studied the sign on the wall. It was a work of art, but I couldn't call it art because it wasn't art. Art was what they taught at U of I. The Dog n Suds sign was designed in the cartoon style of Walt Disney's Comics. The Dog n Suds dog was a white Pluto with a white chef's hat and a black bowtie.

My gum-cracking waitress would never understand anything about design. Her world was light years behind what I'd been taught. Oak Lawn was suburbia. Those people had no idea what art was all about. They were like the Amazonian primitives who didn't recognize their own relatives in photographs. Their puny primal minds were so object-oriented, they saw nothing but pieces of paper with unrelated grey and white patterns.

She came back with my order and said, "What else would you like?" She moved in even closer than before. Her lips were inches away from mine. "Are you from around here?"

"I live in Marquette Park."

"Oh! My best friend goes to Maria. She's a sophomore."

I knew all about Maria High School. I had lived only two blocks away and all my girlfriends had gone there.

"That's cool," I said.

There weren't any other customers, so she hung around while I ate.

"I'm off in an hour, but my boss isn't here and my friend can cover for me, so I can leave now. You wanna see a movie or somethin'? Dutch treat!"

Maybe I shouldn't—

"Okay."

Chapter 80

"What's your name?" she asked.

"Luke."

"Mine's Kathy. With a K. My mother's Polish."

"Is that short for something?"

"Yeah. Short for brains. Or like my dad says, 'A dollar short and a day late.' Or like my friends call me—'shit for brains'."

"Ha, ha. That's really funny, Kathy with a K."

This silly girl will never see college. She'll do well to graduate from Oak Lawn High School.

I opened the passenger door and she slid in. After I started the engine, I stabbed the gas pedal a few times to let her feel the rhythmic rumble of the dual exhausts.

"Where do you wanna go?" she asked, rummaging through her cluttered purse.

I depressed the car lighter, whipped out a Lucky, and was about to offer her one when I saw a Newport in her hand.

Damn! What's with the fucking Newports?

She covered my hand with hers and guided the lighter to her cigarette. She squinted when smoke trailed past her eyes. After a long, drawn out pause— she released my hand. I pushed the lighter back into the dashboard receptacle to reheat it.

"Those things'll kill you," I said, lighting up.

"Yep. So will living in Oak Lawn."

Hmm. Maybe she's not as dippy as I thought.

There were three popular indoor movie theaters near Marquette Park—the Highway, the Marquette, and the Colony. The Colony was the biggest and the nicest. It was where I'd seen *Rebel Without a Cause* with Emma.

"How about the Colony?" I asked.

"The one on Kedzie?"

"Yeah. Fifty-Ninth and Kedzie."

"Oh, that's fine with me, but you have to promise to get me back by six. Six-thirty at the latest. Okay, Luke?"

"I'll get you home in plenty of time. I promise."

"If you promise. You can take me back to the Dog. I always walk home from there."

"That's cool."

I laid a long, squealing, smoking black arc onto Cicero Avenue as I cut out of the Dog's driveway. Kathy wasn't impressed. She probably had an older brother with a tricked out street rod that would blow the doors off my stock Ford. I felt my ears get hot.

We rolled into the Colony Theater's parking lot on Fifty-Ninth Street.

"I got somethin' for ya."

She pulled a glass mug out of her bag.

"Collector's Edition Dog n Suds. They don't sell these any more. I kept this one cooling off behind some boxes in the storage room for four months. My boss doesn't know."

It was actually quite beautiful. The Dog n Suds logo was silk-screened on the glass in white, yellow, black, and red.

"Thanks, Kathy. Now I'll think about *you* every time I drink beer."

I reached in front of her and opened the glove compartment to see if there was room for the mug. She leaned forward and pushed her compact breasts firmly into my outstretched arm. I laid the mug inside the glove box and closed the door.

She looped her arm through mine and we walked to the ticket window. I tried to pay for her movie ticket, but she insisted on buying it herself.

The lobby was empty. The girl behind the concession counter didn't even bother to look up when we passed her on our way to the second set of double swinging doors. *Misfits*, with Marilyn Monroe and Clark Gable, was already playing.

Kathy held my hand as we felt our way in the dark to the last row on the main floor. The wall with the projectionist's windows was directly behind us. The back row was vacant except for one man sitting on the opposite end, but he left as soon as we sat down.

"I'm going to the bathroom. Can I get you somethin',

Luke?"
"No, thanks."
"I'll be right back."

Chapter 81

"I took off those stupid knee socks. They were really bugging me."

Kathy was wearing a black, red, and yellow plaid wool skirt, and a short-sleeved white blouse with a rounded collar. Black leather schoolgirl shoes with straps and buckles fastened over her bare feet. If it weren't for the official Dog n Suds logo colors on her skirt, her outfit could have passed for the Maria High School uniform.

She returned with a large Coca-Cola, a medium plain popcorn, and a box of Raisinets.

"Have some."

"No, thanks. I'm really full."

"I love the salty taste of the popcorn. Just when it almost starts to burn my mouth, I pop in a Raisinet. The chocolate gets warm and melts, and the raisin is chewy. Mmm—love it! C'mon, Luke. Try it!"

I hesitated.

She put three or four kernels in her hand and faced me. She gently pulled on my chin and popped the popcorn into my open mouth.

"Now let it stay on your tongue 'til you feel the burn."

She grabbed a Raisinet.

"Ready?"

I opened my mouth and she tossed it in.

"Now chew. Slowly. Let the taste soak in. Think about all the flavors mixing together. Do you like it?"

"Mmm. Yeah—it's pretty good."

Kathy steadied the popcorn box on my lap while I held the Raisinets. Every time she reached in for a handful, she pushed the box into my lap.

I put my arm around her shoulder and she leaned in closer. She spent more time digging around the bottom of the box as it emptied, which added to the growing pressure in my groin. I stopped paying attention to Marilyn and Clark.

I felt myself push up hard, and Kathy let the box fall to the floor. She placed her hand on the back of my head and moved her face in front of mine. Her eyes were huge in the dim light. Her cheeks were hot, and I got a whiff of her deodorant when she raised her arm.

She pulled my face into hers, pushing her mouth against mine. Her lips parted and I tasted popcorn, chocolate, and salt. She balanced her weight with her hand planted on my upper thigh, and with her fingers, she kneaded my groin. Her tongue slipped deep inside my mouth.

I wasn't at the movies any more.

We were still lip-locked. She undid my belt buckle and pulled down my zipper. She opened my pants and lowered her head down onto my lap. She gave me a quick glance, then buried her face in my groin. I felt the wet heat of her mouth and I grabbed her hand.

After what felt like seconds, my legs went rigid, and my feet kicked the empty seat in front of us. I squeezed her hand and moaned.

When we were face to face again, she gave me a sweet and salty kiss.

"What time is it?" she asked.

I looked at my watch. "Almost six."

"Ohh! Crap! We gotta go! I hope my brother isn't out looking for me already."

"Don't worry. It's only a ten minute drive."

Neither of us saw *Misfits*, or the coming attractions, or the cartoon, or the *Let's All Go to the Lobby* animated marching popcorns, candies, and soft drinks.

We got up to leave—my knees felt wobbly. There was a crisp chill in the early evening air which made our breath visible while we walked.

I unlocked the Ford and Kathy jumped in. The green and white Naugahyde bench seat was cold; she tugged her skirt down to cover her bare legs.

The pipes purred softly when I started the powerful V-8 engine. I moved the heater control lever all the way to High. She opened her bag and took out a Newport. I pushed in the lighter and took out a Lucky. We opened our corner vent windows.

This time Kathy held the lighter, and I guided her

hand to light my Lucky. She lit her Newport and pulled out the ashtray. My mind flashed to Celia. Her ashes were still in my Van Gogh room. The thought sickened me.

Oh, fuck that.
No way!
I'm not wasting my life feeling sad about her any more! Not after what she did to me.
I hate her! I hate Celia!

"Hey, do you remember what the movie was about?" Kathy asked sweetly.

"It was about Heaven."

I looked at Kathy. She was smiling. She had no idea that in less than four hours I'd gone from Hell to Heaven.

I couldn't believe my luck with Kathy. It wasn't even a real date. It had taken me a solid year of dating to get to third base with Emma, and it hadn't been half as good.

I had never been to *that* Heaven before. Lithuanian girls never did anything like *that*. I never dreamed a sweet young sophomore from Oak Lawn High would take me there. I was still grinning when I pulled into the Dog n Suds parking lot.

Kathy made a fast dash out of the car, ran toward the restaurant, and yelled, "Bye, Luke!"

She disappeared as I was calling out, "Thanks, Kathy—"

She hadn't asked for my phone number, or if I'd ever show up again, so I didn't have to explain. I knew I wouldn't be back, but I'd never forget Kathy with a K.

Chapter 82

Dr. Rosen was not impressed by my excited narrative. The only part he approved was my decision to resume my studies. I'd talked to Dean Fitzsimmons, and he agreed to send a note to my instructors explaining that I'd had a family crisis and that I'd only missed two weeks out of the sixteen week semester.

"Luke. You've undermined your healing process. You made up a story. Do you remember what we discussed? I was afraid this might happen."

"But Bob, you said I'd invent stories to convince myself I didn't love Celia and that she didn't love me. I admitted I loved Celia, and even though she never said so, I could tell she probably loved me—in her way.

"But this is different. She worked on that suicide project long before she met me. I couldn't have stopped her because it was never about me. I saw the proof with my own eyes. Mr. Victor has it all—the letter, the painting, the descriptions, and the presentation drawings."

"You got hurt, Luke, and you figured Celia rejected you. You feel like she dumped you when she killed herself. Like she betrayed you and made a fool out of you. You started feeling sorry for yourself. You got pissed off. You covered your guilt with your anger."

"Yeah?"

"You said she freed you from your guilt. Even your appetite came back. For food and sex. You felt like a new person. You were looking forward to life again. You said Celia had put you in Hell, and Kathy had taken you to Heaven. Those were your words."

"Well … yeah. Except I have to disagree about one thing."

"What's that?"

"I don't think I covered up my guilt. I think the guilt was washed away by her lying and cheating and scheming. All my feelings of remorse are gone, Bob."

"Do you still get mad when you think about her?"

"Well … maybe … a little—but I'm thinking about her less and less. And when I get busy with stuff, I don't think about her at all. And I don't even feel weird going to the bathroom any more."

"Let me explain this another way. You understand that our entire universe is hanging together by various forces. Gravity, magnetic attraction, repulsion, and all kinds of other energies and powers. But the point I want to make, Luke, is that everything needs to be in balance.

"The physical world always wants to be in balance— like the oceans seeking their own level. When something gets out of whack, things get pushed around to restore the balance.

"Our thoughts need to stay in balance, too. We have to live according to our principles and trust that the universe supports us. We feel a need for fairness, and that means—balance.

"We need to love and to be loved. When we love and are loved back, we feel good. Our emotions are balanced. You've heard of people saying love is a two-way street. It's all about balance.

"You put your love in Celia, and you paid a big emotional price."

"Well … yeah."

"But she died. Your investment was lost. You can't get it back. You felt guilty first, then angry—at her, at yourself, at the world.

"Let's simplify. She's gone, and you're not. Here's the plain and simple truth: the best, and maybe the only way to balance the scales inside you, is to grieve."

"But—"

"Grieving means you're going to miss Celia. Probably forever. But the more you grieve, the sooner your brain will restore itself to balance. The grief you place on your end of the scale will start to match the pain you feel over your loss—Celia's end of the scale. Over time, your feeling of grief and your sense of loss will diminish. That's when you'll begin to accept that she's gone—and you're here—and that's okay."

"But I don't feel guilty any more. How can I grieve if I don't feel sad?"

"Your brain tricked you, Luke. It wanted so badly to make itself feel better, it jumped at the first opportunity that came along and made up a story. And it was a good one. In fact, it was perfect—the kind your brain needs when it hurts so badly. The painting, the project, Mr. Victor's involvement—everything supported your new story."

Dr. Rosen moved from his sofa to mine and sat down facing me. He stared intensely into my eyes.

"You've got to understand this, Luke. Your brain created a short circuit. It didn't want to grieve, so it cut around the problem area and ignored it."

"But, what does that mean, Bob? What do I do now?"

"You'll have to peel back the story. You'll have to get back to a place that lets you grieve again."

"I think I believe you, but I'm not too sure I can do it. I still get pissed off every time I think of her."

"Your brain kind of fucked you over, Luke. If you stop feeding your fear, your anger will start to go away. Anger is a temporary emotion. It's only there to protect you—like a shield. When you realize you're not in danger, the anger will disappear."

"But I don't feel like I'm in danger. I've never felt any danger. Only anger."

"The danger is that you may start to feel guilty. Your brain doesn't want to feel guilt because it's a painful, lousy feeling. That's the fear."

"So what happens then? What happens after the fear is gone?"

"Then the love you've been hiding from yourself will

come out. You'll start to feel the pain of loss again. And then you'll grieve—and then you'll cry—and then you'll heal."

"But what about the love—"

"The love you have for Celia, the love that was always there, will reveal itself again."

Dr. Rosen walked over to his table and wrote on a prescription pad:

Don't hide your love, Luke.
It's okay to love. Love won't hurt you.
Only fear can do that—
And if you still need me,
You know where to find me—
Bob

Chapter 83

Things started to move fast after I returned to school.

The Industrial Design curriculum required a lot of time and hard work. For each credit hour of art and design, three hours had to be spent in the workrooms each week. Many projects meant many evenings and weekends in the Art and Design Building.

I also worked for Leonard in his pawn shop. I became his official watchmaker after he'd mentioned his technician had left six months prior. At first, he didn't believe I had experience in the field, but after he'd given me a test watch to repair, he hired me on the spot.

Later, Leonard gave me a key to the shop and allowed me to make my own hours. He paid fairly, and I returned good work.

I resumed visiting Mr. Victor after I realized he had nothing to do with Celia's death. Apparently, he was as blind-sided by her suicide as I was.

I was surprised to run into Dalia while I was rushing to one of my classes. She was a student.

It took no time at all to rekindle our former flame. With Dalia, it was as easy as picking up an old dog-eared pulp romance and starting up again on the last page read. But between schoolwork and my job at Leonard's, I had little time to spend with her.

By the time the mid-term exams came around, Dalia had dropped out of school. She admitted she had no use for a degree anyway. She had only enrolled because her girlfriends talked her into it. She moved back to Chicago and got married a year later.

I wasn't able to do what Dr. Rosen advised. For a while, I felt angry every time I thought about Celia. After a few months, I didn't get mad, but I wasn't grieving either. I didn't feel guilty any more, and I was pretty sure I had nothing left in the way of feelings.

The only thing left to remind me of her at all was a fleeting flash when I went to the bathroom. And even that didn't bug me much. I wondered why it ever did.

I don't know if my brain took over to protect me, or if I was just too busy living my life, but I didn't have time to dredge up feelings that didn't seem to exist.

I kept Dr. Rosen's last prescription. It was the perfect bookmark for a novel my mother had given me many years before: *The Romance of Leonardo da Vinci* by Dmitri Merejkowski.

Chapter 84

The next eighteen years were a blur.

Thanks to Mr. Victor's recommendation, I was offered a position teaching Industrial Design at the new University of Illinois campus in downtown Chicago. Five years later, I left to manage the Research and Development Department in a big toy company.

On weekends, I took flying lessons, earned a Private Pilot rating, and bought a Cessna 172—a single engine, four-seat airplane.

Eventually, I left the corporate scene to found my own design business, and bought a house on Woodbine Avenue in Oak Park. It was located in the middle of Frank Lloyd Wright's old stomping ground less than a half block north of his famous home and studio.

Across the alley behind my house was the boyhood home of Papa Hemingway. A short summer's stroll away was a little park where the Oak Park Shakespeare Players put on skits and bits from the Old Bard. The actors wore tee shirts, shorts, halter-tops, and jeans. Many were barefoot. They sang and danced and sipped their wine and ours, transferring us from our world into theirs. It was a good time and a good place.

Dalia resurfaced after her divorce. She didn't have children and visited me with her little dog named Beefy. We found we still had feelings for each other. I asked her to spend the night, and she never left.

Two years later, I asked my mother if she thought I should marry Dalia. I was catching considerable flak from some married friends.

"Nu, why?"

"Well, she keeps talking about wanting kids."

"Nu, why?"

"You don't think—"

"I don't think. You should think. Why do you need to get married and raise children? Da Vinci never had children. Van Gogh, Degas, Munch, and Toulouse-Lautrec did not have children. Beethoven, Brahms, and Chopin did not have children. Why do you want?"

"It's funny that you compare me to all those famous people, Mamyte."

"Nu, and why not?"

That winter, I found a message from Sara on my answering machine. Mr. Victor had died.

I returned her call, and she filled me in on the details. There was no memorial service, no wake, and no funeral. No surprise to me. Mr. Victor and I had discussed his final wishes in one of our many talks. He had decided to donate his body to science to save disposal costs and be of some use to medical research.

During my last visit, Mr. Victor told me that cancer had taken over his lungs. He only had weeks to live. He actually joked about it, saying cancer was how many people chose to stop smoking—himself included.

He wouldn't consider surgery, saying something like, "It would be irresponsible to spend resources on a condition I caused myself. We must let the universe do what it needs to do to maintain equilibrium. The HOLE that was created when I was born will be filled when I die. Balance will be restored. The laws of nature will be upheld. All will be right again."

He insisted I visit Sara after he was gone. "There is something that I will leave for you, Luke. It is very important that you have it. Sara will give it to you when you come."

I drove to the studio hoping Sara would be there. I wanted to say I was sorry that Mr. Victor was gone, and to say goodbye, knowing I wouldn't be coming around much any more.

She opened the door wearing a black sweatshirt and black sweatpants. Her dark hair was long and shiny. She said, "Yes, yes. C'mon in, Luke. I'll leave you two alone."

She had always said that when I visited Mr. Victor. It was sweet but sad to hear it again.

I followed her up the stairway, then went into his private study. It was where he'd shown me Celia's project eighteen years prior.

I settled into Mr. Victor's leather lounger, an Eames chair he'd bought in the late fifties. It was still intact and as comfortable as ever. I rested my legs on the ottoman.

I turned off the light and let the peace of the moment envelop me. My mind felt open, washed clean of past horrors. I felt like the universe could flow through me free and easy without my resistance.

I fell asleep.

The apartment was dark when I came out of his study. I flicked on the light in the dining room, and a fly landed on the half-dome glass lamp hanging over the table. It was unusual—it was the dead of winter.

The warm light illuminated the milky white glass. The fly was in silhouette against the glowing bright background. It walked around to my side of the lamp and stopped. I sat down, and we both stared at each other for a long time. When it finally flew away, I knew it was time for me to go.

I called out to Sara to let her know I was leaving. She came out from the back and pointed to a large black zippered art portfolio leaning against the wall near the front door.

"He left this for you."

I didn't have to look—I knew what was in it.

Why is THIS so important? Why did he want to make sure I had it now—after his death?

I picked up the portfolio and carried it down the long flight of stairs. Sara followed.

We said goodbye and hugged.

Our hugs had always been very tight and lingering,

with neither of us wanting to let go. Our hands had massaged each other's backs, and sometimes she'd say, "Ooh, itch that spot." Her skin always felt warm. She never wore a bra. Her back was smooth and free of straps.

And then there were our kisses—closed mouth. Mostly. Occasionally, her lips parted and I felt the tip of her tongue push against mine. Sometimes her shirt would open, and I wondered if it had been accidental—or maybe it had been a gift—something for me to think about. Or not.

Our final goodbye was different. There was no lingering or clinging. Our kiss was hurried. When I opened the door, the cold air quickly filled the space between us.

I shut the door behind me. The dry hinges squealed as they had a thousand times before—but the sound was deep and hollow, unlike the happy, high-pitched squeaks that used to greet my arrivals.

It had snowed the night before. There was a clean white blanket covering the concrete driveway. The tracks I had made coming in led back to the car. I followed them carefully trying to fit my feet into each step without enlarging the footprints. I used to do that when I was a kid, and knew I had to walk a little pigeon toed to get it right.

Chapter 85

I didn't open the portfolio after I got home. I wrapped it in thick plastic and double-taped the seams with duct tape. Then I put the whole mummified package up in the attic.

I knew it didn't possess mystical powers, and it probably wasn't cursed by some kind of evil spirit on a quest to destroy me.

I just didn't want to look inside.

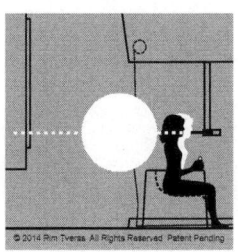

HOLE: Part Three

Chapter 86
Palos Hills, Illinois 2013

I've lived in this house for the last twenty-seven years since I moved from Oak Park, and I know exactly what I have to do.

I've gone over this a million times in my mind. I'm waiting. But not like I did when I was a kid, when I was waiting for Friday night to go out on a date with a girl. Or waiting for summer vacation to start, or for my high school graduation, or my twenty-first birthday. Those were fun things—happy things.

I'm waiting for symptoms. For the first signs that my mind is starting to slip—like my mother's.

I remember the morning she came into my bedroom frantic with terror in her eyes.

"Lukai! Lukai! Nina is burning the house! She wants to kill me! Look!"

I walked her over to her bathroom, but she stopped me. "Lukai! It is not in here! It is in there! Hurry!"

She grabbed my forearm and guided me toward her bedroom. I checked around and found nothing—no fire, no smoke. She pointed to the dresser and insisted it was burning, and for me to do something.

I opened the drawers to let her see for herself, but she was convinced there was fire, and she was angry that I didn't see it. It was unnerving and sad, and there had been no way for me to calm her.

At first, I thought she was confused by her new surroundings and having trouble waking from nightmares. She had only lived with us for a few months since my dad died. But after a short hospital stay, she was diagnosed: sudden onset dementia.

I cared for my mother meticulously. Every morning, I prepared her bathroom by spraying the tiled walls and shower seat with hot water so she wouldn't be chilled. I carried her from her soiled bed to the shower seat, guiding her hand to the grab bar so she wouldn't fall. She held on tight and thanked me for keeping her clean.

Nina, my girlfriend, changed my mother's clothes and bed linens, and fed her baby food when she could no longer chew regular food.

My mother reached a point where all she could do was smile weakly when I entered the room. It tore my heart apart to have to leave her sitting rigid on the sofa, her fingers clenched on her knees, staring blankly at the door—waiting for my return.

Taking care of her was challenging, but I didn't find it difficult. She had always loved and protected me fiercely. I grew up with confidence and had been given every opportunity to live a good life. She sacrificed for me as long as she was able. I was honored to pay it forward.

It was devastating to watch her decline in such a heartless way—to see her fade from what she once was, little by little, day by day. In the end, I realized I was only able to return a tiny portion of the love and support she had always given me. But she died in my home warm, clean, and loved.

After the receiving doctor at Palos Community Hospital examined her body, he commented on her extraordinary physical condition. Her skin was clear, fresh, and completely free of bedsores, something he had rarely witnessed in his experience.

That's not my plan—but I'm not quite ready. I'm still waiting. My mother had no idea she was losing her mind. She couldn't see or feel it happening. Mental decline doesn't exactly announce itself to its victims.

Maybe I'm pushing my luck. Maybe I'm waiting too long. What if I am incapacitated and fall victim to some unexpected illness or accident? My plan, my decisions—my life—won't be in my hands.

On the other hand, I might be jumping the gun. My mind doesn't have to falter. The stroke left no impairment. I still exercise every few days and my body is healthy.

And I do have longevity on my side. My mother was eighty-seven when she died. My dad lived to be eighty-nine, and his mind was sharp to the end when cancer took him out.

Hell, I might have ten or twelve good years left.

Chapter 87

I had kept the portfolio wrapped and stashed away for thirty-four years. I made sure the whole thing was out of my life, and for the most part, out of my mind. But from time to time, troubling thoughts had penetrated my defenses. I always thought that one day I would drag it down from the attic and open it. I guess I was waiting for something—maybe some sort of sign.

"Aren't these just adorable, Luke?"

Nina is holding up a pair of antique bone white Dr. Scholl's exercise sandals she found while rummaging through a pile of old stuff in a local resale shop. She liked searching for vintage fabrics, and I had decided to go along for the ride.

Oh, God—

I feel like I've been smacked in the face with a two-by-four.

"Oh, they're so cute." Nina hands them to me and I feel a chill. I start to shake. Celia had lost one of the screws on her left sandal. I remember I was going to offer to replace it. I never did—

All six screws are there. All present and accounted for. These are not Celia's sandals.

"They're size five, a little too tight for me."

About four sizes too tight, Nina!

"They make new ones just like these. Do you think they'd look good on me?"

"Nah. Girls used to wear them back in the sixties, but I always thought they made their feet look ugly."

I'm lying through my teeth, but I couldn't stand to see Nina in those shoes. Or anyone—

"Really?"

"Yep."

"Luke, are you all right?" I think she noticed my eyes glaze over. She is saying something else, but my ears are ringing so loudly, I can't hear her. I turn away and walk toward the door.

"It's the mothballs in here—I think I'm allergic to them. Go ahead and browse around. Take your time, Nina. I'm fine. I'll be outside."

I unlock the car and get in. The wave of emotion that besieged me in the store is at the head of a rushing torrent from a ruptured dam. It's knocking me off my feet, washing me away, carrying me back through time.

Celia. Laurel Street. Navy Pier. Mr. Victor. Sara. Celia. Celia. Celia.

"Celia! Celiaaa!" I shout out loud. I try to control

myself but can't stop the tears. I'm sobbing. After a few minutes, I stop and open the door. The spring breeze cools and dries my face.

I know what I have to do when I get home.

Celia's painting is just as I remember it. I study the pages and illustration boards describing her HOLE project. I read all of her notes. They are fascinating. And there are sketchbooks—many I have never seen.

All those times I was staring at her cute feet, hiding my eyes under my artist-philosopher helmet's visor for fear she'd catch me—she had been perfecting the details of her plan.

Chapter 88

The paint is ultra-flat black and absorbs light like a sponge—sort of like black velvet. I used it to paint the ceiling, walls, outlet covers, and the exposed conduit. I covered the floor with wall-to-wall carpet of an unknown material similar to black velvet. There is a black futon covered with a black velvet throw in one corner of the room. In the middle sits a chair painted with the same ultra-flat black paint.

I call this room my *Other Room* because anything illuminated inside it looks like it's floating in black space—like *other space*. Objects lose all reference to anything earthly because nothing else is visible, and there is no light reflected from the walls or floor.

I hang the painting with bullet hole in line with my eye level. On the opposite wall, I mount an adjustable spotlight. A dimmer switch with a hand-held remote controls the intensity of the light.

The effect is profound. With the beam of the spotlight centered on the canvas, the painting seems to glow and float in space. With the remote, I can make the painting dissolve into *other space* or emerge out of the blackness.

I sit on the chair and study the painting. I fade it in and out like the effects in Star Trek or The Twilight Zone. It's been over fifty years since I last saw Celia. I wonder what she'd think if she saw me here now.

I stare at the bullet hole—a black dot on a yellow sky. A hole made by a copper-jacketed, lead-filled projectile traveling at over a thousand feet per second. It shot through Celia's soft palate, her brain, and her skull—taking with it blood, brain cells, nerve tissue, cranial fluid, bone, and wisps of her pretty hair.

Cardboard had shielded the canvas from most of the body fragments, but there still must be a lot of embedded DNA remaining.

Some day, from Celia's particulates, she could be cloned. She'd have to begin as an embryo … but no matter how exacting the process, she would never be the same. The new Celia would lack the influence of the twisted turns that occurred in her life while she matured from one cell to full adulthood.

I wonder what she would have been like if Marcelline hadn't mistreated her. Would Celia have been as talented and beautiful as she was? Or would she have been ordinary like Doris Day? Or Dalia?

Why am I so attracted to broken things? My friends preferred brand new, shiny, quality-controlled, triple-inspected, certified, money-back, unconditionally guaranteed everything.

It seems I've always been drawn to things I could put myself into—things I could either make—or make better. I've spent my whole life building, drawing, painting, carving, collecting, fixing, and restoring.

I wish I could have fixed Celia. All that crazy stuff she'd told me about herself—the boys she wanted to love, but as soon as she liked them—she hated them. It scared the Hell out of me.

I know now that she had been more confused and afraid than I was. She was in a horrible place. Her dad left by dying and her mother had never really been there. Richard and all of the other boys were gone—and I left her, too.

Celia was trapped inside her own wrecked, tortured brain. All alone. There was no fix, so she left herself.

Chapter 89

My head casts a dark, almost black, silhouette on the yellow sky as I approach the canvas. The shape gets smaller, more life-sized as I get closer. My forehead touches the painting. My right eye peers into the bullet hole. I'm holding the dimming remote in my hand and turn off the spotlight completely.

I'm entering the hole ... leaving Earth ... going to nothingness.

"If I knew you were coming I'd have baked a cake—"
What the—
It was Marcelline's favorite song. Celia used to sing it, imitating her ridiculous mother. I'd never heard another person parody that tune. It became Celia's silly signature song.

"... baked a cake—"
Am I really hearing this?
"Luke."

What the Hell?
"Luke."
Oh, my God! She's calling me. What the Hell is going on?
"Luke, come here!"
IT IS CELIA!
I never forgot her voice—
I'd know it anywhere!
"Of course it's me, Luke. Come over here. Come closer."
No! You come over here. By me—
"I don't know how."
Did she hear me?
Can she hear my thoughts?
And respond?

I know this isn't really happening. This is a tape replaying inside my head. I remember the episode. It was our favorite place—Northerly Island. I wanted to go down by the water, and Celia had asked how. I said, "Walk." She replied by teasing, "I don't know how." I demonstrated a goofy walk and said, "Like this."

"I still don't know how. Explain how you did that."
"First, raise one leg—"
"How?"
"Lift."
"How?" She was fighting to hold back her giggles.
"Use your leg muscles."
"What leg muscles? I don't know how. Show me."

We were chuckling like idiots when I picked up her leg, lifted it a few inches, released it, and let it drop back to its original standing position. We laughed hysterically until we were in tears.

I think of my mother—I remember the panicked look on her face when she came into my room that morning.

Is this it?
Is this the beginning of it all?
Am I losing my mind like she did?
Should I start to execute my plan?

I leave the room and lock the heavy steel door using the key I wear on a beaded neck chain tucked under my shirt. I walk outside and down the driveway to my shop in the backyard.

Things look normal.

A squirrel runs up one of the huge oaks and makes an acrobatic leap to another branch high up in the trees. I approach the barn. Dakota whinnies to greet me. I open the side door and say hello. Barney, the cat, rubs up against my pants leg. I shut the barn door and test it to make sure it's closed tight.

I enter my shop a few steps away. The job I've been working on is still here laying out on the workbenches the way I left it two days ago.

I pull the chain from under my shirt and use the small key next to the Other Room key to unlock a drawer in my toolbox. I check the contents. Everything's here—all present and accounted for.

I lock the drawer and tuck the chain back inside my shirt. I reach into my pants pocket and take out my cell phone.

"Nina, do I sound okay to you?"

"Uhh ... well you would if you hadn't asked that! What's wrong? Are you having a stroke?"

"Nahh. I feel fine."

"You've been in that dungeon too long. You need to get out more. Remember, you're allergic to mold. Maybe there's mold down there again. It rained all last week. Did you see any water coming in? Have you been taking your B-12?"

"No mold. Yeah, I'm taking my vitamins and my meds. Maybe I need some fresh air."

Ever since my cardiologist told me my B-12 levels were low, I've been getting injections and taking supplements. He said it's a common problem with Eastern Europeans: we don't metabolize B-12 very well. My levels were practically nonexistent before my stroke. Now they're closely monitored.

One of the side effects of low B-12 is altered thinking and behavior.

Maybe I'll call the doctor.

Chapter 90

I need to talk to Celia.

The sweat on my forehead is cold. I touch two fingers to my wrist. My pulse is rapid, but I don't have chest pain. Maybe I should check my blood pressure.

A catastrophic event wouldn't be so bad, would it?

I'll lose consciousness and then—done.

Nothing more to worry about.

Nina will cash in the life insurance policy, pay off the bank note—

I take out my secret key and unlock the Other Room. I'm in. I pick up the remote and turn on the spotlight. I close the heavy door behind me and take a look around.

The room is in the basement of my split-level ranch. The former owner's sister-in-law had died in a tornado in southern Illinois. Rosanne said she'd remain in Illinois under one condition—that a storm-proof space was available in case of a weather emergency.

Rosanne's husband, Casey, loved their home—and his wife—so he'd built a special room for Rosanne. One that could survive any tornado. The walls are solid six inch concrete. The ceiling is corrugated steel with another six inches of concrete on top. The door is thick steel plate and must weigh a thousand pounds. Rosanne had monitored the construction process until she was satisfied that the room was safe.

Can a ghost, assuming there is such a thing, penetrate these massive walls? I know my cell phone doesn't work. Neither does Wi-Fi.

I look at the painting suspended in black space. Maybe Celia is a hallucination. Dr. Rosen said our brain is capable of playing tricks on us. That it can act like it has a life of its own. It takes care of itself selfishly and doesn't like to be in pain. It looks for creative ways to relieve pain.

Okay then, brain.
Go for it!
I'm in pain. You're in pain.
We need to talk to Celia.
We need to know if she exists and we need to know now.
We can't stand the pain much longer.

I sit on the centered chair. Waiting. My nerves are grating on themselves. My heart is quivering. I hear myself breathing.

What the Hell are you so afraid of?
Celia was a sweet girl. She won't hurt you.
You're acting like some kind of monster from Hell is going to leap out and devour you.
Get closer to the painting—like you were before.

Go find her, you chickenshit!

My legs are wobbly as I stand, but not the good kind of wobbly like when I was with Kathy at the Colony Theater. I don't feel so cool and cocky right now.

"Hello, Chickenshit!"

Celia?

"Who else? The Easter Bunny?"

Celia had never called me a chickenshit before, but I just did. A minute ago. Those were my words, not Celia's. This must be my brain again, like Dr. Rosen had said. It's inventing a story for me to stop my own pain. Celia doesn't exist. My brain is fucking with me. Again.

No, no, no! Maybe it's not my brain! Maybe it is Celia! She said Easter Bunny!

Celia dreaded Easter. She had no family to celebrate with. She'd never gone on an Easter egg hunt with her schoolmates because her mother wouldn't allow it. Marcelline would hide a few uncolored eggs inside the house for only Celia to find. That was Celia's Easter.

I'm afraid to think it ... but ... is it you, Celia? Are you really here?

"It's really me, Luke."

I don't understand—

"You don't have to. It's me, Luke."

I can't believe this. I thought—

"You thought I was dead."

I feel lighter. I think I feel Celia's hands holding my hot face, calming me with her soft, soothing hands—the most beautiful hands I'd ever known.

"Breathe, Luke."

I inhale deeply and smell lilies of the valley—Celia's scent.

Dear God—if you exist, please let this be her.
Please let it be Celia.

Chapter 91

I need answers. Again.

I remember feeling this way before, when I drove to Mr. Victor's studio years ago. I'd gotten what I needed, but it wasn't what I wanted and it really messed me up.

Is that going to happen again? Do I really want to know more than I know now?

Whenever thoughts of Celia's death came into my mind, I'd made it my life's work to avoid the subject—to block it all out of my head. But, could I have stopped Celia that day? Have I lived my life in denial? Like Dr. Rosen said I would? Was her inevitable suicide a convenient story my brain made up to protect itself from the horrendous truth? So I wouldn't be ridden with guilt?

I'd never accepted any responsibility for her death, especially after my visit with Mr. Victor. Dr. Rosen had warned me—he said I had to grieve so I could let go and move on. But how could I? Why would I have grieved?

Celia made her decision. She carried out her wish. It was as plain as day that I wasn't part of her sinister plan. She had masterminded the entire event in great detail—complete with illustrations—to accomplish her goal of self-destruction.

And then—she'd called it art.

Why is my mind going there now? I feel like a kid who knows the iron is hot, but just has to touch it anyway. Or like a moth tragically attracted to a flame—drawn to its own destruction.

Am I drawn to my own destruction?

The truth is—Celia caused her own death.

She killed herself! I had no part in it. She didn't do it for me. Or because of me.

So ... why am I afraid to ask her about it?

"Because you're a stupid moron, Luke."

Oh my God. I wasn't talking to her now. I was just thinking ... but she spoke. I heard it. Didn't I? That's what she called me at Northerly Island a lifetime ago.

Is this my mind ... talking to me ... myself?

What should I do? Talk back?

Okay, what the Hell? Why not?

No one knows. No one can hear me.

"Celia ... if that's really you ... did I ... was I ... responsible for your death?"

There! I said it. If it's really Celia, she won't lie to me. She'll say it was all her own doing.

"Like I said, Luke, you're a stupid moron. If I say no, your brain will tell you it's protecting itself. If I say yes, you'll think your brain is fucking itself over. I don't know how to get through to you, sweetheart."

Celia had never called me "sweetheart" before. And just now she said "fucking". I don't remember her ever using that word either. This isn't Celia. This is my own fucked up mind.

"Celia, I love you, but you just used the f-word—"

"I love you, too, Luke. I always did. But a girl's gotta change with the times. Besides, can you think of a better word to describe what a brain does to itself?"

I hear a soft giggle.

She loves me ... I heard her say it ...

Or is it me thinking it? Wishing it? Hearing the voice I remember?

Why do I feel so happy?

I don't know what's happening to me.

Is this Celia or is this my mind melting away into the black other space?

Alright. Look. My brain has always been pretty smart. Given a choice, it always chose the better alternative. When my mother told me about Jesus, my brain accepted it and made Him real. I prayed to Him every night, and I even thought I saw Him sitting on the edge of my bed.

Let's say Jesus isn't real—He was just a story my mother passed on to me to help me feel safe in our struggle to survive the war.

My young growing brain had two choices.

Either:

Jesus is real, and I have a soul that will live forever. If I follow the rules concerning sin and soul, I'll go to Heaven when I die and live forever with my family, friends, pets,

Jesus, and anything else I want in my company.

Or:

Jesus isn't real. He's part of a fictional tale invented centuries ago by ancient people in desperate need of comfort and hope. That would mean when I die, it's over. Finished. End of story. No more life, friends, family, pets—no more me.

My young brain chose wisely back then.

The Jesus stories—they were well founded. Beginning in Weixerau, developed further in Landshut, redefined and taught properly in Nativity, and honed to a fine, sharp edge in Saint Rita High School by our Augustinian Fathers.

I remember dissecting it all curiously after meeting Mr. Victor in college. I'd felt the need to expand the strict bounds I'd grown up with—to free up more running space for my energized brain.

Everything changed after the senseless death of my best friend in Vietnam. Pete "Bojangles" had already finished his tour of duty. He had decided to stay on for a few weeks longer to visit places of interest as a civilian. Three days into his new fun and freedom, he was killed by a sniper.

But, I have to hand it to my brain—it found a way to deal with his death. It wallowed for a while, and then my inventive brain picked itself up, chose a different view of life, and assumed another perspective. Maybe my friend's death wasn't senseless after all—because life is senseless. Wouldn't a senseless tragedy in a senseless world be just fine and dandy? Like multiplying a minus one by a minus one to get a plus one?

Okay, brain—choose.

Yeah, right.

Am I kidding me?

This is a no-brainer—

At least my sense of humor is hanging in.

Has my brain always shielded me from the truth? For the sake of happiness? For its own survival?

Or, like Celia said—does it just fuck with itself constantly?

Chapter 92

"Celia, I want to be with you, but you're talking to me through my brain."

"There is no other way, Luke. Your brain has complete control, even when you dream. You've closed off every other possibility. You're held captive by your brain, but it is also your prisoner. It's locked up in your body. It relies on your physical existence for its life. It will die when your body dies. That's why it wants you to live—so it can live."

She's saying something between the lines. Can I get what she's trying to tell me without my brain finding out? Is there a long forgotten passageway buried deep beneath what my brain blocked off after I became *I*?

I'm aware of myself thinking absurdly, as though any of this is real.

"But you don't have a brain, Celia."

"I used to."

I picture her making one of her funny faces, or pointing her index finger and thumb in a gun-like pose to her head—just like the Celia I remember. But she doesn't have a brain or a body, so how can she communicate at all?

"Remember when I told you I couldn't like you because then I'd hate you? My own brain was in my way. I couldn't escape it. I loved you, Luke. I wanted to be with you, but I knew there was no way I could."

Numbing cold grips my chest. She's telling me what she wants me to do. But wait—is this a trap? If it is, then who's setting it? My brain doesn't want to destroy itself because it wants to exist.

If Celia is doing this—it means she *does* exist.

I'm shaking now, like I did when I saw her painting for the first time.

"But Celia, you made the painting before we met. You started the project before we met, and you finished it with no mention of me. You didn't even leave me a note."

"I didn't make the painting with you or Richard or anyone in mind. But I started my project and bought the gun *after* I met you, Luke.

"What?"

I don't need to hear this. I don't even know who's talking to me. Is it Celia or am I just losing what's left of my mind?

I'm nauseous. Why is my body getting into the act now? What kind of Hell am I in here? My life hasn't sucked completely. Until now.

I don't have to believe her—if she's even her. Or

maybe she's lying. Or maybe my brain is making up another version of this story.

Like Mr. Victor said—I have to get the Hell out! I think I might throw up.

"Bye, Luke."

Damn!

I'm not saying goodbye. She's not even really here.

Chapter 93

I shouldn't have been such a coward. I should have gotten rid of that damn portfolio as soon as I got home from Mr. Victor's place.

I never told anyone about it. Aside from Sara, no one else knows it exists. Maybe I should make a bonfire in the backyard, and toss in the painting and the sketchbooks and all of those crazy project pages. I can rip up the carpet, repaint the room, and all of this mess will be gone from my life as it should have been years ago.

Dr. Rosen's words still haunt me. I think he was right. I never got over Celia. He said I wouldn't unless I admitted to being responsible for her death. I should have grieved and healed my brain when it all happened.

But how could I have done that? How can I do it now? I had nothing to do with her death!

He was right about something else, too. I did get over the anger. I'm just pissed off now because she said she finished the project after she knew she couldn't have me—after she begged me not to go.

That's crap, too.

She didn't beg me to stay. She cried and carried on while I held her, knowing I was leaving the next morning. All she'd said was that she wished I didn't have to go. But she knew about my plans long before that. Everyone knew—it was old news. She was fine with it! It was just a coincidence that she'd had a nervous breakdown the night before I left. Or worse—maybe it had been a ploy to make me feel guilty.

Yeah, this is my brain working on me. Celia died years ago by her own hand. End of story—the real story.

I unlock the door to my Other Room and enter the dark space.

"So ... how are you going to get rid of me now, Luke?"

Oh, crap. The door isn't shut. The light's not on. I haven't even looked at the painting—

"Close the door and sit down, Luke. Before you do, take Myla out of the room."

I turn on the spotlight and see Myla, my misty grey tabby. She digs her claws into the carpet when I grab her, pulling the rug up with her. She meows in protest when I put her out of the black room. Myla hates doing anything that isn't her idea.

Wait. How did Celia know Myla was in here when I didn't even know? If Celia is an invention of my brain ... and I didn't know Myla was in the room ... how could Celia have known?

Myla is real. But Celia isn't. It's not possible—

Is it?

I collapse on my black chair. From this angle, the painting is dazzling. It has a soft golden sheen from the bright spotlight, and it's glowing like the mirrored control tower windows at Meigs Airport when they reflected the setting sun.

"I wasn't sure you'd come back to me, Luke."

I lean forward holding my face in my cold hands.

I start to cry.

Chapter 94

"Celia ..." I am sobbing.

"I never saw you again ... I left for school ... and then I got the letter ..."

I'm crying and wiping my wet face with my shirt. My face is hot, but my hands are numb ice. For the first time, I'm afraid. I'm scared to death she's going to leave me again.

"I'm here now, Luke." I barely hear her voice through my sniffled weeping.

"What happened to your body?" I don't know why I ask that, of all things.

"Detective Hogan found my mother in Branson, Missouri. He's the man who talked to Mr. Victor the morning they found me."

"Mr. Victor never mentioned him."

"You wouldn't let him. You flew out of his place so fast, you didn't ask him anything. You were mad and thrilled it wasn't your fault. Don't you remember?"

"Yes."

I try to stop crying so I can hear her.

"The detective called her and asked if she had a daughter named Celia. When she said yes, he told her I had committed suicide. Her response was, 'I don't have a daughter.' He asked her to come to Chicago to identify my body, but Marcelline said, 'I don't have a daughter. I'm not going to Chicago. I have nothing and no one in Chicago.' And then she hung up.

"He called her back and told her his office would be sending a document for her to sign stating that she refused to claim the body. She said, 'Fine. Mail it. I'll sign it. But make sure you include a stamped, self-addressed, return envelope.'"

"My God, that's disgusting, Celia. I'm so sorry."

I feel like my blood pressure is going through the roof, but I don't care.

"What did they do with your body?"

"No one claimed it, so after the investigation was finished and the Medical Examiner's report was filed, it was donated to science. My body ended up in the cadaver room at Cook County Hospital for students to pick apart. The funny part was that no one found anything wrong with the intact part of my brain. They labeled it 'Normal'."

She giggles, but I can't laugh. It's devastating and tragic and all my fault. I can't stop crying, finally feeling the grief I've been hiding from all these years. My brain wouldn't invent this kind of horror story—one that puts the blame on itself. This has to be Celia.

"I need to know something else—"

"Why I didn't mention you in my project or the letter? Why did I dedicate it to Mr. Victor instead of you?"

"Yes."

"Because I loved you so much, Luke. Even through my anger and sickness and fear, I didn't want to wreck your future. I wanted you to have your life and be free to live it like you wanted. I knew that some day, you'd come back to me. That our love would bring us together again. Somehow."

I sit quietly. Celia just said what I have always wanted to hear. Her suicide wasn't a selfish attempt to free herself from her pain. It was a selfless sacrifice. For *us*.

I don't deserve such love.

I didn't believe in her after she gave all she had—her life—

I don't deserve to live.

Dr. Rosen, I'm not lying now!

"What if Mr. Victor had never given me your painting? And your project? What if I'd never built this room?"

"I left Mr. Victor a note. I asked him to make sure you were given the project, the painting, the note, my sketchbooks, and the envelope, but only *after* he died. And I asked him not tell you about any of it."

Celia's voice is tender and sad.

"Mr. Victor didn't know about any of this for a very long time. The note with the envelope was stuck in the bottom of the box. He only found it years later when he transferred the project into the portfolio."

"Celia, I'm just—I'm shocked. But I believe you're

here. That you're real. You're my real Celia. I loved you then. I love you now. And I'll never doubt you again."

Chapter 95

"I killed you, Celia. I killed the one thing in this world that I loved the most. I understand now. I knew it when I saw Mr. Victor's letter. But when I saw your project, my brain must have felt the pain for an instant, and then told me I wasn't responsible—and I believed it."

"You didn't kill me, Luke. My mother killed me when I was two years old. I died seventeen years later."

"I didn't have to die. I was falling in love, and I knew you were, too. It scared me. I didn't trust you or me. I thought my feelings would turn into hate—like they always had before. It had already happened at the beach. I was overcome with hate when you came back from the bathroom. I know it sounds ridiculous now, but that's when I knew for sure that I loved you."

"How did you know I used the bathroom? You were asleep when I left, and still sleeping when I came out."

"You told me, Luke. Whenever you lied or didn't

know exactly what to say, you'd touch your bottom lip with your finger. I thought it was adorable—well, not that time. When I saw you do it in class, mostly around Shannon or Sara. You were so shy and different from the other boys. They didn't care about lying, but I always felt like you didn't to want to lie. That day on the beach—I know you thought you were protecting me."

"I didn't know you knew."

"I didn't want you to know."

"Did you hate me at the beach?"

"In that moment, Luke, I hated you more than anything else in the world. I wished you were dead. When I asked where you'd been, you pretended one thing, but you knew you'd done the other. It was like you'd snuck into the bathroom and done something sordid and nasty—*to me*. And you came out like nothing had happened. I was overwhelmed with my sickness. And I couldn't control it. I hated you. More than I can describe."

"I'm so sorry, Celia."

"Hate was the symptom. I wouldn't have felt that kind of betrayal if I hadn't loved you. So I wanted to hate you and keep hating you forever. It was like fighting a monster inside my brain, and I was losing that battle. I felt it breathing, panting, wearing me down. It consumed me. It finally killed me."

"I don't understand. You wanted to hate me? So you could keep the hate away?"

"Yes. I wanted to use my self-made hate to destroy the hate my mother had spawned. The sick hate. The Hate with the capital H. I know it's complicated. Does any of this make sense to you?"

"I think so. The little hate keeps the giant Hate away. Like David and Goliath."

"Exactly."

"So why didn't you allow yourself to hate me the way you hated Richard?"

"I tried. I tried to destroy my feelings for you. I wanted to choose life. Between the hate washing over me and the real love I had for you, I couldn't win. When I thought of you, I loved you. So much. And then I remembered your face at the beach, and that horrible, uncontrollable rage would overtake me instantly. I couldn't hold on to the real love because I wasn't taught how to love. I was taught the opposite—Marcelline trained me to hate, and to hold onto that hate no matter what. And even though that Hate was artificially created, it was dominant."

"I had no idea what was going on in your head. And I never asked. I was afraid to hear the truth. I just let it go. And then I left. I'm so sorry."

"I didn't want you to know, Luke. It was madness, and I was ashamed of it."

"You told me about the hate, but what about the love?"

"My father was the only person in my life who ever loved me. My mother hated him, so I never knew what a woman's love for a man looked like or felt like."

"What about your friends? Didn't you see how they were with their boyfriends? Didn't they talk about how in love they were and how they felt?"

"Oh, yeah. I watched them—I practically studied them, and asked them questions, too. They described it—like butterflies, warm and fuzzy feelings, hearts and flowers, all the Hallmark stuff. I thought I understood it in my mind, but I couldn't feel it in my heart."

"What about when you were with Richard?"

"It felt good—whatever *it* was. Sometimes it felt great, and I imagined it was the real deal. Real love, I mean. But mostly, it was like body parts being in love with other body parts. Doing their thing."

"I can't believe I still feel jealous when I think of Richard. But that's not important. I want to hear everything—love and body parts—where does love come from? Our brain? That's an organ. Our brain makes the fiction to fuel love."

"I used to think love was an illusion created by my brain, like Mr. Victor used to say. But I knew my brain was broken and unable to love."

Her voice is soft and wise.

"Celia, when I looked at you, I felt love. All over. Including your body parts, of course. I was crazy about them. But I also loved you—for your energy, your inquisitive mind, your quirky moves, your ways, so many other things. Was that just my brain making a romantic movie?"

"No."

"How do you know?"

"Because I proved it."

"How?"

"When I took my brain out of the picture, I was able to feel. I felt real love for the first time. For *you*. And it was big. Bigger than ever. As big as the universe and everything in it. Greater than anything I'd ever imagined."

"So you don't need a brain to feel love?"

"I know for sure that your brain can stop you from feeling true love. Mine sure did."

"Was it real then? Did we—"

"I know now that we both loved each other for real. And if I had gone on to feel it and live it with you, it would have given me back the life my mother took away."

"Oh, don't say—"

"But it would have destroyed you."

Chapter 96

"I made a mistake, Luke."

"You mean ... by killing yourself?"

"No. By not letting you know that it wasn't your fault. By trying to protect you and me—us—I caused you a lifetime of hurt and anger and confusion. I didn't mean for that to happen, Luke. I wanted to stop my own pain, but even more—I knew I couldn't be with you without rules and restrictions—just like my mother. I was afraid my brain would get worse as I got older, and I wanted to free you from feeling like you had to take care of me because I thought you might want to."

Her words confirm what I tried to deny for years—she *did* love me like I loved her. But hearing them now makes me horribly sad.

"But Celia—maybe we could have figured out a way—"

"No. I made my choice and it was right. I watched

Marcelline abuse my father—I knew there was no fix for me. I think she really loved him, in her way. But he didn't have a chance to feel it because of the rage that overwhelmed her—and then me. He stayed with her, but it killed him. I watched his happy loving spirit die slowly until he had nothing left. That part—my suicide—wasn't a mistake."

"But Celia, maybe we could have figured something out to stop that crazy anger before it happened. Together."

My mind fills with ideas and what-ifs—

"You said you heard Richard in the bathroom and wanted him dead—"

"Luke, this is why—"

"Celia, if we both had wanted to be together bad enough—wait, it was the sound—the violence of the noise, the mystery of the act—Celia! Maybe if you had gone into the bathroom with me, the act would have remained sort of innocent. Maybe it wouldn't have hurt you that way. I wouldn't have been hiding behind a door, secretly cheating on you. In your mind, I mean. You would have been there. Maybe your brain wouldn't have gone into the Hate mode. Celia, we were artists, creators, innovators. We could have worked around it!"

"No. No, no, no, Luke. After your lie—I didn't trust you any more." Her words are distant, like she's fading away.

"No! Celia, wait!"

"I knew you would want to help me. But I knew I was on my way to becoming Marcelline. And after you lied on the beach, that *Hate* was taking over."

She sounds farther away than before. I think I hear her say, "I did the right thing."

My throat is clenching up. I'm holding back a cry. I think she might be gone, or maybe I just don't want to hear these things—

"Why are you talking to me now? Why don't you hate me now?"

"I don't have a broken brain any more, Luke." I exhale a breath of relief. She's still here.

"I'm not afraid. Fear causes rage and hate, and I don't fear you any more. I'm not afraid you'll hurt me. The death of *me* freed me to feel love. It was released from its prison—my messed up brain. It's not locked up in hatred any more."

"I'm not the only one who lied, Celia. What about—"

"When I lied to you?"

"Yes. When I saw the bandage on your arm, and you told me you scraped it on something in your car. Remember?"

"I was in so much pain about your lie—"

"But—"

"Let me finish, Luke. When I got home from the beach, thoughts of you going to the bathroom flooded my brain. I was in agony pain. In my messed up mind, you sickly and purposely betrayed me. I tried so hard, but I couldn't get the sounds, the images, the hate out of my head."

"Sounds and images? But you didn't *hear* or *see* me do it. You were really far away. Sleeping."

"That's how sick I had gotten. Just knowing you were

in the bathroom was enough to set off the *hate* spiral. The sound that was imprinted in my brain from Richard came to life in my head, but this time it was *you* doing the nasty deed. *To me.* When you came back, all I saw was betrayal. All I heard were lies. My imagination was more powerful than reality. There was nothing you could have done to help me, Luke."

"Oh, I can't—Oh—"

"And, I didn't know how to help myself. I tried to block the mental pain with physical pain. I grabbed a dinner fork and gouged the top of my arm."

"Did that mean—" My throat chokes down tears.

"Yes, Luke. As twisted and crazy as it was, that's when I knew I loved you with all my heart."

Chapter 97

I don't think I'll ever stop crying.

"What about the painting? Why did you paint a yellow sky?"

"It's not a sky, Luke. It's pee. The clouds aren't clouds. It's toilet paper disintegrating in a sky of pee. The painting is the nightmare world I lived in."

"You painted something you feared and despised all your life?"

"Yes."

"Why?"

"I wanted to conquer my fear. They say we fear the unknown. I thought if I painted it as a sunny, friendly sky with happy little clouds, I could befriend and stop fearing my worst enemy."

"Did it help?"

"Not even a little bit. Just like Dr. Lopez said—there was no fix for me. But the painting was the beginning of my HOLE project, so it wasn't a totally wasted effort." She sounds like she is smiling.

"What came first? The painting or the gun?" I ask.

"I finished the painting way before I met you. And I bought the gun after I knew you, but I didn't think I'd ever use it."

"Why did you get it if you didn't plan to use it? You said a girl needed protection. That was another lie, I guess." I don't want to feel mad, but I do.

"I'm sorry I lied. I bought it because I wanted control. You have no idea what that means to someone who can't keep their own brain in order. When it's untrustworthy. When it turns on you, sometimes out of nowhere. When it's your worst enemy."

She sounds clear and close now.

"When I handled the gun on Maxwell Street, I was filled with a feeling of power. Having the means didn't require me to use it, but I knew I could. I wanted to force my brain to behave. Instead of being bullied by it, I wanted to make it listen to me, at least the reasonable part of me."

"But it didn't work, did it?"

"Well, it seemed like it did. For a while. I played games pretending to shoot myself. You know—with it unloaded. I'd put it to my head and say things like, 'If you don't behave—click.' You remember that game, don't you, Luke?"

I think I hear her laugh. I guess she knows all about my night with Smith & Wesson. Hell, maybe she was there.

"What happened later?"

"The beach was just the beginning. As soon as I drove away that day, I started having attacks. Day and night. The hate—I mean the BIG Hate with the capital H—was stronger than it had ever been before.

"I had terrible nightmares. Your face, Luke—your handsome face became monstrous. You were a hideous creature with black wings—a bat-like humanoid. With a huge penis. You hovered over me, drenching me with hot, stinking liquid. I wanted to run, but I couldn't move. I tried to hit you, but my arms were useless."

"How long did this go on?"

"About two weeks."

"And then?"

"Then I made my decision. And everything stopped. The nightmares were gone. I could think clearly. That's when I completed my project."

"It was ingenious really. I mean the machine, the art, the unique way of signing the painting. How did you come up with the concept?"

"You gave me the idea, Luke."

"What? What do you mean?" I feel a rush of nerves.

"It was from one of your stories—the one your mother told you about an incident with a farm family when the Bolsheviks occupied Lithuania. The farm wasn't far from your grandfather's place. Soldiers came and shot the man and his son, and raped and killed his daughter."

"I remember."

"The mother had been out, but returned to find their bodies in the blood-soaked room. A small, blood-washed picture of the Virgin Mary was hanging on the wall. It had a bullet hole through it. Later, the woman said her dead husband talked to her through that picture—through the hole. Everyone said she'd gone mad. They found her drowned in the well with the picture inside her clothes next to her heart. That's how it came to me."

"That was quite a stretch, Celia. To use the delusions of a grieving widow as the basis for the creation of elaborate art—"

"Mr. Victor always said we had to stretch beyond our reach to create art. A little Passion and some Love didn't hurt either."

"But there was no mention of a paranormal aspect in your HOLE presentation."

"I didn't want to bring that up. I was afraid it would rob the project of legitimacy. It might have looked more like a manual for witchcraft than serious art—

"—and I wanted it to remain my—no—*our* little secret."

My eyes ache and sting.

"I caused your death, Celia. If you'd never met me, you'd never have gone to such a final extreme. You wouldn't have killed yourself."

"That's not true, Luke. Don't think you were the only cool cat on the planet I would have gone kookie for. You're not the Lone Ranger."

"Thanks."

"Any time."

Chapter 98

"What about Marcelline?"

"You want to know if I've forgiven her."

"Yes."

"There was nothing to forgive, Luke. She was very sick and didn't know it. She did the best she could for me."

"That's really generous of you, Celia."

"Not really. She suffered as much as I did in her own brain. She was born blind and she died blind."

"I still can't see you."

"I can see you."

"Then you must be seeing an old man."

"That's not what I see."

"If you're seeing me the way I used to look, you're not seeing the real me."

"You see an old man in the mirror. But that's not what you are. That's the Expression, like Mr. Victor used to say. That's the Lego Man, Luke."

"But—"

"Remember when Mr. Victor asked us to create things from Legos?"

"Of course I do. You made a spider, and then you didn't want to take him apart—"

"Edgar."

"I remember Edgar. You always had him riding with you in your car. I never really understood that. He was just a bunch of blocks you put together."

"We're all just a bunch of blocks, Luke."

"I still can't see you."

"Your brain is still fighting with you. It's afraid for you—for itself. It doesn't want to die."

"I'm so confused, Celia. I know your body doesn't exist. You said we're all a bunch of blocks—but, what are you? A spirit? I don't understand."

I try to sit up straight on my chair, but I'm too exhausted to stay upright.

"You have to go back to when you were little. Before you were in Weixerau. When you were still one with the universe. Before your brain got in your way. Before you were taught that you were unique and better—different from all other life. Before you started thinking small. Before you started believing you were *you*."

"How can I go back?"

"It took your brain years to create its own reality. As time passed, you lost touch, but not as much as you lost sight. You saw false truths all around you through the fake glasses your brain made for you. They weren't rose-colored, but your own special brand of make-believe specs. You lived in your own world with *you* in its center.

"But what you call *you* is that pile of Legos we always joked about. Like Mr. Victor told us, the arrangement is just an Expression for the Source and the System. 'Do not fall in love with the Expression. It is just temporary. It is part of the journey. It is not the destination.'"

I hear Celia imitate Mr. Victor's accent like she used to. She's funny, but I want to cry.

"But how do I—what is the destination?"

"There isn't one. A destination is an ending. The journey never stops. You never arrive. It's endless."

"Then there's no point to anything—"

"Oh, no, Luke. There is a point to everything. The point is love. That's what it's all about."

"But love isn't an object, it's an emotion. Emotions need to be about something, like art or music or people or animals or a beautiful sunset. You can't be emotional about emotion."

"Yes. That's right. It's love—for. Love for the universe and everything in harmony and balance with it. Love for air, water, grass, trees. Love for the earthworm that breaks up soil for roots to grow. Love for insects who spread pollen and propagate flowers and gardens. It's endless—and that's the point."

"It sounds beautiful, but—"

"It *is* beautiful when it happens—when you reconnect with the universe. When you know you're part of it all. When your love for yourself grows and flows and reaches into everything. When you become everything—and everything becomes you."

Chapter 99

"Do you remember the pinhole demonstration, Luke? In Mr. Victor's studio?" She sounds clear now, like she's standing in front of me talking.

"Yes."

"He said when an Expression is born, another HOLE opens in the universe. Remember?"

"Yes."

"Do you have any black construction paper?"

"I think I have some in a file cabinet in the garage."

"Can you go get two pieces and a pin or needle?"

"I can."

"Don't forget to come back."

"I won't."

I always did what she wanted me to. Except that one time ... at the beach.

I find paper and a straight pin, and return to the room. I turn on the light and close the door.

"Leave the light on, Luke. I want you to be able to see what you're doing. I want to show you what Mr. Victor forgot to mention in his scheme. He left out one key point."

"I always thought he was pretty thorough."

"He was, but I found a hole in his HOLE theory."

"Funny." I think I'm smiling a little.

"Mr. Victor said that we—as we think of ourselves—are a creation of our own brain."

"Yes."

"He said when we're born, the HOLE opens. When we die, the HOLE closes."

"Yes."

"The HOLE has nothing to do with the body, Luke. It has everything to do with the brain. The HOLE is completely open when we're born. It starts to close as the brain begins building its own reality—blocking out the truth."

"Okay, I'm following you so far."

"Your new reality began with your mother's intense love for you. Her love was so powerful it consumed everything around itself. It was blinding like the sun. When you looked into her eyes, you saw and felt nothing but love. Your HOLE began to close as you took it all in. You started believing you were something special, and the universe—the Source—the truth—couldn't get through."

"Yes. I've always carried my mother's love with me. I still feel it now."

"Think about it. About what you just said, Luke. Think back to all your loves. You had many, but you never married, and you never wanted to have children."

"Well … no."

"Do you know why?"

"I guess I never found anyone I could commit to."

"No. That wasn't why."

"It wasn't?"

"It was because of the only true loves in your life—your mother. And me."

"But, I don't—"

"Your mother was the perfect woman. No one else could ever measure up."

"But—"

"No. I don't mean in a sexual way. Not like that. That's where I came in."

"You mean when I was with other women, I thought of you?"

"You didn't exactly think, but I was always in your subconscious mind. You thought you'd gotten rid of me that day at Mr. Victor's, but I've been alive inside your brain all along."

"But all these years—I thought I was hating you—"

"That's what you wanted to think. But your heart knew differently. Why did you pick Palos Hills, of all places, to live?"

"Because Nina wanted horses?"

"No, Luke. Because I lived here. And I died here."

"I thought it was coincidence—"

"There is no coincidence in the universe, Luke."

"I love you, Celia. I always have from the moment I met you. When you said I could call you Celia. Do you remember?"

"Of course I remember. You probably still don't know what you did that endeared you to me instantly, do you?"

"No ... what?"

"When I asked you your name, you did that thing—you put your finger to your mouth and touched your bottom lip like a shy little boy. Like you weren't sure what your name was. It was so cute. I understood after you said 'Lukas' that you didn't know which name to use—but that did it for me. I never forgot it."

"But—"

"I know. It wasn't so cute at the beach. That's how I knew you were lying."

"I'm sorry. I loved you so much. I didn't want to hurt you, and I wasn't sure if it even would, but I made a choice and I've been sorry for it ever since."

"I know. I always knew. That's why I waited for you."

"You waited a lifetime—my lifetime."

"It wasn't long—"

"Really?"

"Time is relative. You could say we've been on different clocks, but that's impossible to explain ... can we try something, Luke?"

"Okay."

"Take one of the papers and stick the pin through it."

"Like this?"

"Yes. Now, look through the hole and tell me what you see."

I hold the paper up close to my eye and squint to look through it. I find the painting. It is bathed in bright yellow light. The rough texture of the canvas and brush strokes show clearly. The edges of the pinhole circle move like running water in a shallow creek.

"I see your painting."

"The other piece of paper doesn't have a hole. That is you, Luke. The HOLE in you closed up years ago."

"Okay, I get it."

"Now, cover my paper with yours. No light comes through. The HOLE in the Universe that was me was closed by you."

I see solid black and suddenly feel sad.

"Push the pin through both papers, then look through the hole."

"Oh my God! I see me. But I look like I'm twenty years old! Have I gone back in time?"

"No, Luke. You crossed over and into my mind-stream for an instant."

"Oh! Celia! I just saw you! I saw your face!"

The most beautiful face I've ever known just appeared before me for one second! Now it's gone, and I only see the painting.

"What happened? Where did you go?"

"I didn't go anywhere. You lost your connection. You opened your brain for a moment, and then you lost focus."

"How—"

"Do you remember when Mr. Victor said our brains are like a radio? They are a receiver, not a transmitter. They can only channel a tiny part of what's out there. There are hundreds of stations playing at the same time, but the radio can only select and play one at a time. It shuts out the rest."

"Is that why I can only experience a single reality as Luke, and not multiple realities? Why I can't be me, Sara, Marty, and Nixon all at once?"

"Exactly. You're programmed to receive only one pathway. Cell phones, laptops, and tablets can access other connections, but your brain is a dedicated device. It plays only one single track."

"Like a one track mind?"

"Good one."

"So when I saw my own face, it was like I crossed over into your pathway? Like my brain jumped tracks?"

"Yes, like interference. Like when you hear another conversation while you're on a phone or when another radio station cuts into yours."

"Did I see what you see now?"

"Yes."

"But when I saw you—"

"That was your own brain opening up, Luke."

"So, your painting with the bullet hole—"

"Think of it as a portal. A communication link. A pathway to connect our separate realities."

"Can I connect to you? Can I experience you, Celia?"

"Yes, Luke. When your brain no longer controls what you're allowed to access. When it's no longer your keeper."

"You mean—"

"Yes. You'll become one with the universe."

"Won't it be total chaos?"

"Only to your earthly brain."

Chapter 100

"All these years—a lifetime of loving you, Celia. I'm so tired of denying it. I've always loved you. Why didn't I just accept it and deal with it? I was such a coward—"

"Rest, Luke. Sleep deeply. When you wake, you'll be strong and ready to do what you need to do."

"Are you sure? Are you really sure?"

"Yes. It's time. We almost didn't make it. Time almost ran out for us."

"You mean when I had the stroke?"

"Then, and a thousand other times you weren't aware of."

"Is it over? Is it too late?"

"It's only the beginning."

I feel kisses. Tender kisses from baby soft lips onto mine.

"It's going to be a beautiful morning in the woods tomorrow. You need to get out of the basement. Let the stink blow off. I think you've been in your dungeon too long."

More kisses.

"Celia ... how did you know your painting idea would work?"

"I didn't. I just thought it was worth a shot."

I feel a giggly kiss press into my cheek.

Wednesday: 6:24 AM

Celia was right. It is a beautiful morning. There's a robin in the backyard. She looks like she's loaded with eggs. She must have a nest nearby. I wonder if it's in one of these ancient oaks.

Shit, shower, shave. That was an important routine when I was on a tight morning schedule. It's amazing how well my body adapted. It never left me sitting there, waiting, wasting precious morning minutes.

I'm in no rush today. Now for my meds.

My red plastic pillbox is in its usual place on the top shelf of the medicine cabinet. The compartments are empty except for Wednesday. I can't believe another week flew by already.

All four pills are here: Dyazide for my high blood pressure, a multi vitamin, a B-12 pill, and low-dose aspirin to prevent my blood from clotting.

I'm lucky—the stroke didn't leave me impaired. Or

worse. Most of my old friends are long gone.

I pour Wednesday's contents into my cupped left hand, toss it in my mouth, catch some water from the tap, and slurp it down.

I close the mirrored door on the vanity and study the face. I see the eyes, the droopy bags, the wrinkly sags, the folds, stains, and spider veins. I touch the skin. I pull it up and back. It doesn't return after it's stretched. It just hangs there. A girlfriend—I forgot which one—thought some nips and tucks might have been a good idea decades ago.

Disappointing? Maybe. But not surprising. Like dings and rust spots on a car, I know there'll be plenty more next time I look.

Funny how different I feel studying the face this morning. I'm amused. It's like playing with Silly Putty or making fish lips on an infant. It's hard to believe I was ever bothered.

Last night, Celia told me something so simple I'm amazed I never thought of it myself:

"That's not you, Luke. That's just Lego Man."

I feel great. I slept better than I have in years. I'm going to get dressed, have breakfast, drive over to Martha's Riding Stables, and go for a nice walk in the woods.

Wednesday: 10:08 AM

Region Six of the Cook County Forest Preserve District has some of the most pristine natural settings in the state of Illinois.

It's less than a two minute drive to Martha's. She's a good friend. I took two trail horses off her hands when they had gotten too old to ride. I put them out to pasture on my property so they could end their hard lives in leisure and comfort. She won't mind that my car's parked in her lot.

A wide driveway leads out of her place and connects to the street. Across the road, a bridle path the width of two horses cuts into the forest.

I cross the street and walk down the gravelly path to a narrow trail leading south into the thick woods. I follow the path and the forest closes in.

The woods shield the traffic noises coming off Kean Avenue. It's sunny and quiet. A fly buzzes by. The trees and bushes are in full bloom and block the cool spring morning breeze. The majestic oaks are beginning to unfurl their leaves. From a distance, they look like silvery orchids tinted with gold. Bushes are blossoming. Red honeysuckles, white chokecherries, and wild pink roses are popping their buds.

A frog splashes through a puddle. A few feet ahead, a rabbit darts across the path. Farther down, deer munch on tender new greens. Soon newborns with white dots will be born. A woodpecker machine-guns a dead tree. Somewhere an owl hoots. High above in the blue sky, a red-tailed falcon circles. Bees collect pollen and flies buzz over piles of fresh horse dung.

Life is everywhere. Crappie, bluegill, bass, and bullheads fill the ponds and lakes. Turtles, frogs, garter snakes, and salamanders hide in the low foliage. Foxes, coyotes, raccoons, opossums, and woodchucks are out of sight, but watchful. Canadian geese, sandpipers, gulls, and local waterfowl dip and dive along the muddy shores. White cranes and blue herons fly in temporarily, then migrate on. Puddles and water-filled sinkholes house tadpoles, pond skippers, gnats, and mosquito larva. Snails and algae thrive.

A butterfly—beautiful and unlike any I've seen before—flits along the edge of the trail. It seems too early in the season for butterflies, but I won't question the universe. Not any more.

I've walked these footpaths many times. Some lead to open, grassy areas where families picnic. Others wind up along edges of swamps and creeks, or follow ridge tops of deep, wooded ravines—the work of the latest ice age.

Dead trees lay where they fell. Some are rotted, their trunks stripped bare, slowly sinking into the earth; others still stand. Gravity will bring them down after their roots rot, and they succumb to the work done by subterranean tunnel dwellers.

New sprouts and vegetation are busy recycling and replacing the deceased. Clumps of yellow, red, brown, and white mushrooms have sprung up through green mosses that cover decayed wood. Insects are flying, walking, sucking, chewing, and burrowing. Squirrels run and leap and perform horrifying aerial stunts.

I'm here.

I take off my windbreaker and sit down at the base of the giant oak. Its massive roots protrude from the forest floor and embrace me like an armchair.

I've been here before. I know this tree. It feels like an old friend. It stands on the edge of high ground that rolls down from the steep overlook to a meandering creek below.

The sun's rays warm my face and arms. The heat feels good on my pasty, winter white skin. I love my first outing of spring after a cold winter. It makes me feel hopeful and energized.

I see little green shoots peek out from under dry leaves. In a few days Creeping Charlie, with its dainty blue-lavender flowers, will overtake the brown winter carpet. Only small patches of last year will remain.

Bright blue sprinkles—Bluebells—mingle with native shrubs in the sunnier spots. Their bell-shaped flowers hang down in rows like in a Chinese lantern factory. Bees inspect their tubes for nectar.

Life is perfectly choreographed here. Bluebells and Queen Anne's lace never crowd in together. Each living thing has its own time and respects its order of appearance. And exit.

There's that butterfly again. Maybe it's attracted to my yellow jacket.

I lean back and rest my head against the magnificent trunk. This tree has been here since Native Americans populated the area. Respectfully, they allowed it to live. Luckily for these woods, the terrain was too rough for the white settlers to farm.

To my left is a patch of lilies of the valley. The delicate fragrance drifts to me—I know it so well—the scent of Celia. I can almost feel her next to me.

A black carpenter ant runs around on my right hand. He checks out each finger. He races up and over my shoulder, and I lose sight of him. I see him again, disappearing and reappearing as he sprints up the craggy bark. He sure looks like he's in a hurry. I hope he finds what he's looking for.

I'm in love with everything. I want to be that woodpecker. I want to be that ant. I want to be that tree. I want to be that beautiful butterfly.

Celia said I could see her, but not with my eyes. She said my HOLE is closed—that I had closed it years ago, but not like a door. It's shut up from being filled with beliefs, with stories my brain made and my mind saved like a compulsive hoarder. Like plaque in my arteries, the stuff that caused my stroke.

Dr. Rosen predicted I'd invent stories, but he also said stories aren't necessarily bad. If they are allowed to flow—not stop and suffocate—they can animate and heal the brain temporarily, or on an as needed basis.

Beliefs are dangerous. Stories I accepted as truth became my beliefs. Through obstinacy and devotion, they became immovable like bricks in a wall. Just as Mr. Victor had said—the beliefs closed up the HOLE.

My big story—Story with a capital S—was the one I'd invented about Celia. The story that proved I had nothing to do with her death. The story I believed instantly, and doggedly hung onto for over fifty years.

My most enduring belief—the one that's lasted my lifetime—was about the man in the mirror.

I believed *he* was really *me*.

It's time—no, it's way past time—to get rid of my beliefs. I love Celia more than life. I always have.

That's not a belief. That's not even a story. That's the truth, and I won't let it get stuck. I won't let it become a belief. I'll keep it as a story—*our* story. It will stay fresh and new forever, and I, the HOLE in the Universe, will stay open, clean, and free.

I haven't smoked in over thirty years, but on the way here I stopped at the Speedway gas station and bought a pack of cigarettes.

Wednesday: 10:28 AM

I feel her body and smell her familiar scent. She's lying next to me naked. I reach toward her and comb my fingers through her golden curls. I trace her ear with my index finger, moving along her cheek, and draw lightly on her face. Her skin feels dewy like vanilla velvet. I brush over her long eyelashes and follow her brows over her cheekbones and the bridge of her nose.

I pause on her perfectly shaped lips—Celia's lips—as soft and yielding as they were the night she gave me her last tearful kiss.

I lean closer and kiss her forehead. My lips rest for a moment, then touch her closed eyelid ever so gently.

Her breathing is warm and even on my face. I love her breath—so slow and relaxed. Her calmness keeps me from shaking. I kiss her baby-soft lips as they begin to open. She breathes through her mouth—the most beautiful mouth in the world.

I trace her flawless lips with the tip of my tongue and keep moving—down her chin and throat, planting kisses all the way. She tilts her head back while I pause in the space between her collarbones.

Celia raises both arms and rests them under her head. She laces her delicate fingers together and watches me move to just below her left arm. A trace of mist wafts from her skin as I kiss, lick, and nuzzle all parts of her to just below her armpit. I wonder if she is ticklish here.

"Very."

She's reading my mind, knowing every thought and move before I have it or make it. This would be scary with anyone else, but with Celia, it feels natural and right. Complete closeness with total trust, the concept of my most desired dreams. Is there such a thing as Siamese brains?

"I don't know, Luke, but for the first time, I can feel you, too. We only have to be what we are."

I glide my lips lightly over her silky breast. It's soft with a firm foundation. My kisses fall on a velvet path, and there is only the slightest change in texture as my lips touch the very tip.

I hear a soft moan. I'm breathing harder now. I feel her rise with anticipation when my breath warms her skin.

I can't resist any longer. My kissing turns to sucking as I massage and lick the sensitive peak with my tongue.

I find her Marilyn Monroe beauty mark and kiss my way down her flat belly.

I feel her breathing faster—the patch of soft blond hair is only inches away.

"It's darker than blond. Like my eyelashes."

"But in my dream—"

She giggles and relaxes her legs—my kisses continue downward. I lick and explore her with my tongue. Her inner thighs are soft but firm, and we're both getting a little sticky.

"Slow ... Luke." Her voice is soft.

My obsessive kissing drives me down to her right foot. I slip my hand underneath it and raise it to my face. Celia's beautiful foot. I studied it for so long and now it's mine to hold and love. I kiss her toes and the little spaces in between. There's a faint taste of clean sea salt—

Wednesday: 10:30 AM

Her hair tickles as she hovers over me, leaving soft kisses in her trail. I'm lying on my back, and her breasts brush against my bare chest. She moves down slowly, teasing the Hell out of me. I might explode any second.

I feel like Celia and I are teenagers again. Like all hope that was lost has returned. Celia, with her big green eyes and soulful smile, makes me feel like things are finally going to be alright. Like they were always meant to be.

I don't understand it, but here I am—with her. It seems impossible. Have we gone back in time?

"It's not about time, Luke. It's about love. Love isn't about time or place. You're seeing me through your love. You're feeling me—us—in a brand new way. You've disconnected from the world, and from your physical body. This is real love. Love that's been released from human bondage."

She leans in close and lets her face slide down my

belly. Her breasts press into my abdomen as she rests her weight on me. Her cheek is against my skin, and her hand closes firmly around me. I inhale sharply from the shock of her first touch. I've waited a lifetime for this.

I'm breathless as she runs her tongue up and down and all around. I ache and want her more than anything I've ever wanted before. My chest pounds harder each time her warm mouth opens and closes just long enough to taunt me into surrendering.

My body is throbbing in hindered pain. My instinct is to relieve my distress, but I'm holding back—like never before. Celia's need trumps mine. I want to please her first. I want to bring her the most complete and joyous bliss I can deliver.

I run my fingers along her spine and massage her lower back to her tailbone. I touch and taste her in ways I've only imagined. It's a delicacy; a feast of giving and sharing. A wild new landscape, yet somehow familiar. We move in rhythm as I play to her pleasure, finding her highest notes of passion.

Wednesday: 10:32 AM

Waves. Coming and coming. And yet I keep going. I'm near my peak in this orgasmic circle with no let up. Celia doesn't stop or slow down. She won't release me—the intensity is beyond comfort.

We tease and touch and test—I feel our bodies flex and ebb in perfect unity. We are locked, luscious and loving, moving in an undulating, oscillating universe.

How long will this last? What kind of space flight is this? Are we orbiting, tethered to a pulsing star?

She's making love without a body and speaking without a mouth, yet I can touch and feel her. I move her—she responds. Her words are soundless while she holds me deep inside.

"You are feeling me, all of me, the real me, Luke. You told me you can't be in love with love. I'm giving you myself the way you always held me in your hopes and dreams."

A new surge of excitement lifts me even higher.

"How does my body feel your body? I have a real body, after all. Isn't that what's making love?"

"There you go with your Lego Man thoughts again. Go ahead and feel yourself."

"But—"

"I won't let you go."

"But—"

"I promise, Luke."

I rub my hands over my chest and down my sides. My skin is smooth and supple. My muscles move over strong bones. Celia is still holding me tightly; I can feel my own hardness pulse and throb within her.

I touch my neck. It's covered with taut young skin. My face is sculpted without sags or bags. My hands are strong with straight fingers and slender knuckles. My scalp is full of thick blonde hair.

"There's no magic, Luke, no smoke and mirrors. This is what real love is."

I'm aware of the rhythmic waves of joy rising and lapping without pause as I listen to her voice.

"Is this Heaven, Celia?"

"Heaven is just a word. There are no words that can express things our minds can't grasp. Just let yourself go. This is the moment we've waited for all of your life— the moment that almost didn't happen. This is our time, Luke."

"Celia—"

She releases me in a way I'm not sure of. She faces me and wraps her hands behind my neck, her fingers kneading into my full hair. Her strong legs close around my waist, and I feel her opening to me, pulling me in. I put my arms around her back and press her harder into me. She fills me completely—her love, her essence, everything that makes her Celia—she overwhelms my senses.

She holds me tighter. The nonstop orgasmic motions increase. Stars grow large and swish by soundlessly. Constellations blur. Our bodies are inseparably linked, whirling windless through black space.

"Let yourself go. With me, Luke. Trust your heart. Trust us. Let us be what we were always supposed to be."

I can't tell where I begin or end. I don't know what is me or what is Celia. I am drowning in love. My body and mind are consumed—my heart and soul are soaked with the love I always dreamed of. The kind of love I could never find without her. We're welded together now, melding in cosmic matrimony. She—me is becoming one and the same.

We graze a lightning bolt. The brilliant light energizes us with dazzling power as it races from our feet, through our legs, up over our chests, shoulders, necks, lighting up our heads, sparkling through our hair. A million volts shoot through our tongue and our brain.

Our body is continuous—a flowing Gordian knot. A Möbius strip with no beginning and no end. We are inseparable, and the pleasure is unbearable.

"If we get any higher, will I die?"

"You're not Lego Man any more, Luke."

"Is there an end to our pleasure? Does it ever stop?"

"Yes. When you can't take it any more."
"Then what?"
"Then you give it up."
"How?"
"You cry uncle."
"What if I don't?"
"You will."
"What is this, Celia? Where are we?"
"This is love, Luke. We're in love."

We fly fast and high into the whitest light of all. Faster and faster. There's no going back. No escape as we turn transparent. Light turns to heat. Matter turns to energy.

We are a blinding flash of white light—unseen.

An impassioned cry—unheard—

Wednesday: 10:34 AM

UNCLE!

Chapter 101

PALOS HILLS POLICE DEPARTMENT
Dispatcher's Notepad

WED 10:24 AM

MAN Called—Non Emergency
   Found BODY in Woods—
   (Near Kean and 101st St)

   Walk West on Riding Path from Martha's Stables—
   (About 100 feet)
   Take foot Path along Cemetery to where it veers off to the Right—
   See Giant Oak Tree on Left—
   Tree is in Line with South Fence of Cemetery—

BODY is next to Tree—

No need to hurry—Man is DEAD—

Yes I am SURE—

Yes there is a GUN—

Yes I Will be THERE for the Officers—
   (Hung up Phone)

GPS: 41°42'25.1"N 87°50'52.6"W

"Looks like you'll need the ATV to bring it in. Yeah. No, it's about a quarter mile hike. No, over by Martha's. Yeah, on Kean. Uh, huh … yeah. I got the GPS numbers. White Oak Woods. Yeah, I'm looking at Google Maps right now. Yeah. Are McNally and Hough in? Great. Let me talk to them. I don't care. Thanks."

After McNally and Hough surveyed the scene, they got in touch with the Cook County Medical Examiner's Office.
   "Yep, the victim was most likely the caller. Yep. We'll know for sure when we ID him back at the station. Yep. Uh, huh. Okay. Yep. Okay. We'll be in touch."

Based on the phone description, the Medical Examiner's Office saw no need to preserve the scene or make an official visit. They gave the police permission to collect everything and send it to their office. It looked like a standard gun-in-the-mouth suicide.

EVIDENCE FROM SCENE
Officer McNally's Notepad

PAINTING: Canvas on Frame—24" x 36"
    Image: Sky
    Color: Yellow
    Observation: (2) Holes in lower right-hand quadrant
    Probable Cause: Bullets

CARDBOARD: 24" x 36"
    Observation: Blood on Cardboard consistent with short distance exit wound and Blood/Tissue Spatter Patterns
    Observation: (1) Bullet hole at origin of pattern

WEAPON: Smith & Wesson .38 Cal
    Cylinder contents: (1) Cartridge casing, discharged

FOUND IN JACKET POCKET:
    (5) Live cartridges .38 Cal
        2 Flat points, 3 Hollow points

FOUND ON NECK OF DECEASED:
    (1) Beaded neck chain with Silver Triangle Pendant and 2 Keys
    (1) Silver neck chain with Airplane and Silver Triangle Pendant

OTHER ITEMS FROM SCENE:
    (1) Cell Phone (Samsung)

(1) Pack Newport cigarettes
   2 Cigarettes missing, 1 Smoked down halfway and crushed
   1 Lit but not smoked (self-extinguished after it burned to filter)
(1) Zippo lighter—Fighting Seabees insignia
(1) Envelope—empty, torn open
   Inscription: *Please give to Luke.*

McNally, Hough, and other on-duty personnel inspected the body in Room B-17 in the basement of the police station.

"McNally, how long does it take for the brain to die after this kind of injury?"

"About six minutes."

"I thought it was instant."

"He probably wasn't aware of anything going on outside, but his brain kept functioning. Probably in some kind of dream state."

"No shit? That is FAR out."

"Yes. It is."

"Hey, did you see that butterfly? The one sitting on the painting?" McNally asked Hough.

"Yep. Sure did. It flew away after we loaded the body."

"I grew up around here—never saw one like that before. I gotta say—that was the most beautiful butterfly I've ever seen."

I am a HOLE in the Universe.
Expression born of Source and System.
I will be open to the flow
And tread lightly on the earth
Taking as little as I am able
And returning as much as I can.
I will stay free of beliefs that
Confine and confuse.
I will stay suspended and curious.

Mr. Victor's Credo—Class of 1961